7XN

D0409455

F/0123978

Schlee, A.

The Time in Aderra

Also by Ann Schlee

Rhine Journey
The Proprietor
Laing

Ann Schlee

The Time in
Aderra

F/421350

MACMILLAN

First published 1996 by Macmillan

an imprint of Macmillan Publishers Ltd
25 Eccleston Place
London SW1W 9NF
and Basingstoke

Associated companies throughout the world

ISBN 0 333 65680 6

1 3 5 7 9 8 6 4 2

A CIP catalogue record for this book is available from
the British Library

Phototypeset by Intype London Ltd
Printed and bound in Great Britain

To Nick

Chapter One

O N THE NIGHT before she was to fly out to Aderra, Flo stayed in London with her mother's friend, Daisy Mayhew. At six in the morning she was called to breakfast.

'Always an egg before a journey,' Daisy told her. While Flo struggled to eat it, she went on, 'My father always used to make us say, "Money, passport, tickets." '

'I don't deal with any of that,' Flo said. 'Major Denbigh does.'

They had eaten in their dressing-gowns. Back in the bedroom, Flo packed her nightclothes, dragged on the crumpled cotton dress she planned to wear in Africa and covered it quickly with her out-grown school tweed coat, all but the two bottom inches of the hem, which hung below. She brushed her thin brown hair until it lay smooth and fastened it with a plastic clip. The room was unheated. Only a faint smell of gas suggested there had once been warmth. Still, rather than have to talk again to Daisy Mayhew, she sat shivering on the edge of her bed and waited.

Her journey had had a wretched start. Two days

before the end of the school term she had contracted chickenpox. The original flight had been cancelled and, having no family in England to look after her, she had spent Christmas in the sanatorium, too feverish much to care. Then another two weeks must pass before she was deemed out of quarantine and safe to travel. She had spent this time reading by the small coal fire in her room, but once the fever had gone, nothing could alleviate the cold she felt. Her breasts had shrivelled with it. An ineluctable chill had pressed between her shoulder-blades.

At night she had lain awake and talked to herself in an agitated way. The sense of genteel sinfulness so carefully instilled by the boarding-school had caused her to feel as though set endlessly before a stern tribunal. The brilliance with which she was able to answer these accusations astonished her, the more so that during the day her efforts to make conversation to the kindly women who looked after her had seemed increasingly perilous and strange.

All that time her mind had been distracted by her longing to be on the aeroplane and the fear that some new accident would prevent her from reaching it. Constantly she thanked people without any sense of gratitude.

It was a great relief when at seven thirty precisely Major Denbigh rang the doorbell of Daisy Mayhew's flat. From whence he came each year to escort her to the airport Flo had never fully understood. He was attached in some way to the Foreign Office; to do with transport perhaps, for in addition to his military cap and tunic he wore riding boots and jodhpurs. More interestingly he wore a monocle. Now he stood on the landing directing his driver to take Flo's two suitcases down in the lift. Still colder air blew past him into the flat while Flo said her goodbyes. Daisy Mayhew hugged her briefly, pleased to find that at the last she could summon up affection for pretty Lydia Morgan's sad child. 'Dear Flo,' she said. 'You'll have a lovely time. Of course you will. Lots of parties. Lots of devastating young men!' For Flo, although she scarcely looked it, was almost seventeen.

She doesn't really like me, Flo thought. 'Thank you,' she said. 'Thank you for having me.'

The lift had rattled to the ground floor with the luggage. The sound of its doors clanging open and shut carried up the shaft. Major Denbigh prodded the button with his swagger stick, and when the lift reappeared, bowed Flo elaborately into it. He saluted Miss Mayhew, stick to visor, climbed in with Flo and stood in silence during its juddering descent. A black car was waiting by the kerb. The driver saluted and opened the back door. Flo smiled at him and said, 'Thank you.' Then she said to Major Denbigh, 'May I sit on the little seat please?'

'Really?' he said, gripping the monocle in a frown. 'There's no need, you know.'

'I'd like to.'

'As you wish,' he said, prising down the folding

jump seat with his stick. 'Thought you'd grown out of that sort of thing.'

Outside, the adult world plied past the window. Flo sat tensely forward, watching the small blunt cars, the women walking in the streets with set, powdery faces. The Major reached his copy of the *Racing Times* from behind his back and began to study it. At Hounslow he laid it on his knee and said, 'Aderra's a nice place by all accounts. Apart from the troubles, of course. I expect they write to you about it – at school. Tell you what goes on there? Not long now, of course, until the handover.'

'I've left school,' Flo said quickly.

'Have you now,' said Major Denbigh, glinting his monocle at her. 'Thought there was a change. Glad, are you?'

'Oh yes.' She smiled completely. Sweet thing when she smiles, he thought. She was alarming, too; wanting something; so watchful and intent.

As they waited to go through passport control he said, 'You'll give my regards to your father, won't you?'

'Harry's my stepfather.'

'To be sure. Of course he is. Nice chap, I've always thought. Kind.'

'Did you know him in the war?' She spoke so hastily and watched him so attentively that he grew cautious.

'Not really.' A moment later when the flight had still not been called, he said, 'I came across him once though at Mersa Matruh. I'd been sent there. A chap in his unit had been killed. A rum business. I had to take him back to Cairo for the inquest. Had to spend the night in a tent with him.'

'With Harry?'

'No. With this dead chap. Funny thing,' he said after a moment's thought. 'He was remarkably noisy.'

'Wasn't he really dead then?'

'Oh, he was dead all right. Very. Just settling in to it, I suppose. I couldn't sleep a wink.'

Flo smiled at him. No one had ever mentioned death to her before in such a practical and interesting way. She felt that he had done her a kindness and would have asked him more about the dead man had not the loudspeaker started to crackle and bray notice of the plane's departure.

'Well, there we are,' said Major Denbigh. He tucked his stick under his arm and bowed gravely over her hand as he shook it.

'Regards to Harry Morgan then, and to your good Mama. Happy landings!'

Flo sat in the plane and sucked the barley sugar sweet the hostess had given her. England, grown small and manageable, had tilted past the wing and vanished under thick cloud. It seemed in that exalted moment that she, Flo, had achieved this with powers that she alone knew were hers. The great surge of energy that drove the plane up into the sky had seemed to issue from the base of her own spine. Now she need only sit and wait. Nothing more would be required of her. She spoke to no one during the long flight, sitting, even at mealtimes, with a book open. She had read in a magazine the advice to do so if forced to eat alone in a public place. It was a signal to other people, men in particular, that they were not wanted. But she scarcely read the story in the book at all. It was her own story she recited again and again like a spell, for the school must be obliterated and she, herself, restored.

In those days, in the early fifties, the flight to Aderra was broken for refuelling at Rome and again at Malta, where the passengers were taken for the night to an hotel. At dawn they were called to an elaborate breakfast and taken back to the aerodrome. The plane refuelled next at el Adam. Outside the windows of the concrete waiting-room rolls of barbed wire and empty jerrycans shifted in the dust. It was cold, even though by now they were in Africa. Flo kept her school coat huddled about her. Only at Wadi Halfa did the passengers face an alien heat stacked solidly against the open door of the aeroplane as they climbed down on to the tarmac. At Khartoum the London flight continued on to Nairobi. The few passengers remaining boarded a smaller plane and flew east to Aderra over a flat brown landscape which, as the mountains approached, was erased by cloud.

They never did descend; or so it seemed to Flo. At one moment they crawled over the brilliant surface of the clouds. At the next stony earth, sparsely set with eucalyptus trees, was scudding just below the window at a tremendous rate and the plane landed with a series of diminishing jolts. It taxied past low buildings roofed with corrugated iron and paths marked out with white-washed stones. A Union Jack drooped on a flagstaff. In front of it a group of people waved like survivors on a rock. Parked a few yards to one side was a large black car and standing beside it, waving, righting the world by her presence, was Flo's mother.

'There she is! There she is!' Lydia Morgan cried out to her driver, Haile.

'Praise be to God!' the Aderran answered. He clicked his tongue and beamed with pleasure. He approved unreservedly of mother love.

At partings and at meetings Lydia Morgan permitted herself to cry. Now unashamedly she snatched off her dark glasses and began to run across the tarmac with tears streaming down her cheeks. Flo watched her come, a small urgent figure, whose face, at this moment of joy, was contracted with grief. I am taller than she is, she thought with wonder. It had been so for several years but again it surprised her.

They sat together in the back of the black Chevrolet. Lydia, turned sideways, gripped her child's hands so tightly that the pressure of her rings was painful to them both. 'I can't get over this,' she was saying. 'My darling Flo, you are here. You really are here. I just can't get over it.'

'How's Harry?' Flo asked. She felt shy with happiness.

'Harry's a dear. He's at the office now, or he'd be here.'

'He doesn't mind my coming?'

'Don't say that,' Lydia said sharply. 'Why say that when you know he adores you?' Then hearing herself she switched her tone to one of mock despair. 'Oh Flo, you don't change.' For Flo was watching with the same expression she had worn as a child, at once uncertain and intent. 'Oh, I just can't get over you.' Tears still shone on the swollen skin beneath her eyes.

She always cries when I get here, Flo thought. She saw her mother with an intense recognition, her broad pleasing features, the frown between her eyebrows, the freckles on her bare arms which merged towards the shoulders. When they had clung to one another those arms had given off their own dry incessant heat. But she had changed too. For an instant Flo could see that something had spread and loosened in her. Then, in the next instant, like something held too close to the eye, her mother was again too familiar to be seen at all.

'How ridiculous we are,' Lydia was saying, laughing and letting go Flo's hands to wipe at her face with a handkerchief. Now she unclipped her handbag and felt inside for her cigarettes; shook one from the pack, tapped it on her thumbnail, held it between her lips, found her lighter, struck it, dipped her head towards the flame, blew smoke from her nostrils. She began at once to talk about people whom Flo did not know. 'She is my friend. I knew the moment that I met her that she was one of the few people whom life provides. You will love her, Flo. Oh, how can I describe her?'

'She's Frant Road?' Flo suggested. It was their highest term of approbation. It meant she would have been at home in Granny Franklyn's house. It meant 'one of us', the 'us' referring only to the two of them. The expression pre-dated Harry Morgan.

'Oh, she's Frant Road all right,' Lydia said. She began to cry again, for the secret term had laid its finger on the separateness and intimacy that had for a time been theirs but had vanished with Flo's childhood. Now she spoke of someone else who would make Flo laugh. 'I knew him years ago. Daisy would remember him. He's lost really. The war has done for him, but still he makes me laugh.'

Flo made no effort to absorb these people. It was always like this, whenever she arrived – at Khartoum for the last three years, at Nairobi the three years before that. Lydia had gone before, created each new place, populated it, passed judgement, before ever she arrived. 'Oh, the war!' her mother was saying now. 'The war's to blame for everything.'

They could not at that moment look at one another. Lydia turned to crush another cigarette in the ashtray on the rear door. Flo stared out at this new place. Now concrete villas glided past, some with green shutters, some with brown, some fronted with a row of eucalyptus trees, some with oleanders. The driver blared his horn and swung out, now to overtake a flock of doomed sheep being driven into town, now a lorry with a flapping canvas cover which in its turn had swerved to avoid four towering loads of firewood being jerked forward by what means it was impossible to know. Donkeys probably. She strained to see but failed.

'This place!' her mother was saying. 'It isn't real. When I first saw it I said, "I won't believe this until Flo comes and tells me that it's true." ' She leaned back laughing as if the laughter had been trapped inside her until now. 'And the house! You won't believe it, it's so grand!' The car had swung into place again and looking back Flo could see that there were no donkeys, but people, bent over until their backs formed platforms for branches of wood stacked higher than themselves. Could that be? Glancing at Lydia she saw that her mother had not noticed them.

They had reached the centre of the town. Now the concrete buildings rose to three storeys or even four. Flats perched above shops. Slatted wooden shutters sloped out over their windows. The streets were lined with oleanders, their trunks made uniform by white-wash. The pavements were thronged with people saun-tering along as if their only purpose were to display themselves: Aderrans swathed in white, the women with violently coloured chiffon scarves tied around their springy hair, sallow Italians in narrow suits, British sol-diers with pink knees protruding between their long khaki shorts and knee socks.

'You may feel strange at first,' her mother was saying. 'People do. It's the altitude. Lack of oxygen. Every-thing's blamed on it. You mustn't worry if you're not yourself for a while.'

Oh, but I am myself, Flo thought with utter satisfaction. She wiped her damp upper lip against her wrist and sniffed at her dusty skin as if it had grown anew. She watched the eager movement of her mother's face and thought, it's all come right.

'You're going to have a marvellous time,' her mother was saying in just the way that Daisy Mayhew had. 'You can't help doing.' She shook Flo's hands slightly as if by doing so she might transfer her own vitality and make the thing she said be true. They had turned at that moment past a sentry box and up a gravel drive towards a handsome shuttered villa with a flight of marble steps.

Chapter Two

THE VILLA DELLA Pace stood in a quiet backstreet
in an area of the town where, in the thirties, the
more prosperous Italian colonists had built their homes
and planted their bougainvillaeas. It had been the Aderran residence of the Italian Viceroy, whose state palace
was in Routa Routa, the capital of the Northern Province. Here he had stayed for two months of the year
during his tours of duty in the south. Harry Morgan
had known it as a British officers' mess after the invasion
and collapse of the Fascist regime.

Since then, like himself, it had reverted to civilian
status and in recent years been used to house the head
of the British caretaker government. On his return after
ten years in other parts of Africa, he found the villa
little changed. Fascist symbols were set with dreadful
permanency into the terrazzo floors, so placed that
any attempt to cover them with the furniture looked
impossibly awkward. The walls of the front sitting-room
were still painted with a hectic scene of thick-lipped
monkeys disporting themselves in brightly painted trees.
On the linen slip-covers of the many square upholstered

chairs armoured warriors marched and countermarched in red and green. The effect was agitated and entirely ugly.

Still, there was a suspect glamour about the place. Some relics of the old regime even gave an amused pleasure to Harry Morgan whose own origins had been simple enough. In the confused days before the final surrender of the Italians at Routa Routa, the Italian Viceroy's chauffeur had had the presence of mind to drive a magnificent black Lancia through the mountain passes, and surrender both himself and it to the British headquarters in Aderra. Sitting stiff and silent in the front passenger seat had been the Duke's Aderran major-domo, too shocked by his master's inexplicable overthrow to realize how little his life was likely to be worth to the victorious patriots. It was the chauffeur, Colomboroli, who had taken pity on him and brought him to sanctuary. Now ten years later, the Lancia, with Colomboroli still at the wheel and Union Jacks fluttering from the mudguards, was the grandest of the three vehicles at Harry Morgan's disposal.

The major-domo, with his cropped curls turned grey, his silence and his air of puzzled gravity more deeply settled, still waited at table in white cotton gloves, and ran his reduced staff of eleven servants to an immaculate standard, as if at any moment his true master might return and ask account of him. It was wiser, Lydia found, once she had overcome an initial zeal to change things, to surrender to the benign rule of the major-domo. It had been foolish to suppose that he

would permit any whim of hers to alter the smooth
routines established long ago. Her very death would not
have been allowed to delay lunch. Without a word
exchanged they had settled into a peaceful coexistence
based on mutual respect.

Such as it was, the villa represented the climax of
Harry Morgan's career. At the end of this mission he
would retire from public service in Africa. It puzzled
Lydia, and she knew it disappointed him, that she had
never really settled here. It was the first house they
had shared where she had failed to unpack the six black
wooden ammunition boxes in which were packed their
personal possessions. Their marriage was still compara-
tively recent, barely six years old. Among the relics of
Lydia's former life in Frant Road were items with some
particular and private memory attached to them: a set
of ebony elephants diminishing in size, a silver ashtray
beaten out around a Maria Theresa dollar, his shy early
gifts.

She knew, without his ever saying so, that he would
like to see such things scattered about the villa to establish that it was really his. Nevertheless the ammunition
boxes remained stacked in the corner of the upstairs
sitting-room with their metal bands nailed in place. As
Flo's arrival approached, Lydia had wondered if she
should hunt out a few of the old treasures from Frant
Road to make her feel at home, but she delayed and
told herself there was no point now. Their stay in Aderra
had never been intended to last more than a single year.
From its start Morgan's task had been directed towards

the day, now only six months hence, when he must hand over his administration in the south to an Aderran governor from the Northern Province. Aderra was to be federated to its more powerful neighbour. Without an army, with little more than a subsistence economy, its frail autonomy was to be ensured by a United Nations charter. The British mandate was to avoid bloodshed before the handover; to hold an election and establish a constitution that might hope to lessen the near certainty of bloodshed afterwards. To be packed in readiness to leave from the very start, Lydia told herself, was merely prudent.

In truth the villa was so impersonal that, until Flo's arrival, Lydia had simply ceased to see it. She lived in it as she might have done aboard an ocean liner; one upright steamer trunk wedged open in the corner of the cabin, friendships made recklessly because they need not endure, the days filled with unproductive activity, all sense of being at sea lost for hours at a time. Then one would catch the primitive smell of heated paint, or wake to hear the creaking strain of the great ship at night, or see the placid disc of soup lurch without warning and spill on the starched white tablecloth and know oneself to be in a position that was both abnormal and dangerous. So it was here, if ever Lydia Morgan permitted herself to think too closely of her husband's job. Therefore, although she was an intelligent woman, she did not.

Instead she filled her days as best she might. In the mornings the major-domo came to receive his orders for the day. What was she to say to him? She knew nothing of this viceregal style of life. He was expert in it. Besides, he was her friend. She trusted him. They smiled at one another. It sufficed. He was followed by the cook. She would finger the pages of her mother's *Mrs Beeton* and explain the recipes to him in a patient mixture of Italian and Arabic, neither of which languages he would admit to understanding. Twice a week there was a dinner party to arrange for the senior British officials and their wives, the colonel of the regiment, consuls of the various foreign legations, members of the United Nations Commission and occasional visitors from London or the Northern Province. The table sat fourteen. '*Va bene?*' she would say to the major-domo. '*Va bene, Signora.*' He saw to everything.

In the week preceding Flo's arrival, seeing her life through what she imagined might be Flo's eyes, she was shocked to discover the extent to which she had withdrawn from all but official engagements. Her friends, the people she had mentioned in the car to Flo, came privately to see her, usually for a drink before lunch on Saturdays when the work of the week was ended. With the rest she shunned daytime meetings as being too prodigal with what little there would be to say in the evening. Particularly she avoided contact with the wives of the other British officials, who, it seemed for want of wider issues, talked endlessly of gynaecological dramas within themselves. She resisted invitations to tea and bridge, although she loved the game, and in the afternoon retreated to the villa's upstairs sitting-room.

There, with a cotton dressing-gown over her slip and her hair pinned high on her head to free her from its heat, with dance tunes crackling over the unboxed wireless set, she played the games of patience by which she attempted to ward off evil from those she loved.

'If it comes out,' she had told Flo at the card-table in the drawing-room at Frant Road, 'we will win the war.'

If it comes out, she had told herself in the grim sixth winter of her widowhood, Harry Morgan will marry me.

Now, on the rare occasions when she permitted herself to think of Harry Morgan's present job, she was tempted to say, If it comes out, Harry will bring it off . . . But that seemed too precarious. What if some error of hers, some fumbling of the black six on the red seven should bring all he had accomplished crumbling down? She would not risk it. She swept the cards over the edge of the table, caught them in her other hand, tapped them side and bottom and set them out again. But she was not without courage. If it comes out, she had told herself that very morning, Flo will get here safely. I'll have her back again.

And now it was so. The double doors of the villa were thrown open as they came up the steps. The major-domo appeared, smiling and bowing to greet them. 'This is my child,' Lydia said to him. 'My child has come.' It will be different now, she told herself, hurrying past him. There will be a purpose to it. It was as if, in showing the villa to Flo, she too was seeing it for the first time. She found herself thinking with a real regret how soon it would all be over.

Flo felt the old man's light dry touch on her hand and watched the painful shift of wrinkles when he smiled. The hallway behind him smelt of beeswax and continental cigarettes, of water freshly dried on marble floors; the smell of the hotel in Malta, a pleasant transitory smell. She followed as her mother ran forward, throwing open door after door. A dining-room, a study, a sitting-room. 'Isn't it incredible?' her mother said. 'Would you believe those monkeys? And wait till you see this!'

On the far side of the sitting-room she pushed open a pair of glass and wrought-iron doors. When Flo followed her through them she found that they were standing on the dais of a room that stretched the entire length of the house. The walls and floors were lined with pale pink marble. The tall windows were shielded with thick net curtains. Set between them pink-tinted mirrors faced others on the opposite wall. Three elaborate cut-glass chandeliers hung from the ceiling. 'Isn't it dreadful?' Lydia said. But it was wonderful too. They both knew that. It touched on something one supposed one wanted, but never thought to be confronted with.

'What is it for?' Flo asked her mother. Her voice scarcely rose above a whisper for awe.

'It's for dancing,' Lydia said recklessly. 'We'll have a dance. A kind of coming out. For you, Flo.'

Flo walked down the shallow steps as cautiously as

someone entering an untested pool. Immediately the facing mirrors snatched at her, so that it seemed on either side there curved away a queue of other Flos, each one smaller and less distinct than the last. She did not care to look at them. She did not care to listen to her mother who had run back into the sitting-room to ring for lunch and now called out to her something about a man she had met at a party. It all might wait, another day and another day while the world regained its sanity and the old, child's sense of being secure and central to the scheme of things might be restored.

That evening when Harry Morgan returned from the office they celebrated their belated Christmas. After that for a week they never left the villa and nobody, except of course Harry Morgan, intruded on their privacy. 'Will you forgive us?' Flo heard her mother say on the telephone. 'Could we soon? You do understand? It's just so long since I've had her to myself.' Each time it seemed to Flo she had been issued with a reprieve from an outside world in which she had no interest.

They talked, or rather Lydia talked. It seemed that she would never come to the end of the things that over the past months she had wanted to say, but had had no Flo to say them to. 'Oh, Wendy Waller is intolerable,' she could say to Flo, and repeat the foolish thing that Wendy Waller had said. And Flo watching her attentively would smile unquestioning agreement. All the hurtful things that rankle in the mind came out. The

cruel thing a man had said to her years ago, when she
went out a bride to Nairobi, about a hat she was wearing. Why tell Flo that? And yet the moment she did
she felt relieved of it. And a woman at a party just a
week ago. No one she knew, but British, and drunk,
would you believe it? And wearing such a dress! 'Why
Flo, you could see where her navel was!' The words
seemed crude even as she spoke them, but Flo was
shaking her head in amused disapproval. Oh, the comfort of her! Why do I never ask her about herself? the
mother thought. But what should she ask? And besides
Flo was looking at her with the same eager attention
she had had as a child to anything that Lydia might say.

The days were all the same. The sun shone until
noon. Then clouds surged up the mountainside and
overtook the town. For two hours it rained. The odour
of wet dust clung in the throat and disturbed the shuttered afternoon. It was then that Lydia pinned up her
hair and set out her cards. Now there was no need for
the wireless. There was Flo, sitting with her long legs
hanging sideways over the arm of a chair. They had
begun to talk about carefully selected portions of that
past of which they alone knew the existence.

'Do you remember that dreadful flat?' Lydia said
once.

'Oh yes,' said Flo and laughed, although secretly she
had loved that flat. She and her mother had lived there
undisturbed for an entire winter after the war. Granny
Franklyn had died. The house in Frant Road had been
sold. The furniture and ornaments which had stayed in

their appointed places since Lydia was a child had been packed away and sent to the depository. Later Flo had come to understand that this was the nadir of their fortunes. At the time she had only been aware of an intense happiness which she had supposed would not end.

A single box had been withheld from the depository, containing Flo's collection of china cats. Each had its name and distinct invented character. Over each, as over nothing else before or since, she exercised complete control. Once they had been set out on the mantelpiece of the ugly little sitting-room she had felt entirely at home. She and Lydia had walked about the threadbare carpets in stockinged feet and dressing-gowns. Her mother's hair had been shorter then, russet coloured and springy. She would sit with remarkable patience while Flo brushed it and arranged it this way and that. Lydia would sit watching her altered image in the glass, smoking steadily and thinking thoughts that Flo might not be privy to.

They had done everything together then. They went to Harrods on the bus and looked at the cats and parrots in their cages. Flo wore a tweed coat with a stitched velvet collar and its matching velvet beret, handed down from Daisy Mayhew's sister's child. They went to the National Gallery and searched for the lion that always lurked somewhere in the paintings of St Jerome. Lydia read her a poem about a lion, and Flo to please her had secretly learned it off by heart and said it to her on her birthday.

Only once had Lydia suddenly put on her coat and gone out alone. Flo, lying on her stomach reading in front of the gas fire, had felt a mild alarm as the yellow twilight thickened and settled in the street outside. She had turned on the lights, but not drawn the curtains, liking to imagine her mother hurrying towards the lighted windows. Later, uncertain as to how much time had passed, she had leant on the sill with her breath clouding the glass and her nostrils filled with the cold metallic smell of leading.

When Lydia came back she merely said, 'I went out to buy some nail varnish.' Without taking off her coat, she sat on the sofa, pulled off her shoes, rolled down her stockings and, with her knees bent up under her chin, began to paint each toe with blood-red varnish. Then she had painted her fingernails. Her absorption in the task, the effort needed to keep the little brush steady, excluded Flo entirely, but Flo had been aware that it excluded something else that threatened them both.

Later she came to understand that these were months of ultimatum when her mother had refused to see Harry Morgan until he broke off an engagement to another woman, formed before the war, and married her. As soon as that letter came the little china cats had been packed up again; the flat locked up; the keys returned to the agent; her mother's passage booked to Cairo and Nairobi and Flo dispatched to the boarding-school.

All this in all its detail came back to her between

one sentence and the next. Now she said abruptly, 'Why haven't you unpacked the boxes?'

'There isn't time,' Lydia said.

'I could do it.'

'Oh, there's too much else to do,' her mother said, rising with sudden energy. It was four o'clock already. Sunlight again fell from a cloudless sky. It was time to go down to tea. Through the open windows of the downstairs sitting-room they heard the crunch of the Lancia's tyres on the gravel drive and presently Harry Morgan's gruff exchange with the major-domo in the hall and the clip of his heels on the marble floor. He came into the home rubbing his hands as if to raise a lather, saying in a pleased voice, 'Ah, tea!' as if he had not expected to find the coffee-table spread with a white cloth, or known with an absolute certainty that at just that moment the major-domo would enter with his rattling tea tray.

'How did it go today?' Lydia would ask him, always with a note of alarm in her voice that begged to be assuaged.

'Not too bad really.' He would begin to tell her what had happened at the office and immediately Flo would cease to listen, although their voices accompanied her thoughts like the wash of a distant sea. Sometimes Harry Morgan caught her eye and, without interrupting what he was saying, winked at her in a companionable way. She smiled at him.

Promptly at six night fell. They went upstairs to bathe and change for dinner. In the dark Flo ran the length of the balcony outside her bedroom and hung over the balustrade. Brilliant naked light-bulbs illuminated the sentry boxes. The invisible garden released its scents. 'Are you all right?' they asked her repeatedly, Lydia and kindly Harry Morgan. 'Are you sure you don't feel the altitude?' When she breathed in, her lungs felt shallow. She did feel strange, but relished this strangeness.

At night, in the moments before sleep when the mind still keeps some control of dreams, pictures of the past appeared without warning. Perhaps that too was an effect of altitude. She might have asked but did not, to avoid being questioned. Once, just as she fell asleep, her real father, Edward Wharton, stood behind her throwing bread to a swan whose black feet trod the dark waters of a shallow pond. The bread lodged on its back between the wings. Its neck writhed like a snake in the frustration of being unable to reach it. Its black beak snatched again and again. She thought that Edward Wharton had aimed it there on purpose. Behind her she heard him laugh.

There was a stiffened flap inside the lid of her suitcase where she kept a cardboard sheet of forty tiny photographs of Edward Wharton, taken in a Polyfoto booth, with his head turned this way and that way, smiling and serious. One of the smiling ones had been enlarged and stood in a frame on Lydia's dressing-table until she married Harry Morgan when it had been put away. Nor did Flo study the little images as once she had. Neither separately nor together could she make them into the man who tormented the swan in that solitary memory.

Next morning she said to Lydia, 'Did Major Denbigh know my father?'

'Do you mean Edward?'

'Yes.' She had been so young and he had been so much abroad that she had had no childish name for him.

'Whatever makes you ask that?' Lydia said. She bent the cards slowly and deliberately as she set them down to ensure the line was absolutely true. 'Did he say something?'

'He said that he knew Harry,' the girl said vaguely.

'Ah, Harry. Yes, I think he did. Not well. He's not Harry's type really, is he? Isn't he a card?' She began to tell Flo something one of the secretaries in the London office had told her about Tommy Denbigh at a race meeting before the war. What a thing to tell the child, she thought. But Flo had laughed.

'Won't you be bored?' Lydia said to Flo. 'Won't you be lonely?' For after the first rush of talk between them was exhausted she found Flo quiet. But Flo was entirely content. Still in the seconds of half-consciousness before she was fully awake, it seemed that the boarding-school, with its mingled odour of wallflowers and girlish sweat, its particular blend of piety and malice, must lie in wait to repossess her. Then she would hear the cheerful banging and clattering from the servants' quarters and know that she was safe, her former life left far below under the thick protective wadding of the clouds.

Chapter Three

THEY COULD not go on like this, not seeing anyone, fending people off. 'We'll have a party,' Lydia said. 'Just a few friends. You must meet Gerda.' She had not talked with Gerda for a week now and already she missed her. 'And Geoffrey and the Wallers. We must, you know. Bridie's just a year or two older. She'll be a friend. Besides, they know so many people. They'll introduce you.'

The girl was looking at her doubtfully. It's her hair, her mother thought. Perhaps if it were cut well. She looked speculatively at Flo, arranging in her mind the straight brown hair one way and another. Instantly she saw her own anxiety reflected in the girl's expression and continued bravely, 'I've just the young man for you. I met him at a party and I thought at once, he'll do for Flo.'

Flo sat there with her legs thrown over the arm of the chair and, it seemed to Lydia, an utter lack of some necessary awareness. She must try, the mother thought. She'll get nowhere if she doesn't try. 'Of course, he's far too old,' she added quickly, 'but he'll make you laugh.' Later that morning Flo heard her mother on the telephone. 'Thursday week, then,' she was saying. 'Yes. Yes, she is.'

Putting down the receiver she said suddenly to Flo, 'Do you remember that lovely coat you had, with the velvet collar? There was a hat that matched it.' The sight of her child dressed as other people's children were came back to her. 'How sweet you looked.' Looking at her now she thought how it said in magazines that overnight they changed at this age. Overnight they became enchanting. But not perhaps by Thursday week. Nevertherless a good frock could do no harm. She dialled the number of Signora Ponticelli, the best Italian dressmaker in the town, and made an appointment for that very afternoon.

Haile drove them in the Chevrolet to a street behind the Corso and Lydia rang the bell of what might have been an ordinary house. The signora greeted them eagerly and led them upstairs to a sunny workroom lined with shelves of untouched fabric wrapped in bolts. There was to be a dress for the signorina to wear at evening parties and to dances. Signora Ponticelli cocked her head to one side and regarded Flo. '*Cara,*' she said to Lydia. '*Carissima!*' It seemed a hopeful beginning. Now the dressmaker began dragging from the shelves bolts of fine tulle. She snatched up fistfuls of the stuff and held them up to Flo, while their bolts went rattling across the table, blues, pinks, greens. 'You must choose for yourself,' Lydia cried.

Without hesitation Flo's hand went out to a rich

water-melon pink. She dared not crush it as the signora had, but lifted it cautiously to her cheek and stared, awestruck, into the signora's long pier-glass.

'Oh, too strong, too strong,' Lydia cried. 'It would wipe you out. Don't you think so, Signora?' Over her shoulder in the mirror Flo watched the signora's face grow thoughtful. 'Perhaps not yet. Perhaps in a year or two.'

'Oh no,' the mother said. 'Never. It isn't you, Flo. It would take such living up to.'

Flo stood with the flagrant pink still held to her cheek, seeing only the imaginary dress, unable to see herself. Now the tactful signora darted forward with a crisp white organdie and held it up to the other cheek while gently releasing the pink. '*Bella*,' she said decisively. '*Bella*.' Care must be taken, the two women agreed, lest the finished effect appear too bridal. They sat in armchairs by the window and consulted Italian fashion magazines. Eventually it was decided that the dress should have no sleeves and a high-standing collar. They were to come again for a first fitting in two days' time and a final fitting four days after that. The appointments and Flo's measurements were carefully noted down. There was no question of its not being ready by the following Thursday. Then, just as they were leaving, Lydia's glance fell on a turquoise linen of a shade she had often worn at Flo's age. Feeling in an obscure way that something more was owed to Flo, she ordered a short frock to be made up from that, at the signora's convenience, when the other was finished.

Just as promised the white dress, sewn, pressed and wrapped in tissue paper, was delivered to the villa on the following Thursday afternoon. Flo tried it on. She found she liked the crisp feel of the stuff and the intimacy of its perfect fit against her back when she did up the buttons. She studied the dress in the glass and was entirely satisfied to find it seemed more real than she. She looked at her face. That was unchanged, but perhaps the unknown people approaching the villa through the darkened streets might see her in ways that she had never seen herself. She looked away. A burden was lifted from her. She had become invisible again.

In the morning and the evening birds had racketed in the rhododendron thickets in Granny Franklyn's garden. Flo had wanted then to be invisible so that she might move closer and closer to them without sending them battering off through the leaves. She listened to them. 'Cat. Cat. Cat,' they shouted sometimes, but no single other word they spoke would yield its meaning to her. She learned phrases of their song and practised whistling them, taking great care with the pitch and timing. A pause. Then miraculously from out of sight behind the leaves the sound would be repeated. Immediately she feared the unknown words she had spoken. Perhaps they had been wicked or insulting. When the birds pitched their voices all together, like marbles shaken in a jar, she thought they jeered at her. Later, in the boarding-school, the fear of saying the wrong thing to the other girls had grown acute. She spoke as little as she could and found that as she grew more silent, their inexplicable hostilities, the constant babble of their voices grew indistinct and nearly tolerable.

Now, in Aderra, she sat on the edge of the bed with her arm across the lap of the white dress so that she could watch the minutes pass around her wristwatch. She waited for Harry and Lydia to finish dressing for the dinner party and wondered what it was that these people would find to say to one another.

'Is there time for a cigarette?' Harry Morgan asked his wife.

'Just,' she said over her shoulder. 'If you're quick.'

Not worth it, he thought, and slipped the cigarette case back into his pocket. He had had the first whisky of the evening brought to the upstairs sitting-room and drank it, leaning in the open door to the large balcony that lay above the ceiling of the ballroom, half of him in the lighted room, half in the mild, dark night.

Through the door of the bedroom he watched his wife burrow in a drawer for a scarf, take an earring from a box and hold it questioningly to her cheek. She came alive at night. He liked to watch her like this when she was unaware of him. It felt like spying and awakened a tired sensuousness that made these glimpses of her seem like memories. Her back, bare between the straps of her evening frock, was turned towards him. He liked to watch the delicate line of bones just showing through the depth of freckled flesh. He liked the coarse sweet-smelling hair which she let loose in the cool evenings. He felt the impulse to cross the room and lift it to his face and smell it, but he thought, No, better not, no time. The guests would be there soon, 'Will Flo cope all right?' he called across to her.

'Why shouldn't she?'

'I only thought that she might be bored with everyone so much older.'

'Bridie's not *much* older.'

'Oh God, are they coming?'

'I told you,' she said, glancing across her shoulder. 'Flo must meet them. They know all those subalterns. I don't.'

'Has that begun?' he said and laughed. 'For Flo?'

'Don't be unkind. She's only shy. She has to learn. Everyone does. It has to begin somewhere.'

'I suppose it must.'

'I've asked Roland Routh tonight,' she said. And then as if the two things were in some way connected, 'I thought we'd have our coffee in the ballroom for a change.'

'Why him? He's not particularly young?'

'You don't like him, do you?'

It startled Morgan to discover that no, he did not. Routh had been foisted on him by the Foreign Office quite recently, too late in the proceedings to be easily integrated. Someone's relative, he guessed, who needed to be got abroad. He had that look and yet so far had worked hard and efficiently enough. So far so good and God knew, he needed all the help he could get. To make amends for his dislike he said, 'He's damned good at his job.'

Then, rather than discuss Roland Routh further, he went out on to the balcony.

The image of his wife was still powerfully with him. Passion had come late to him. It had seemed a miraculous thing. Now he sometimes thought, I shouldn't have to feel, not at my age, not with all the rest there is to do.

One step, another and he was startlingly alone, staring up at the dark sky and the close bright stars. He was a big man, whose blondness, so striking in his youth, was growing indistinct. He had been a cricketer. People still said to him, 'Were you *that* Harry Morgan? I hadn't realized.' It always pleased him. Now all that former prowess hung unneeded from his heavy frame, but you could still see it in the conviction of his bearing: that early knowledge that he was stronger and more skilful than the other boys, at the thing that mattered most. It was there in his ease of movement, his lack of haste, his withheld anger.

Now, when for a moment no one watched him, he polished up an imaginary cricket-ball along the corded seam of his evening trousers, took three long skipping strides and bowled it into the night with a final twist of his straightened fingers. He thought he'd have a cigarette after all and leant over the balcony to smoke it.

The haze of light about the sentry boxes quite obscured the town beyond, but knowing that it was there, he seemed to hear a hum of expectancy rise from it; a babel of voices demanding from him some indistinguishable benefit. My God, but I'm tired, he thought. But tiredness had ceased to worry him. It was his familiar, his wartime comrade. He had the measure of it; could trust it in a way. He continued to stand there taking slow swallows of the warm smoke, letting nothing hurry him. He imagined the lighted Corso and the great darkened mass of the plateau lying beyond the town; the sheer drop of the escarpment to the sea on one side and the desert on the other, all of it so vast that it swallowed up any human movement, any human voice. But they were there all right, as he well knew, squatting at this very moment about their low aromatic fires, sitting on pavements under the poor light of street lamps, crowded in beershops, wanting God knew what of him; hoping God knew what would come to them on the day of his departure.

This morning there had been a set-back, the first in months. Two women had been reported murdered in a village in the great hinterland beyond the road that ran between the town and the sea. By some fluke the bandits had been captured. The police corporal at Heziga had phoned through to say that he was on his way there to organize the clearing of a runway. He would, he had promised, do his best to keep the suspects alive until Morgan himself could get there. Of necessity the women must be buried but he had instructions to take careful note of their injuries.

He must fly down there in the morning and deal with it. There was never any telling which way these things would go. A fresh outbreak of violence might hold up the election by a month, two months. Now he seemed to hear another sound, a persistent ticking like a clock buried under a pillow. It's the tiredness, he told himself. It's nothing. They won't stay late tonight. I'll take something. I'll sleep. He tossed the cigarette away and watched its bright trajectory into the darkened garden. Then he went back into the sitting-room and said, 'I forgot to tell you. I'm flying tomorrow.'

'Trouble?' Lydia said. She put down her hairbrush with a clatter and turned to look at him.

'Not really. An incident in a village near Heziga.'

Her face was blank with alarm. 'You'll be safe?'

'I'll have Broad with me. You're not to worry.'

'I can't help worrying. You know I hate it when you fly.'

'You have Flo.'

'Yes,' she said, with an odd little laugh that he could not interpret. 'I have Flo.' Then suddenly turning to the travelling-clock on her dressing-table she said, 'Oh God, look at the time. They'll be here any minute.' She snatched up her little golden evening purse and ran ahead of him out of the room calling, 'Flo, Flo, hurry. We'll be late.'

Downstairs the major-domo had already opened the front door to the first of the evening's guests. Earlier he had chosen the wine and supervised the gardener while he laid out a pattern of crimson bougainvillaea blossoms

on the white tablecloth. He had overseen the elaborate
arrangement of cutlery and glass, and had himself folded
the starched napkins into fans at the centre of each
setting. Now encased in white cotton tunic, trousers
and gloves he stood by the front door with Amde, the
third boy, a few paces behind him. They talked to one
another in the quiet sporadic way of two men with
much in common.

The door into the drawing-room was open and
through it the second boy, Hassan, could be seen
intercepting Roland Routh's efforts to light his own
cigarette. It was Routh's first summons to the villa.
Fearful of being late, he had arrived absurdly early. What
could he do? Pace up and down in the full glare of
the sentry boxes? He had braved the steps, the hall, the
major-domo, and now this empty room. To his relief
he heard the doorbell ring.

Geoffrey Wheeler had arrived, the number two in
the legal department. He always came a little early,
partly out of a feeling that it was very good of them to
ask him at all, partly to lay claim to that family intimacy
which he needed to feel accepted anywhere. 'Major-
domo,' he said genially, *'come sta?'* The old man gave a
twitch of a smile and bowed a number of times.
Wheeler walked noisily across the marble floor, nodding
to Amde and Hassan. 'God, it does one good, all this
bowing and scraping,' he said to Roland Routh.

What's he doing here? he thought. He had met
Routh a number of times in meetings about the legal
aspects of the forthcoming election, but had not

particularly warmed to him. Now, he supposed, if Lydia had taken him up, he would have to try to like him. How odd of her, he thought. Where is she? Why doesn't she come down? Then he remembered the daughter and his obscure discomfort vanished. Of course, she had asked Routh for the daughter. He held up a restraining hand to Hassan who had sprung forward with a heavy alabaster box of cigarettes. 'I've given them up,' he explained to Routh. 'It's so I can take them up again at the end, when the panic's on.'

'Need there be a panic?'

'There usually is.' He had sunk back into his chair in a posture of exaggerated ease, with one black shoe and sock cocked over the other black knee, his head thrown back against the uncomfortable upholstery so that the light caught the lenses of his spectacles and made his eyes invisible. 'You heard about the incident?'

'I thought that sort of thing had stopped,' Routh said.

'Well, of course it never stops. Not entirely. Bandits, patriots, whatever you care to call them. They're always there. It's how they live. But this was ugly. Two women finished off rather unpleasantly.'

'I'd gathered,' Routh said. 'But surely it's all much better than it was? From what I hear.' He was a small, neat-featured man, good-looking in his way, hiding his nervousness with that brittle self-esteem that the public schools could still provide. Which one? Wheeler peered at Routh's tie, but found it told him nothing. Not open, he thought. More complicated than that. He cast a shadow of some sort. Wheeler remembered someone had said he was RC or had been. 'Indeed it is,' he said. 'Harry's clamped right down on them. You wouldn't think it of him really.'

'Oh, I don't know,' Routh said.

'Not that he has much choice. He has to have it all tied up by June. That's the job.'

'You don't think people choose their jobs?'

Wheeler laughed. 'That's too deep for me.' He held out his empty glass towards Hassan. There were sounds of fresh arrivals in the hall. Wendy Waller's commanding voice could be heard saying, 'Hello, Major-domo. How are you?' Dreadful woman, Wheeler thought. And he's such a stick. And Bridie, a prune of a girl. How England breeds them!'

Behind them came the Wertheimers. He heard Gerda Sondheimer exclaim, 'Oh, those monkeys, they fill me with despair!'

What a collection, he thought and remembered ruefully how slowly the day had passed in expectation of an evening at the villa.

Then he heard Lydia's breathy voice call over the stairs, 'Oh, do forgive us. We're late! We're late to our own party.' Immediately he felt the braced-up contentment her presence always gave him, and thought, Well, here we are again. How very jolly!

Lydia too was wondering whatever had induced her to ask this particular group of people to spend an evening in each other's company. What an error! She could imagine them standing in the room below, expression-less, indifferent to her, indifferent to one another, indif-ferent to Flo, who had at that moment come out of her room and stood at the head of the stairs, awkward and unappealing in her virginal frock. Even the white organdie was a mistake, the mother thought, smiling and hurrying past her down the stairs. For so long she had been sustained by the thought of Flo, the repository of all that was good in her, safe between the laundered sheets of the boarding-school. Now as she crossed the hall the casual cruelty of the world caught her by the heart and she thought, To what have I exposed her?

But there was no turning back. 'You're here, you're here,' she cried, hurrying into the room and seizing each hand as if it offered her only hope of rescue. But it was she who must rescue them; must lift from them the weight of their resistance to being good to one another and, glancing at Flo, she saw her as something alien and intractable that added to the weight.

'How sweet Bridie looks,' she said to Wendy Waller at the same moment that Wendy Waller fixed her preda-tory eye on Flo and said, 'What a charming frock. Ponticelli, isn't it? I thought it was.'

'It was awful when I first came out,' she heard Bridie say to Flo. 'Before I knew anyone.' The girl's plump face appeared quite stricken.

That is why I asked them, Lydia thought: because of Flo and Bridie and all those subalterns. Out of the corner of her eye she noticed Roland Routh leaning

against the mantelpiece, drinking his whisky too
quickly, looking as if when he had drained his glass he
would walk out in disgust. He isn't young at all, she
thought. Whatever made me think he was? 'You came,'
she said and smiled at him.

'I'm most impressed,' he told her in an undertone,
circling his eyes around the vulgar room. He mocked
it, of course. Still she thought he was drawn up a little,
uncertain how to speak to her, and she for the moment
was too distracted to stay with him. Her ears gauged
the strength of conversation in the room. How frail it
was; how hesitant still. 'More drink, more drink,' she
said to Hassan as he passed her with his tray.

Now, just as she might have lost heart altogether,
her dear Gerda Sondheimer cried out, 'So this is Flo!'
and caught Flo's chin on her finger to turn her face to
the lamp. She said across the girl's shoulder, 'I did not
know such faces still existed. So empty, so innocent of
everything!' And Lydia caught her friend impetuously
by the arms and kissed her for understanding that. This
is my child, she wanted to say to Gerda Sondheimer,
whose mind is my mind; who is my witness, as I am
hers, that the world is how we think it is. Instead she
turned to say to Rudi Sondheimer, 'I thought you
might not manage it.' He had been in New York, but
he kissed her hand and assured her that he had come
back especially to be with her tonight. He had brought
her a record, of the latest Broadway hit.

'Oh, how lovely! Flo, look!' Perhaps if she directed
the girl to put it on the gramophone, animation would

flood into the room and Flo appear to be the source of it. But what if everyone stopped talking altogether to listen to it? 'Oh, thank you, thank you,' she said, kissing him on his scented cheek and setting the record firmly on a side-table.

Now Geoffrey, who could always be counted on, had come across the room and was saying to Flo, 'I scored tonight. Do you know the rules yet? Five points if the major-domo recognizes you at all; ten if he smiles.'

And Clive Waller was saying to Harry, 'I say, weren't you in Cairo at the end of the war? I had a letter today from a chap . . .' And Rudi Sondheimer was kissing Wendy Waller's hand. Still she must not rest. The germ of silence might yet catch and spread; might stifle the bright forces of talk and laughter. 'Won't you have a peanut?' she beseeched them each in turn. Then seeing Bridie standing patient and alone she handed her the dish and said, 'Bridie, dear, would you mind passing these around? Just while the servants are busy with the drinks.' For the risk of anyone staying still and silent for a moment was too great to take.

To Routh as she passed him she said out of the corner of her mouth, 'Go and talk to Bridie Waller.' Surely he was taller than that, she thought, or were we sitting down? No, she remembered he had walked beside her down a corridor in the Circolo Italiano; buoyant then and unabashed, talking eagerly about his work. What energy he had put into talking! It was that that had made her think him young. He had carried in his pocket a novel which she had liked and he, he said, detested. Nevertheless, when she defended it, he had cried out, 'Point taken. Point taken,' with evident delight. And when she had asked him about himself, she had seen that other thing: that pause, that wistful consideration, some disproportionate sorrow, like a child's.

Remembering that, she took pity on him and said to Rudi Wertheimer, 'Do go and rescue Roland Routh. You'll like him. He's very bright. You can talk to him.'

Just for a moment Geoffrey Wheeler laid his warm hand against her back. Just for a moment she allowed the tension to go out of her. What a touch he had, that gave and asked for nothing. She had known him in Nairobi before the war. 'Is it all right?' she asked him.

'Of course it is. It always is.'

'And what do you make of my Flo?'

'Who *is* she like?' he said. He was shy of asking if she were like her father whom he had never known.

'You don't think she's like me?'

'In some ways. The smile,' he said, smiling himself. 'When it comes.' He wondered if she would expect more, but apparently that satisfied her. 'Will she find enough to do here?'

'Oh, it will be wonderful for her! Don't you believe that every life has one special year in it? One marvellous year that is the making of all the others?'

'I'd never thought.' His own life had been a chequer-ed affair, much of it unknown to Lydia, who supposed she knew him well. But she was not thinking of him at all. She was thinking how this was to be Flo's year;

how Harry's year was the second year of the war before she ever knew him; how hers had been long before that.

'Oh, that year in Nairobi,' she said to him. 'Do you ever think of it?' He laughed to cover the fact that he did remember, with astonishing force, an episode in the passage of the clubhouse in Nairobi. That the same recollection might be at that moment in her mind seemed almost an indecency. She was saying, 'Do you remember that play?'

'I try so hard to forget it!'

But her attention had reverted to her party. At last it seemed that the sound of voices in the room had reached a pitch that might generate its own energy and keep aloft without her. It was safe. She reached for the first drink of the evening from Amde's tray and swallowed the clean, cold gin, thinking, How could I have doubted them? It's what we want, all of us, to be given the chance to be good to one another. The major-domo bowed before her and said, 'Dinner is ready.' She clapped her hands above her head to make herself heard and called out, 'Dinner! Dinner is ready!'

The ritual was set in motion. There was nothing more required of her other than to talk to her right and to her left, while the deft white sleeves of the servants reached between, shifting plates, pouring wine, providing just that necessary punctuation, so that it was possible to break off the conversation to the left before it flagged and turn quite naturally to the conversation on the right.

Immediately Clive Waller began to tell her how his

friend in Cairo, the one who had written to him, had been in Shepheard's Hotel on the very day the mob had burnt it down as being a symbol of Foreign Imperialism. 'The British Council offices are fair game,' he said. 'But dear old Shepheard's!'

'Shepheard's,' she said. 'What a shock that was!' and she smiled down the table at Harry, thinking of a time they had stayed there just after their marriage. But he was attending to whatever Wendy Waller was saying with that particular brightness of eye that meant he longed to be asleep. Clive Waller was telling her how his friend had thought, Oh, it's just another riot, and settled into the bar to wait until it was over; but in the end they had been lucky to get out alive. 'Lost all his kit, though,' he said indignantly.

'Shepheard's,' she said again. 'Who would have thought it?'

'What next?' he said. 'That's what I'd like to know. If Shepheard's goes, what's next?'

From the corner of her eye she saw that Flo was staring at the candles in the middle of the table and not talking to Roland Routh at all. What can have possessed me, she thought, even to have thought of it. She's still a child.

'What next indeed?' she said to Clive Waller.

Now, as Hassan extracted her plate with the knife and the fork, the fish's spine laid neatly side beside, she turned to Rudi Sondheimer saying, 'How was New York?' He told her how beautiful it was; how untouched, how ignorant, how bold the flags were in the streets, how the steam still rose out of the pavements and the air still smelt of coffee. 'How lovely,' she said and glanced again at Flo, and saw her this time as she might have seen some stranger in a foreign street and thought to her astonishment, How pretty she is! For the miracle appeared to have occurred. Flo had turned her eager look on to Roland Routh and he was talking so intently that his fork, with a piece of chicken speared on it, hung motionless above his plate. Thank God, she thought; then, What does he find to say to her?

Chapter Four

SIMPLY, ROLAND Routh had turned to Flo and said, 'We are expected to talk about something. What shall it be?'

'I don't know,' Flo told him. 'I find it most awfully difficult.'

'Do you?' he said with apparent interest. 'I've always talked a lot.' He gave her no opportunity to answer but hurried on. 'What can you possibly make of all of this? But perhaps you're used to it. Perhaps it all seems perfectly normal? Perhaps you've always lived like this.'

She laughed then, a loud childish laugh, so that her mother, catching her eye from the other end of the table laid her finger affectionately on her lips. Flo's own fingers immediately slid upwards like bars across her mouth but from behind them she continued to smile at Roland Routh. He was looking at her so cleverly and attentively. Rather it seemed he looked right through her for the thing her words must presently reveal. 'It's much better than school,' she said.

He laughed as if she had said something remarkably

witty. 'I hated school,' he told her. 'But then the other
boys disliked me so. I don't even think about it. I forgot
it the moment I left.'

'I think of it sometimes when I first wake up.'

'Oh, so do I. Of course I do, along with other
things.' His voice had become thin and detached.
'When I'm particularly low I think there might have
been something in it after all. That they might have been
quite right about me.' He smiled at her. 'That's only
when things are very bad.'

She said in sympathy, 'The headmistress where I
went was mad.'

'Yes,' he said. 'I believe they often are. You rejected
it, of course. You rebelled.'

'No,' Flo said.

'Of course you did. You're too intelligent. Tell me
the worst thing that you did there.'

She had no difficulty in choosing. There had been
a long blue runner on the altar steps. It had been her
duty, on one particular day, to sweep it with a dustpan
and brush and then fold the ends to the middle. 'Why
do you suppose it mattered so?' she asked him with her
puzzled frown.

'Bats might defecate?' he suggested. 'Mice might
copulate?'

'Oh,' she said. 'I hadn't thought of that. It seemed
to do with God.'

'And you refused?'

'I forgot.' She felt her whole body flush under the
thin dress at the remembered shame of it. She had

woken in the night and thought, That was all God asked of me and I have failed Him even in that.

'Is that all?' he was saying.

'Yes.'

He laughed, throwing back his head so that Amde, who was clearing away the dinner plates, had to skip to one side to avoid him. And Flo too began to laugh with her fingers now clamped over her mouth for fear that the laughter might become uncontrollable.

'Now,' he said, 'you're going to ask me what was the worst thing I ever did.'

Something in his look made her wary. 'No, I'm not.'

'How very wise.' But she had disappointed him, forfeited his attention. When Amde reached his arm between them to set down the dessert, he turned easily away to talk to Gerda Wertheimer.

Clive Waller was sitting on her right. Now he leant towards her to ask, 'Were you in Cairo with Harry, or was that before your time?' She turned and listened while he told her how he had been posted to Cairo after the war and seen a most inferior gully-gully man on the veranda at Shepheard's. 'There were riots then,' he told her, 'only we never thought anything of them. Just a bore not being able to go to the cinema. Someone did go and got stabbed for his pains. Silly beggar should have known enough to sit in the dress circle.'

All the time he talked, she was aware of Roland Routh's black sleeve reaching for the glass of wine which Amde from time to time refilled.

And at the same time Rudi Sondheimer was telling Lydia how, in New York, at the end of the war, they had locked the audiences in the cinemas to force them to watch the newsreels of the concentration camps and of the Warsaw Ghetto. 'With the evidence before their eyes some of them still could not believe it. Could you believe such ignorance is left in the world, such innocence?'

'How terrible. How terrible,' she said, but she could not let such images haunt her table. She looked across it to her husband. He leant towards Wendy Waller with his hand cupped behind his ear, listening patiently to whatever she said. His eyes were brilliant now. His wife laid her napkin on the cloth and rose. All the chairs scraped back in answer. Everyone was on their feet. She smiled and led the ladies out of the room and up the stairs. They followed with their long skirts lifted in handfuls and their little evening purses dangling from their wrists.

'All right?' she whispered to Flo outside the bedroom and was startled at the smile the girl gave her in reply.

Afterwards coffee was brought to the clusters of tables and chairs grouped on the ballroom floor. It was possible now to sit in twos and threes and say the things there had been no time to say before. Harry Morgan stood by the curtains talking shop to Geoffrey Wheeler. She would let them be. Roland Routh sat by himself on a sofa with a look of slack detachment about his face. She thought, He's had too much to drink, but he

could not be left there. She would make it the final
duty of the evening to talk to him. At her approach he
sprang to his feet with an exaggerated courtesy.

'Oh don't,' she said, sitting beside him and crossing
her legs briskly at the knee. She reached across him to
the table for a cigarette. He produced a lighter from his
pocket and flicked it several times before the flame
caught, saying, 'I'm not very good at this sort of thing.'
She shook her head dumbly with the cigarette between
her lips, and drew in a warm steadying breath before
she turned to smile at him.

Routh said, 'I must thank you for all this.'

'Oh,' she said, looking around the room to limit
what he might mean.

'It's pretty, isn't it? With the lights. It's rather awful
too. Still, we don't make enough use of it. I should
thank you.'

'Why?'

'You were sweet to Flo.'

'She's charming,' he said quickly.

These were the words she had come for. She had
them and might take him over to rescue Gerda from
Wendy Waller, but sensed, by some relaxation in him,
some alteration in his voice, that he wished to hold her
attention and keep her there. He had begun to talk quite
seriously, looking down into his hands which he held
loosely clasped on his knees, glancing up, almost shyly, as
if for reassurance that he did not bore her. He told her
how he had spent a year in Italy after the war, teaching
English to support himself while he wrote a thesis.

How old does that make him?, she thought. Twenty-eight? Thirty? Is that possible?

There had been no food, no fuel. 'You can't imagine how they suffered,' he told her. But they had been incredibly good to him. He would never forget it. He was looking at her quite unguardedly, at the age that he was then, bewildered and pained by what he had seen. She sat very still, very composed, infinitely older than he. 'I think your heart was involved,' she said and smiled at him.

'How could you know that?' He seemed in some way grateful, but by a slight movement gave her to understand that he would risk no more.

Nor would she ask. They were silent until he said without the least impertinence, 'You love all this, don't you?'

'Do I? Yes, I suppose I do. Some of it. Does that surprise you?'

'It's just that you don't question any of it.'

'What good would I do by questioning it? Besides, it's almost over.'

'No good,' he said quickly. 'None. Look, don't misunderstand me. I have the greatest admiration for him. Everybody has. He'll bring it off if anybody can.' He was looking across the room at Harry Morgan. Seeing, she supposed, the thing which she had always seen. The thing which did not flinch when other people would have flinched; that saw things through. Tears she could not account for had come into her eyes. He was watching her without pretence. 'I'm sorry,' he said quietly. 'Whatever it is, I'm very sorry.'

'I'm being ridiculous,' she told him, laughing slightly in case anybody noticed them. 'It's just that when this is over, I don't know what I'll do.'

'What will happen?'

'Harry retires. We go home.'

'One's meant to want that.'

'Of course. But it's changed. England. Hasn't it?'

'My mother says it has.'

She laughed more easily then. 'And you?'

'Go back? Get a job? I don't think about it.'

'But you must.'

'She says that too.'

She had forgotten the room, forgotten her guests, forgotten what frock she wore. Now with a feeling of strangeness these things came back to her. He was saying, 'I make my mother very unhappy. There is absolutely nothing I can do about it.'

'No,' she said. 'I don't suppose there is.' His hand which was small and quite unworn rested an inch from her hand on the sofa. The black hair seemed outrageous on it. She reached out and laid a single finger on his wrist: an admonition, no caress. He would understand that. Her composure was returned. She must exert herself; make everything move forward. Now she caught the eye of the major-domo who at once passed on her signal with a slight motion of his gloved hand. Tumblerfuls of water and lemonade were carried in, the sign that the evening was at an end. Wendy Waller took her cue and shortly afterwards rose to leave. The other guests rose with her.

Geoffrey Wheeler walked by Lydia as she followed them to the door. 'However did you come across Routh?' he said.

'By chance. With Harry. I couldn't think who he could possibly be. Harry never mentioned him.'

'I don't suppose he would. He hasn't been here long. You like him, don't you?'

Wheeler was an old friend. She might pause to consider what it was she had felt about Roland Routh. She said, 'He's the sort of person one wants to help in some way. Not that one ever can, of course.'

'What sort?'

'Bright. Self-damaging.'

'And you like that sort of thing?' It was unfair to ask. To save her answering he said quickly, 'I tell you who I *am* prepared to like. Your Flo. I'm prepared to let her grow on me. I think she will.'

She kissed him for that, as he had known she would.

In the hall the guests lingered while the men took turns to sign the visitors' book. Bridie whispered urgently to her mother who turned a beaming smile on Lydia and said, 'It's awfully short notice, but won't Flo come with us to the Friday hop? What about you, Rolly? Are you on?'

Routh gave a curt bow. 'Sorry, I'm spoken for.'

'Never mind,' said Wendy Waller bravely. 'We'll find someone. One of the subalterns. It's always easier to get them when one has someone new.'

The Wallers climbed down to their waiting car, but the others lingered briefly in the hall as if they needed to summon energy or resolution to set out. The Wertheimers, who lived on the far side of the town, offered lifts. Geoffrey accepted. Routh said he would walk. 'Get Geoffrey to bring you over for a drink,' Lydia said as they shook hands. 'Some Saturday,' she said as she kissed Geoffrey again on the cheek, and he said, 'Perfect as always,' against her ear.

'Goodbye.'

'Goodbye.'

'Goodbye.'

'Goodbye.'

She stood there waving at the top of the steps until the cars had drawn away and then went back into the house calling, 'Flo! Flo!'

But Flo had already run upstairs. She had undressed without turning on the light and climbed immediately into bed. She did not kneel to pray. What might she say to God when she had so recently laughed at Him? Nor did she wish to comment on the evening which was in some way precious to her. She lay under the thin sheet, with each event held tightly in her mind. When her mother tapped on the door and then opened it a crack to whisper, 'Are you all right?' she lay quite still. The door was pulled to. Lydia's footsteps diminished in the corridor.

At the foot of the stairs Harry Morgan was saying to the major-domo, 'Put out my bush shirt for the morning, will you?'

Chapter Five

O N THE MORNING after the party, just as Harry
Morgan was fastening the buckle on his khaki
bush shirt, Lydia came hurrying into his dressing-room.
The sun shone through her nightdress and her hair
was bunched in confusion on her shoulders, but she was
quite unaware of all of that in her alarm at what the
day might hold for him. 'What time is it?' she said.
'Have I overslept? When does the plane go?'

'Any time,' he said. 'They expect me any time. Did
I disturb you?'

'But I wanted to get up,' she said, running back to
find her dressing-gown. 'I wanted to see you off.'

They had breakfast brought upstairs to the little
sitting-room. 'It went quite well last night,' she said to
him, after a moment's silence.

'First class!' But his mind had embarked already on
his day. Though briefly he tried, he could remember
nothing of the night before to distinguish it from many
others.

'Flo enjoyed herself, I think.'

He remembered then that Flo had laughed. 'Of

course she did,' he said. 'She had a whale of a time.'
He ate his toast hastily and drank down his tea. 'Look,
I'd best be off.'

She leant over the banisters, clutching the thin stuff
of her dressing-gown about her throat. 'We're due at
the American Consulate,' she called down to him. 'At
eight. You won't be late? Oh, do be careful, won't you.'

The major-domo handed him his dispatch-case and
the stitched cotton hat he always wore when he must
be out in the sun for any length of time. He turned to
wave up at her from the door. At the bottom of the steps
Colomboroli reached over the bonnet of the Lancia,
plucking the leather sheaths from the flags on the mudguards. He straightened, and smiled as he saluted. 'To
the airport,' Harry Morgan said.

Lydia waved until the Lancia drew out of sight and the
door was closed. Then she went back to the sitting-
room. Breakfast had already been cleared away and
without pausing to dress she sat down and spread out
the first hand of cards that would keep Harry Morgan
safe throughout the day, though from what particular
peril she realized now that she had never asked him.
She seldom varied from this particular game. Occasionally she tried others requiring some modicum of skill,
but that part of her that loved the stern play of math-
ematics always compelled her to return to this one,
which depended merely on the chance layout of the
cards. With it, she could be sure her agile mind might

not outwit and falsify the intentions of chance and fate.

'You slept well,' she said to Flo when the girl came into the room. She smiled briefly at her, but was too preoccupied in setting out the long unwavering lines to talk.

Flo stood behind her and watched her lift out the aces and set them one below the other along the left-hand margin. There were four gaps now by which the cards could be manoeuvred into sequence: the three after the two of diamonds, the six after the five of hearts. 'It's a good one,' Lydia said. 'It'll come out.' She moved the cards briskly and hopefully. It was always so at first. Then one by one the spaces for manoeuvre became blocked. A gap beyond a king could not be filled. That was the rule. It was then that Lydia felt the power of that adversary who controlled the game. She felt his strength. Her own was powerless against it. On the whole, although she hated him, she liked to know that he was there. Still, she must try to win for Harry's sake and played on doggedly, queen of spades after the jack of spades, until she reached stasis. She had failed and had set the world and everyone she loved at an intolerable risk. She swept up the disordered rows and bent the cards together in the waterfall shuffle a gambling man had taught her on a ship once. Then she set them out again and would again and again until the adversary relented.

Flo had begun to move discontentedly around the room, hating its signs of impermanence, hating her mother's absorption in something other than herself.

Sleep had scarcely distanced her from the events of the night before. Her eyes still smarted with tiredness and cigarette smoke. The confused surface of the dining-table, the animated faces mouthing across the candle flames, stayed with her, demanding now to be talked about before they were in some way lost.

Lydia said, 'Switch on the wireless, would you?'

The unboxed set stood on a table in the corner of the room. Its exposed tubes and wires gave it the appearance of an architect's model for some vast industrial complex. They were uniformly coated with a thick soft dust, but when Flo turned the knob, light could be seen to flicker along the wires and the sprightly tune of 'Lillibullero' came crackling out, followed by the chimes of Big Ben and a man's voice reading the news from London. Flo did not listen to him. That world had already grown too remote for interest. She stooped to blow at the dust, but it was long established and would not shift. A moment later Lydia said, 'Oh, how depressing. Switch it off.' Still in the same preoccupied, card-playing voice, she said, 'What did you make of Roland Routh?'

'I felt sorry for him,' Flo said after a moment.

'*Sorry* for him?' Her mother had looked up, but now went back to placing her cards deliberately, matching her words to the movement. 'Of course, he's entirely out of place here. He drank too much last night. We have to be careful who we ask. You'll have to be careful too.' Her hands were moving quickly now. She broke in upon herself to say, 'Oh look, Flo. It's coming out! I've done it!' And indeed the cards had suddenly yielded to her and lined up in perfect sequence. The war was won. The little plane would not fall glittering from the sky. She might lean back and light another cigarette and feel for a moment she had achieved; was in control.

Flo, her sweet frock and courage at the party, immediately filled her mind. Now she wanted to talk about these things, but Flo, she found, had gone from the room in those few seconds when she had been too preoccupied to notice. That too was a relief. She drew deeply on the cigarette, and enjoyed for a moment an obscure pleasure in the morning which she did not trace to any source.

Flo went downstairs and ate breakfast alone at the emptied dining-table, waited on by Amde. The smell of cigar smoke was still faintly discernible in the room. When she had eaten she went into the ballroom where the windows were open and the last gleaming traces of a wet mop were drying on the floor. She found Rudi Sondheimer's record and put it on the turntable. Then she lifted the weighted head of the gramophone and set the needle on the record's shining outer rim. Tense vigorous tunes leapt out into the silent room. She listened seriously through to the end before she went into the drawing-room. Her mother was dressed and talking to the cook. She sat swinging her legs over the hard square arms of her chair. There was nothing to do. Before she had not minded but now it seemed that something had happened to which this new day had failed to respond. When the phone rang she listened with a startling eagerness.

It was Wendy Waller saying how much they had enjoyed the party. Later, a bunch of roses was delivered at the door with a note of thanks from Gerda. Amde was sent for to fetch a vase of water. '*There's* something you could do,' Lydia said when he returned with it. Flo set the roses stiffly in the vase and moved them this way and that with her finger. She sniffed at them, but they were shop flowers and hardly smelt at all.

Harry Morgan had walked briskly into the empty departure lounge where Sergeant Broad was waiting for him. 'Who's flying us?' he asked as they walked together out on to the runway.

'Sawley.'

Morgan shook his head. 'Do I know him?'

'Quiet chap. No one knows him that well,' the sergeant said.

He added, 'I've brought along a spare revolver, sir. Will you be carrying one?'

Morgan shook his head again. 'Much good it would do us if it came to that.'

'Oh, I don't know, sir,' Broad said, and grinned at him.

They climbed aboard: Broad in the back seat, Morgan up behind the pilot with his long legs bent uncomfortably in the cramped space. A mechanic spun the propeller into action, gave a thumbs up and darted

back. They set off down the runway eastwards into the
sun. Morgan had supposed the pilot might point things
out to him. When Sawley said nothing, he thought it
wiser to let his silence run its course. The din of the
engine made it impossible to talk with any ease.

He stared alertly at the little town spread out like a
map below him. The plane banked. They flew to the
west now, following the single road out over the stony
surface of the plateau to the edge of the escarpment.
The valley at this hour was free of cloud. Morgan turned
to Broad and pointed silently downward to the Italian
road looping up the side of the mountain. Up this road
they had both followed the routed Italian forces;
Morgan a young staff officer, Broad an even younger
conscript. They had been quite unknown to one
another then. Now it was a bond between them.

They had been all set, Morgan remembered, for
some show of force at the top; some defence of the
town at least; snipers, as they drove up the main
thoroughfare. As it was, the civilians lay low behind
their shutters while every last one of the military and
their hangers-on had fled down the far side of the
plateau to the port. There was no transport waiting for
them there. The victors could afford to let them go and
follow at their ease once they had the town secured.

As that day went on they had uncovered more and
more evidence of a panicky departure. Especially,
Morgan remembered entering the military hospital to
discover two Aderrans abandoned on the operating
table. One was already dead of thirst or shock. The

other had lain there in agony for God knew how long after the anaesthetic had worn off. He died before they could get morphine to him. Morgan was a doctor's son. This of all things he had found impossible to forgive. Even now he felt a stir of nausea when he thought of it.

Sawley turned to shout at him. 'We're nearly there.'

'Right,' he said. 'They've cleared an open space of some sort. The policeman speaks quite good Arabic. He says they've marked it out for you as best they can. We'll deal with the whole thing right there. It shouldn't take long.'

Minutes later they spotted the village, a cluster of circular huts with smoke seeping through their thatch. Sawley brought the Auster down neatly enough. 'Well done,' Morgan shouted to him. They taxied over the rough ground with small boys and dogs racing along beside them. The plane was drawn up, as Morgan directed, where a crowd of people stood grouped in front of a large tree.

Broad jumped down first, stood to attention, saluted Morgan as he appeared at the door of the plane and gave him a hand down. Morgan put on his hat and carried the dispatch-case in his left hand while he shook hands, first with the headman of the village, then with the police corporal, then with five or six of the younger men who crowded forward. With the policeman interpreting, he told them in Arabic that they had acted courageously in capturing the bandits and correctly in sending for him rather than taking justice into their own hands. The corporal then directed him to a wooden chair set in the shadow of the tree.

'Is there another for my sergeant?' Morgan asked him.

'Not to worry, sir,' Broad told him. 'I'd as soon stand.'

'Never mind then,' Morgan said and made a slight negative movement with his two fingers. He sat down on the chair. Sergeant Broad stood tensely behind him. The men all came and squatted two deep in a semi-circle in front of him. Behind them, to the left, a group of women stared out from the dusty cloths they held across the lower portions of their faces. One of these women keened mechanically. The rest stood silent and ignored her. 'Right,' Morgan said. 'Let's get on then.'

First three rifles and three bandoliers were laid out neatly on the ground before his feet. Then the three prisoners were led forward from somewhere behind the huts. The first had his hands chained in front of him with a pair of rusty manacles. The other two had theirs bound behind with what looked like strips of leather. They were lean, but far from starving. They all wore leather kilts of some sort. One had a ragged khaki shirt. Their hair grew wildly from their heads and was oiled with rancid butter. Morgan could smell it from where he sat. He noticed the dullness of their skin and the utter remoteness of their expression. 'Would you say they'd been knocked about a bit?' he said quietly to Broad.

'I shouldn't wonder, sir,' the sergeant said. 'It's hard to tell. They being dark like that.'

'Let them sit down,' Morgan said. The policeman shouted and when one of the prisoners hesitated he poked him with his rifle butt.

'That's enough of that,' Morgan said sharply. Immediately the man began to repeat some phrase in a low hoarse voice. 'What's he saying?' Morgan asked the policeman.

'He says he's thirsty.'

'Well, bring them water then.'

A woman was dispatched to the huts. He could not look up without encountering the prisoners' eyes. Instead he watched the bracelet jogging on her ankle and the little puffs of dust from under her feet as she ran. She came back with a jug. 'Free their hands,' Morgan told the policeman. They drank with an eagerness that was uncomfortable to watch. Morgan signalled that they should be left unbound and pointed to the headman. 'Tell him,' he said to the policeman, 'that my Government wishes to deal justly with all men; that he is to be entirely truthful in what he tells us; that I and my Government would be very angry if I thought he were, for any reason, trying to settle old scores with these men. Ask him if he ever saw them before they were captured.'

The headman heard out the translation and denied all knowledge of the men.

'Ask him why that woman is crying.'

'She is the mother of one of the women who was killed.'

'Right then. Ask him to tell me what happened.'

The old man told his tale dramatically enough for Morgan to follow the general drift of it before it was translated. They had been attacked in the night. They did not know by how many but they all agreed there had been many men; more than these three. They had stolen six goats and hamstrung three of the cattle. They had taken the two women who had been sleeping in a hut near the edge of the village and stolen the mead that they had brewed. The child of one of these women was pushed forward between the squatting men and made to bow his head to show the weal where he had been struck unconscious. At dawn the villagers had set out in pursuit and come upon the bodies of the two women.

He was bound to ask, 'How were they killed?' The old man detailed the nature of their injuries. While he spoke Morgan studied the faces of the captives. They remained impassive. The corporal translated. 'They did understand that?' Morgan asked him with distaste. 'They do speak the same dialect, I suppose?'

'Yes, sir.'

Later they had come upon these three, dead drunk, having drunk the mead. Morgan called on two other villagers to corroborate the story. Each spoke at length. He listened carefully to the translation. Their accounts were substantially the same. Then he asked, 'What proof is there that these are the men who did this dreadful thing?'

'They are bandits, sir,' the policeman said indignantly. 'Anyone can see that.'

'Yes,' Morgan said. 'But I must be certain that they are the men who committed this particular crime. Do you understand that?' Privately he thought, Of course they did it. There can be no doubt.

Nevertheless he studied patiently a clay jar that was alleged to be one of those that had contained the mead. A cloth that had belonged to one of the women was laid across his knee. One of the prisoners, they told him, had been sleeping with it under his head when he was taken.

'That can't be,' Morgan said. 'It's too clean.'

The corporal shouted a question at the wailing woman, who stopped at once and broke into vehement speech. 'She washed it, sir,' he said to Morgan. 'It had her daughter's blood on it so she washed it.'

Although he spoke Arabic fluently, Morgan was unable to read it. He had the corporal read aloud to him his deposition on the condition of the bodies when he saw them. Then he had him translate what he had read, so that the villagers too might hear it. When it was finished Morgan waited a minute and then asked, 'Does anyone else have anything to say?' There was silence. He nodded towards the prisoners. The policeman spoke to them, but they gave no indication of having heard. 'Are you sure they understand?' he asked again.

'Yes, sir.'

'Well, that's that then,' Morgan said. He lifted his dispatch-case and, settling it on his knee, opened it and took out the necessary papers and his fountain pen. He had each of the prisoners repeat his name slowly and distinctly so that he might write it phonetically into the typed warrant. He signed it, and had Broad witness it. As he took back his pen he said, 'Get on with it then, but see that it's done properly.' He said to the corporal, 'I'll leave my sergeant here to see that things don't get out of hand at all.' He turned and walked back over the dusty ground to the aeroplane.

Sawley was leaning against the far side of the plane in the shade cast by its wing. Morgan stood beside him and lit a cigarette. 'We'll be out of here in thirty minutes,' he told him.

'It doesn't take long then,' Sawley said.

Morgan couldn't gauge his tone. 'It's the only way to do it,' he said. 'Fast. Where they can see it done. It's what they understand.' It's a pity, he might have added. But why talk cant? Pity didn't come into it, except on so grand a scale that they were all included in it. When Sawley said nothing, he thought, Damn him. What does he know?

He walked away and while he waited stood staring across the parched glittering floor of the valley to the opposite hillside. There was a total silence there that made the murmur of activity in the village behind him seem remote and meaningless. He stared at the face of the hill from under the brim of his hat, watching intently for what? A puff of dust. The flash of light on metal. Trouble. There was nothing until a kite glided along the length of the valley, its wings tensed, the feathers splayed and tilted upwards at their tips. A beautiful sight. It moved with apparent freedom. Then he thought how desperately its life was tied to that of some minute creature that cowered between the stones. Its shadow trailed behind it, distorted by the rocky surface of the ground. He dropped his cigarette and crushed it with his shoe. He consulted his watch. 'We'll be off in fifteen minutes,' he said to Sawley as he passed him. 'Have her ready, will you?'

The three men were hanging nod-headed from the tree. He wondered if the chair, which was still standing there, had been used in the proceedings. He stood by Broad, appearing to watch, but not watching. 'Dead, do you think?' he asked him quietly.

'Quite, sir.'

Ten minutes later he gave orders that they be left hanging for another half-hour and then be cut down. He made the corporal responsible for seeing that they were buried intact. He had Broad hold his dispatch-case while he extracted the reward money and counted the soiled notes into the headman's hand. He told him he might keep the rifles and the ammunition and again congratulated his men on their courage and restraint. He pointed to the money and said, 'You see, this is how my Government keeps its promises.' He pointed to the tree. 'This is how my Government treats those who break the law.' He glanced over the headman's shoulder as he shook his hand and saw that Sawley was winding the propeller.

'You get in first,' he said to Broad as they walked slowly towards the aeroplane. He thought, There mustn't be a hitch at this point. If the engine should stall, if he should stumble as he climbed aboard, they would see him as a tired man whose body failed him. Broad scrambled in and gave him a hand up. Sawley gave the propeller a final turn and hauled himself into the pilot's seat. 'Off you go then,' Morgan said. He turned to wave through the window as they taxied off through the dust.

None of them spoke until the plane was airborne. Then Morgan said again, 'Well, that's that.'

'It was that kiddy I felt sorry for,' Broad said disgustedly.

'Quite,' Morgan said. He wiped his hands over his face which he found was cold with sweat. 'Well, justice was seen to be done by their lights, but was it done by ours?' He spoke to Broad, but half-hoped that Sawley might hear him.

Broad said, 'Well, if they didn't do it, as sure as hell they'd done something just as bad. Christ, sir, who'd have thought six months ago they'd take matters into their own hands and fight back like that, let alone send for us? He must be damn good, that corporal, to keep them alive until we got there.'

'Damn good,' Morgan said. 'We'll get promotion for him.'

They were silent after that. The small distance that had removed Sawley from their afternoon's activities had removed him utterly. It was impossible to speak in front of him even though it was unlikely that he could hear. Morgan passed around the major-domo's sandwiches.

Sawley indicated that he had had his own food. Morgan himself found that he had little appetite, but Broad ate eagerly.

At the airport Colomboroli was waiting with the Lancia. Morgan shook Sawley by the hand and thanked him. Then he clapped Broad on the shoulder and, letting his hand remain there, steered him a little way towards the car. 'Rather a sullen fellow, isn't he?' he asked, nodding back towards the plane. 'What do you know about him?'

'Keeps himself to himself,' Broad said with a shrug. 'He has a wife out here. There's been some talk – there always is.'

'I wondered if he drank.'

'He seemed sober enough just now.'

'That's so, but perhaps someone else next time?'

'Perhaps there won't be a next time, sir.'

'God willing,' Harry Morgan said and climbed into his car.

He sat with his arms stretched out along the back of the seat, his head thrown back. Once he caught Colomboroli watching him in the mirror and forced himself to smile.

'*Grazie. Buona sera,*' he told him when Colomboroli held open the car door at the foot of the villa steps. '*Buona sera,*' he said to the major-domo who was waiting at the top. He was aware that Colomboroli had not driven off and turned to see him slowly polishing the dust off the bonnet with a chamois leather. 'Tell him he may go,' he said to the major-domo.

'He is to wait and take the Signorina to Colonel Waller's house,' the old man told him in Italian. 'Then he must come back and take *Sua Ecellenza* and the Signora to the American Consulate.'

'Right,' he said. 'I'd forgotten. Tell the Signora I'll be down shortly.' Without speaking to his wife, he went upstairs to bathe and change into the fresh evening clothes that the major-domo had laid out for him.

Chapter Six

A T PRECISELY seven twenty-seven Colomboroli drove Flo the short distance to the Wallers' house. From there she went with them, in their black Cadillac, to the English Club on the Corso. An open door led off the street and revealed a flight of marble stairs. Two young officers in their evening blues were waiting on the pavement. They were introduced to Flo as Richie South and Simon Philpotts.

In the ballroom at the head of the stairs, dancing was already in progress. Wendy Waller led her party, in single file, around the edges of the room towards a corner table. Drinks were ordered in the same penetrating tone above the beat of the music. The dancers circled past. There was much cheerful jigging up and down, especially with the arms, but relatively little movement forward. They talked, if at all, directly ahead across one another's shoulders. A pallid Italian photographer, with stubble on his chin, darted in and out among the couples, twitching thick black electric cables between his feet and dazzling their faces with flash bulbs. By the time Wendy Waller had established that everyone had the drink he or she had ordered, the last tune was ending with a flourish. The dancers stood back from one another. There was a patter of applause. The cameras flashed again. Everyone trooped back to their tables.

Flo sat lifting her glass, taking small cold sips and setting it down again. She stared around at the other people in the room. There was no one there she knew. Bridie sat protectively close to her. She fingered the stuff of Flo's dress and asked her what it had cost. The two subalterns muttered to one another. It was unsafe to look in their direction.

The quartet from the regimental band who played on these occasions shuffled their sheet music on their metal stands and struck up another tune. Immediately Richie South stood up and asked Flo to dance with him. 'We tossed for you,' he said as they set out. 'I won.' It made her laugh, but she was pleased too. No one had ever paid her a compliment before. After that she danced with Simon Philpotts. It did not seem to matter at all that she did not know properly how to dance. He shouted in her ear that it was nice to dance with someone tall. Then she danced with Richie South again.

At the end of that dance the musicians rose and, laying their instruments carefully on their chairs, went together to the bar. Wendy Waller signalled to a waiter and a fresh round of drinks was ordered. Just as the tray was set down on the table a party of new arrivals came into the room. They had not noticed the hush that had fallen in the absence of the music and hurried across the floor talking and laughing at the tops of their voices. Wendy Waller waved gaily at them while she said in a significant voice to her husband, 'Our theatricals!'

It embarrassed Flo, the more so since she had instantly recognized Roland Routh among them, that none of the theatricals waved back, except a tall young man in army blues.

'Good heavens,' Wendy Waller now said. 'Why is Jamie Renfrew in amongst that lot? He's not doing the play this time, surely? I hear that Rolly Routh has talked them into doing *Hamlet* and filled it with some socialist claptrap.'

'Typical,' Colonel Waller said and lapsed into silence.

The musicians had returned and, taking up their instruments, had launched into a medley from *South Pacific*. 'I'm going to wash that man right out of my hair,' Wendy Waller hummed, tapping with her hand on the edge of the plastic tabletop. Then she said, 'I don't expect anything will ever come of it. That sort never sees anything through.'

The theatricals, all fresh to the dancing, rose as one. Even when they had separated into pairs and begun to whirl about the room, they continued to call back and forth to one another. Other couples rose now. It was Richie South's turn to dance with Flo. As they shifted about the floor, she watched over his shoulder to where Roland Routh danced elaborately with a woman in a bright red dress. He swung her round the corner of the room with her little waist bunched up under his arm and her bright skirt clinging to his trouser leg. His small handsome features were set with concentration. They said not a word to one another. Even before the music stopped they went back to their table.

When the music sprang up again Routh rose from his table and walked across the dance floor, frowning slightly, as if he came to deliver a message. After the curtest of greetings to Wendy Waller and the others, he bowed to Flo and asked her if she would care to dance. She went with him quickly before anyone could tell her not to, and a moment later he was steering her briskly through the dancers. 'I'm afraid I'm not much good at it,' she told him. 'I always had to be the man at school.'

'Why ever was that?'

She was reluctant to say, 'Because I am tall,' when it might draw attention to the fact that she was quite as tall as he was. She said evasively, 'I had to wear a yellow band to prove I was a man.'

He laughed. It pleased her to have made him laugh again. At the same time he gripped her dispassionately by the waist and whirled her so quickly around the corner of the room that she had no time to resist him. For the remaining minutes of the dance she gave up all attempts to talk and watched, as if in a dream, the other faces spinning past her.

It was over. As he led her back to the table the others stared. Wendy Waller called out, 'Very *palais de danse* tonight, aren't we?'

'Oh, isn't Wendy Waller awful,' Routh whispered, giving Flo's waist a slight squeeze. 'Poor you.'

She was sweating. She sat between Richie South and Simon Philpotts, dabbing with a handkerchief at her upper lip.

'What a cheek,' said Richie South when she danced with him next. 'Do you *know* him?'

'A little,' Flo said.

When she sat down she smiled across at Routh. She would have liked to dance with him again so that she could tell him what Richie South had said and hear him laugh.

'You mustn't smile at him like that,' Simon Philpotts said. 'He'll get the wrong idea.' But her smile had done no harm. It had not even been noticed. Just as the music began again the entire party of theatricals gathered up their stoles and purses and pushed their way annoyingly across the centre of the dance floor so that several couples had to dodge aside. 'Good riddance,' Wendy Waller said.

After that Flo danced with Richie South and Simon Philpotts turn and turn about. There was a waltz. Then everyone linked arms and charged about the room in groups of six or eight, shouting and yipping while the band played 'The Post Horn Gallop'. Then they froze to attention for 'God Save the King'.

The Wallers delivered Flo back to the front door of the villa. Amde had waited up to let her in and turned out the lights behind her as she went upstairs. The house was silent, but an oblong of light reached through the open door of her mother's sitting-room on to the upstairs landing. Lydia was playing cards. She beckoned, smiling, moving her finger quickly to her lips and then pointing to the bedroom where Harry lay asleep. 'Did you have a good time?' she whispered.

'Oh, yes,' Flo told her. Directly she sat down, energy ached in her arms and legs and made her want to move again.

'Did you dance?'

'Yes.'

'Who with?'

'Richie South and Simon Philpotts mostly.'

The names meant nothing to Lydia. 'And were they nice?'

'Yes.'

'Anyone else?' the mother said, going back to her patience.

'With Roland Routh.'

She didn't look at Lydia, but heard her say cautiously, 'Well, that was nice.'

'No one was very kind about him.'

'Who wasn't?'

'Well, everyone,' the girl said in an aggrieved voice.

'Flo, my darling, who on earth is everyone?'

'Well, Wendy Waller. All of them.'

'And are they everyone? Are you surprised? He's scarcely one of them. I think he's Frant Road, don't you?'

Flo had looked up then and smiled at her so brilliantly that Lydia took alarm and going back to her cards, said, as if she counted under her breath, 'Did he dance with you more than once?'

'No.'

'Well then,' her mother said as she bent her card in place. 'There you are. I expect it was just his way of saying thank you for the other evening. And you really enjoyed yourself?'

'Yes,' Flo persisted. The brightness of the dance, her modest sense of being sought after, had seemed a gift that she might give her mother; something surely that Lydia had wanted and would take pleasure in, but already the feeling of elation had died away like something held too tightly in the hand.

Chapter Seven

IN THE MORNING Flo again woke with the feeling that sleep had given insufficient respite from the night before. Light fell too brightly on the empty expanse of the balcony outside her window. The events of the dance, which had seemed so satisfactory at the time, had lost their power to reassure. Immediately it was necessary for something else to happen. It seemed that she was scarcely awake before she was waiting again, though for what she was not certain. At ten o'clock promptly, as if the caller had waited for that considerate hour, the phone rang. Lydia answered it and held the receiver smilingly towards her. It was Bridie suggesting that they walk down to the town to look at the photographs of the dance. Lydia gave her some money and told her not to buy more than one. Flo could see it pleased her that she had made a friend.

Because she could not be sure of remembering the way to the Wallers' house, Bridie called for her at the villa and together they walked to the shops off the Corso where the photographs, taken the night before, were already on display. They peered through the shop window at rows of minute, startled faces, turned to meet the photographer's flash. 'I can't see you,' Bridie said. But Flo had spotted herself directly, standing in her white dress, smiling uncertainly in one at Richie South and in another at Simon Philpotts.

Inside the shop they were a long time in making their choice. The photographer, more ill-shaven and exhausted than ever, grew irritable with them. In the end Bridie chose four. She glanced sharply at Flo's and said, 'You liked Philpotts best then.' It was not particularly so. Flo had looked quickly for one that might give proof that Roland Routh had crossed the room to dance with her, but there had been none and to purchase one of him dancing with the woman in the red dress would have been too perverse and revealing a choice to lay before her mother. Instead she had chosen the one in which she judged that she looked the prettiest and happiest as being the most acceptable.

As they walked along the dusty pavements she looked through Bridie's chosen photographs. 'You're not in any of them,' she said. 'No,' Bridie said, darting her a look. 'But Jamie Renfrew is.' It was true. She had had none of Flo's scruples. In each there appeared the good-looking captain whose presence among the theatricals had so offended Wendy Waller. 'I have a thing about him,' Bridie told her. It was a curiously sedate statement: a pledge of the new friendship, Flo supposed. She glanced sideways at Bridie's plump, tense face and wished that she had something to proffer in return. 'It's hopeless really,' the girl went on. 'Still, he might get keen on me. Mummy says they do sometimes, just like that; come to the boil.'

The brief afternoon rain had begun. They could feel the big drops flatten on their bare arms. Dark rounds appeared on the warm pavement and were instantly absorbed. They hurried on in a solemn silence. Bridie's love had in some way aged and distanced her. Flo was awed by it and shyly pleased when, at the gates of the villa, the girl said, 'Will you come to the dance again next Friday?' Then she added artlessly, 'If you come it's easier to ask the other people.'

'I'll have to see,' Flo said.

Lydia seemed quite agreeable to her going. She looked quizzically from the photograph to Flo and back again. 'I shouldn't get *too* friendly with them,' she said. 'Of course we are thrown up against them here, but Bridie's not really for you, is she?' Flo shook her head, accepting that it was so, although she had thought Bridie pleasanter than the girls at school. She did not tell her mother about Captain Renfrew, more because she did not want the information to be dismissed as uninteresting than out of loyalty to Bridie. It was a new sensation to have a secret from her mother. She sat watching Lydia play cards, testing out the feel of it.

On Sunday it was necessary to go to church. Harry must go and Lydia, although she believed in nothing, would never have shirked the duty of going with him. Although the Catholic, Muslim, Greek Orthodox and Jewish congregations were all handsomely accommodated in Aderra, there was no Anglican foundation.

The English community worshipped in an upper room of the town hall, chosen, perhaps, for the coincidence of its having stained-glass windows. There seemed nothing else to recommend it. Even for so small a gathering there was not sufficient space and its position under the tiled roof made it hot and stuffy. The regimental padre took the service. Harry Morgan read the first lesson. The Colonel read the second. Clive Waller carried the collection plate. A detachment from the regimental band played hymns that deafened in the crowded room. In that interval of private supplication for sufferers known personally to the worshippers, flies could be heard to buzz against the coloured window-panes.

Flo had, by now, abandoned altogether her stream of anxious requests to God that she should not fail at this and that. Instead she prayed for Bridie and her hopeless love, and then, as an afterthought, for Harry Morgan, that he would succeed in doing what they expected of him. For herself and Lydia there seemed in those weeks nothing to ask.

Sunday was completed. The week with its round of engagements had begun again.

On Monday the Aderran Wolf Cubs were marched in past one sentry box, around the crescent drive, and smartly out past the other. Harry Morgan, whose gravity could always be relied on, took the salute from the villa steps.

On Tuesday Lydia and Harry went to a reception at the embassy of the Northern Territory. Flo stayed behind and listened to her record. The major-domo brought her sandwiches on a tray.

On Wednesday Lydia took her on a visit to an orphanage. Little boys in clean white shirts sat at three long trestle-tables while Wendy Waller, her voice pitched high, gave them instruction, in English, as to how to place coloured wooden beads on a piece of string.

On Thursday she accompanied Lydia and Harry to a high mass for the souls of three Italian soldiers whose skeletons had recently been disinterred in the desert that stretched eastward from the foot of the escarpment.

On Friday evenings it was now accepted that Flo went dancing at the club. Sometimes Wendy Waller made up a party; sometimes she collaborated with a Mrs Bynge or another of the majors' wives. Different subalterns were asked in strict rotation, but always after the first two dances Richie South and Simon Philpotts appeared from the direction of the bar, and Flo found herself partnered by them turn and turn about.

Whatever arrangement had been come to, she was agreeable to it. The effort to make conversation had largely been abandoned. They danced with damp cheek pressed against damp cheek. Flo closed her eyes and sniffed their pleasant soapy smell and listened to the music's deeper promise of older men in other rooms. Sometimes she forgot which one she danced with, Richie South or Simon Philpotts. Pressed close as she was, she could not easily tell one from the other. There was the identical feel of damp blue serge against her hand, the hot stiff ear against her brow, the smell of Imperial Leather shaving-soap. Even if for a moment she opened her eyes, there was the identical epaulette. She was quite unmoved by either of them, but felt gratitude for both, that they should disguise her absence of heart and give her the necessary semblance of success. So that when Lydia asked her, 'Did you have a good time?' she might say, 'Wonderful,' and catch the minute shift of relief at the back of her mother's eyes that told her she had done what she was meant to do.

After that first dance she never saw Roland Routh at the club again, although during the week she often imagined his coming, on his own perhaps, crossing the room to Wendy Waller's table, and insisting that she dance with him. These dreams compensated, nearly, for his not being there. They took away the need to question whether she was sad or happy. In any case that was unimportant. It mattered only that she should not seem to fail at the thing that was expected of her. What that was had not been clearly stated. She was guided only by a long and delicate knowledge of Lydia's need to know that she had made her daughter happy in the way that she intended.

On Saturday morning, with the different rhythms of Rudi Sondheimer's record beating through the empty ballroom, the small events of the night before gave way to her imaginings of what might happen on the Friday night to come. She drank the lemonade which Hassan brought her on a tray and let the glib words of the songs imprint themselves upon her mind.

A ritual had been established. Promptly at ten she walked through the back streets to Bridie's house and the two of them proceeded arm in arm into the town to select their photographs. It was too anxious a pursuit to be classed as vanity. Time must be taken over it, at least an hour. Often the shop was crowded. Perhaps they were not the only ones who needed proof that the evening had succeeded, or found this a means to snatch at other people's partners.

As the number of these mementoes increased, Flo began to keep them in an album, which Lydia had bought for the purpose. Each new entry she handed solemnly to her mother. Lydia would put down her cigarette to study it and nod approvingly. But Flo could sense that already this was not enough. Something had been set in motion that was expected to keep pace with her mother's more urgent sense of time. She had begun, as she looked at the photographs, to question with a gentle, but intrusive voice, 'Does he like you?'

'Which one?'

'Well, this one. Richie South.'

'Simon Philpotts,' Flo said; then, more hesitantly, 'Yes. He seems to.'

'Has he tried to kiss you yet?'

'I think so.' For in the moist pressure of the dance surely his lips had rested on the line of her hair.

'You must *know*,' her mother said and would not shift her glance away.

She did not care for Flo's association with the Wallers, though as far as she could see these evenings were harmless enough. 'It's good for her to get out of the house,' she said to Harry. 'Besides, it's good practice.'

'For what?'

'Well,' she said defensively. 'For England.'

And on the whole it suited her that Flo should disappear on Saturday mornings and sometimes stay on to lunch with the Wallers. It was on Saturdays that she occasionally permitted herself a little party, but only of the people she enjoyed. To square her conscience that government money must pay for it, she confined these gatherings to drinks on a Saturday lunchtime, and told herself that their purpose was to strengthen the morale of the office. Not all the office came, however; the Wallers were never invited. Nor only the office: the Sondheimers always were; they and Geoffrey, sometimes Nigel Harrington from the education department and his wife, and of course Harry Morgan himself, appearing like any other guest when the office shut for the weekend. For a few weeks after Flo's arrival this ritual had been suspended. Now seemed the time to reinstate it. Flo heard her on the telephone, 'Tomorrow as usual? Oh, so have I. Yes, twelve as always.'

It was at just this time of day that the cloud rising up the face of the escarpment overspilled the town. The air cooled and held the faint scent of the approaching rain, so that the visitors climbed from their cars and hurried up the steps as if in search of shelter. And shelter it should be, the Villa della Pace in more than name, for these few, dear people who had suffered. For all of them had. Geoffrey had lived out a wretched war at his post in Kenya, despising himself that he was not in uniform and imagining, still, that everyone despised him for it. The army might have saved and sobered him.

Yet his had been by far the kindest fate. The Harringtons had been interned by the Japanese in Burma and lost their only child. Gerda Sondheimer had simply told her, 'There is nobody left of my family but me.' What they woke to in the night, what rose up in their dreams was theirs alone. None of them spoke of these things, but hid their suffering in a world that, in seven years of peace, had already lost the stomach to contemplate what they had known. There was nothing that Lydia could do, other than order Hassan to set out the peanuts in their plated silver bowls and open up to them this peaceable kingdom where for an hour they would be distracted and entirely safe. The title of a novel she had read, *Where Love and Friendship Dwelt*, came to her mind as all that she wanted of the Villa della Pace. It was what she had, on impulse, wanted to extend to Roland Routh.

Now she waited for her visitors in some cool, brightly belted frock which she had carefully chosen the day before and sent down to old Gidea to be freshly pressed. To keep it fresh she sat upright in her chair with her arms stretched out along its square sides. Her hair was knotted up to bare her damp neck to any gust of air that managed to penetrate the muffled room. The first drink of the day stood cooling on the table at her side, but she had left it scrupulously untouched, waiting for someone to come and join her.

It occurred to her that Routh might well come, with Geoffrey, although she had made no attempt to remind him of her casual invitation. He had, she had heard, been out of town inspecting the designated polling stations in the south. She had no idea whether or not he was back, but when the first voice in the hall was not immediately familiar, she guessed at once that it was he.

'I didn't hear a car,' she said. 'Did no one bring you?' She was disconcerted by the speed with which he had entered the room and come right up to her. I shed tears, she thought in astonishment. In the ballroom. But the sight of him in daylight dispersed all that.

'I walked.' He was slightly out of breath. Smaller than she remembered him, younger. She pictured him hurrying along the street, feeling bound to keep an invitation she had half-forgotten.

'It is all right?' he said. 'You said I might.' But she did not think he was at all unsure of her. She was touched by his trust. It was that and his haste that had made him seem younger than he could possibly be.

'Isn't Geoffrey with you?'

'No. Is he coming too? Am I in the way? I am. You're expecting other people.'

'Don't be silly,' she said. 'Have a drink.'

'A whisky. Thank you.'

'At this time of day?' But at the same time she gave a nod to Amde.

'Does that shock you?'

'No.' If anything she was amused by her shifting sense of him. While his drink was poured he prowled about the room as a cat will to take possession of a place. She sat down again, sipped at her own drink and watched him.

'May I take my jacket off?' he asked her next. 'It was rather hot coming along.'

Instantly she feared the odour of his sweat might reach too intimately out to her; imagined the others arriving to find him so unaccountably at home. She said, 'You may want to put it on again.' But already he had shrugged it off and slung it over the back of a chair, all in one swift movement that forestalled Amde's attempt to help him with it.

'What a pity Flo's not here,' she said.

'Oh, isn't she?' He had sat down opposite her and seemed to toast her with a quick nod before he drank too large a gulp of whisky.

'You've been away. Harry mentioned it.'

'Yes,' he said. 'I'd have come before otherwise. Look, I'm sorry I never wrote. About the other evening. It was very nice. I've just been busy.'

'How was it, your trip?'

'It was interesting.' Immediately he began to talk to her without caution, about his tour of the provincial towns in the south; about the rusty battered ballot-boxes sent out from England because nothing could be made locally to serve the purpose; about the inadequate schoolrooms he had had to commandeer for polling-stations; about the young schoolmasters with radical politics, who must be appeased, talked to for hours, helped with their own studies for the British School Certificate, before they would allow him to get out his measuring tape and work out the dimensions of the room. 'No one else of voting age can read,' he told her. 'Isn't that extraordinary?'

She sat forward in her chair listening to him, picturing each incident as he told it to her, adding the thing which he omitted, which was himself: the serious young white man listening courteously. It struck her pleasantly that until this moment he had had no one to whom to tell these things. How well he spoke. She had been right about him. With an odd regret she caught the sound of crushed gravel as the first car drove up the drive.

He had heard it too and broke off what he was saying. So intently was she watching him that it seemed a shadow had fallen on the bright scenes he described. She rose quickly and stood with her back to him as if to look out of the window, although it was too thickly swathed with net to see anything but the blurred shape of the approaching car. When she turned again, he too had risen and was smiling at her with what she sensed was an accustomed charm. 'Look,' he said, 'I should have said at first, I really came to ask a favour.'

'What's that?'

'We've decided to put on *Hamlet*. Did you know

that? We need H.E.'s permission to put it on in the public theatre and rehearse there. I said I knew you. Do you mind that? I said I'd ask. That's what I came for.'

'Ask Harry,' she said. 'He'll be here in a minute.'

'I have. At least, I don't suppose it ever got to him. Clive Waller's against it.'

'Why on earth?'

'Against me rather.'

'Surely not!'

'Oh well,' he said. 'You know . . . You know how people are.'

She thought at once that she did, but what if there was something she did not know? 'But *Hamlet* surely is . . .'

'Is *Hamlet*,' he said smiling again. 'I promise you that's all it is. That's all it can be, but the production must be of the here and now, you know. Someone must have said something. There's always someone.'

'But *Hamlet!*'

'He seems to think it might be disrespectful to the Royal Family.'

She had laughed aloud, so that her drink, which she had hardly sipped, spilt slightly, chilling her leg through her skirt. How closely he was watching her. She bent to brush at her skirt and avoid his look. 'I think it's very brave of you to tackle it.'

'Not really. I found a batch of unused copies in one of the schools. They were quite unread. I doubt they'll be wanted after June. I liberated them.'

She had laughed again. But to steal . . . To steal
Shakespeare from schoolchildren. Voices could be heard
in the hall. Geoffrey Wheeler and the Sondheimers.
There was no time to deal with this. Already they were
filing into the room, and instantly her mind was taken
over by them.

'No Harry?' Wheeler said and kissed her more
warmly than he might have done had Harry been there.
'Good God, Routh, half-dressed, swilling whisky? She's
corrupted you already.'

'I haven't seen you,' she said to Gerda. 'Not for
days.' They filled the room with their decisions as to
where to sit, their explanations to Amde and Hassan of
exactly what they would have to drink. When she
glanced back at Roland Routh, he was diminished by
them. He must wait. Just for this moment before everyone arrived she would talk to Gerda. She held tightly
to her friend's ringed hand and sat her down beside her
on the sofa. 'What have you been doing?' she asked
her. 'I feel so out of touch.' For normally until Flo
arrived they had spoken daily.

Even above the added voices in the room she heard
the gravel, heard Harry's voice. He came through the
door rubbing his hands together and saying, 'Ah, Saturday!' Everyone stood up till he was seated. His drink
was brought. The peanuts went their rounds. The men
talked of the troubles in Kenya. The women turned
their heads from side to side to listen brightly to each
one as he spoke.

The Harringtons came. The men rose. By slipping

her arm around Nell Harrington's plump waist and steering her to the place where Geoffrey had been sitting, and at the same time sliding his glass along the coffee-table next to Gerda's and saying firmly to Nigel Harrington, 'You may not know Roland Routh,' she contrived that everyone sat down next to someone else.

'Well,' Harry said. 'How very nice this is.'

Nigel Harrington said to Routh, 'I hear you're pumping new life into our theatrical society.'

'I'm trying to,' Routh said. He seemed sullen, almost rude. It was a mistake to have asked him with the others, Lydia thought. He should have come on his own, when Flo was there. The hard-cornered fact that he had forgotten her invitation and come only to ask a favour lodged in her mind. There was a pause while everyone waited for him to say something else about his play. Am I supposed to ask Harry here and now? she thought. Rain was just audible outside the muffled windows. Then Rudi Sondheimer said, 'How very English. So much at stake, and you decide to put on a play!'

'Oh, there's nothing frivolous about it,' Wheeler told him. 'It's all in deadly earnest. *Hamlet*, no less. Very modern. I've heard all about it. Claudius rigged out like the Duce. Gertrude a floozie. Hamlet mows down the entire cast with his service revolver. Stirring stuff.'

He shouldn't mock, Lydia thought. Never mock the young.

'Quite so,' Sondheimer said. 'A serious play about assassination, about corruption in high places, about political collapse, just when all this is coming to an end.' His gesture was extravagant, and seemed to extend beyond the present room to take in the British Empire as a whole. He looked at their thoughtful, unresponsive faces and said, 'Do you not agree? Am I wrong about your play? Why does no one respond to me?' In the pause that followed he began to laugh in the harsh humourless way of foreigners.

'I think it's a great mistake,' Nell Harrington said suddenly. 'Nobody wants to be made to think of things like that. Not now especially. Not ever.'

'Nobody's obliged to come to it,' Routh said. He stood up and said to Lydia alone, 'I'm afraid I must go. I'm going out to lunch.'

Because he was too young and brusque, because he slung his coat too casually across his arm, because his appointment in some complex world outside these walls disturbed her, she said to the others, 'Don't move,' and followed him out into the hall. There, with the servants gravely watching them, they shook hands. 'You're absolutely right to do it,' she said. 'I'll speak to Harry. You mustn't mind the others. It's he that matters and I'm sure that he'll agree.'

'Look,' he said, spreading his hands helplessly, 'if I can do anything in return. I can't imagine what it might be.'

'You can,' she said. 'You can find something in it for Flo.' Then seeing him look dismayed, she said, 'Oh, she doesn't act. Nothing like that. Only there must be something. Behind the scenes. Just something.'

'I'll try,' he said, nodded curtly and left.

She stood for a moment where she was, telling herself that it was a relief that he had gone; that he knew no better; that she had dealt with him. Then, because nothing must unsettle the peace of Saturday mornings at the villa, she ran back into the room, interrupting their talk to say, 'Oh, I am so sorry,' and at the same time rolling her eyes in mock despair as if to say, The young!

'But they should put on something pleasant,' Nell Harrington persisted. 'Something people would enjoy.'

'Of course,' Lydia told her, beckoning Amde to fill up her glass. 'Of course you're absolutely right.' And sitting down beside her she began to talk some nonsense about the play that she and Geoffrey had acted in in Nairobi, all those years ago.

'That play!' he called across to her in mock horror.

'Do you remember? You had to carry that woman and lay her on a *chaise longue.*'

'Was she dead? I can't remember. She was fiendishly heavy.'

' "Play something, Mother," ' Lydia intoned. ' "It might bring her in from the garden." '

'No one could have made me speak a line like that,' he cried clapping his knees with both his hands. 'Never, never, never!'

And at last they were able to laugh.

Chapter Eight

OVER LUNCH Harry Morgan said, 'What ever came over Routh, rushing off like that? Was it wise to ask him again so soon?'

'I didn't ask him. He came because he wants to put this play on in the theatre. He needs your permission.'

'Why didn't he ask for it?'

'He did. Clive's put the kibosh on it. He disapproves.'

'Of *Hamlet*?' He gave a grunt half of amusement, half of contempt. 'There's nothing wrong with it, is there?'

'It's just more highbrow than they're used to.'

'Well, I don't see why not,' Morgan said.

'Will you sort Clive out then?'

'Yes, if you wish.' She wondered if he would ever remember so trivial a thing. He had risen and tossed his white starched napkin on the surface of the table. 'Upstairs?' he asked her, and when she nodded he told the major-domo to bring the coffee tray to the upstairs sitting-room.

At mealtimes, between the serving of the courses,

the servants waited at the edges of the room. There was no possibility then of discussing more personal matters, but over coffee, in the upstairs sitting-room, they were left alone. They sat in easy chairs facing each other across the round glass-topped table on which Lydia played her games of patience.

'Tired?' she said, smiling at him.

'End of the week.' He dragged his hands down his face, shaking his head slightly to rid it of the need for sleep. 'Where's Flo?' he said, as if only now aware of her absence.

'At the Wallers'.'

'I'm glad she's out here,' he said. 'It's company for you.'

His affection for Flo was real enough. Her dead father, his never-to-be-born son, their mutual inability to compensate one another, formed a bond of a particular kind. Nevertheless he found her presence in the house disturbing. He would have liked to say, She's so quiet. I can't find anything to say to her. He would have liked to be reassured that he was not to blame for that; to ask, What will become of her? How long will she be with us? – things he found he could not ask.

Instead he said, 'I've been thinking, when this is all over, we might not go directly home.' The sudden eagerness of her look surprised him. And Lydia herself was shocked to hear her heart cry out, Anything, anything but England! They had never talked in any practical way of the future. To do so had seemed to venture into some promised but forbidden land; perhaps to invite disaster.

She was smiling at him. 'Do you remember how we used to say, "After the war . . ." all the time. Everything would happen, "after the war".' He gave the curt upward nod of his head, the intimate grunt at the back of his throat, that meant, Yes: he too remembered the shining promise of that time, which was this time, before it came.

Still, he had ventured across the border and would not turn back. 'I'd thought of Kenya, but it's too unsettled now. Rhodesia, maybe South Africa. Malcolm Parkes has always wanted me to come and see his set-up out there.'

'A job?' she said quickly.

He shrugged. 'It wouldn't hurt to have a look. Let Parkes know we're coming out there. Just a trip, a holiday, a rest, then if something came up, we might think about staying on.'

How could she be so eager to exchange the dream of home for what: the promise of continued light, the pressure of the sun on her bared arms, this life she could have sworn meant nothing to her? Immediately her pleasure conjured up its shadow.

'And Flo? What would become of Flo?'

'Well, yes. Of course, Flo too. I was assuming that.'

But he had spoken too quickly for her not to know that Flo had had no part in this bright vision, in his mind or in hers, though both might wish it had been otherwise.

They were silent for a moment. Then Lydia said, 'I can't ask that. Besides, she should go back to England. Get established there. Do something. There's not enough for her out here.'

'Do what?'

'Well, something.'

'She'll marry,' he said quickly. 'Of course she will.' But he could not suppress the thought, And if no one marries her? What then? Will she always be with us? A need to cloak this lack of generosity made him say gravely now something he had hesitated to say before. 'Look, don't be alarmed, but really you know, it might be for the best. Whatever happens in the long run, she should go back to London a few weeks before we do.'

He watched Lydia's face fill with a fear that knew no limits. 'Has something gone wrong? Is there going to be trouble?'

'No, of course not. But you know how it is.'

'But it's not dangerous, is it? For you I mean.'

'No,' he said wearily. 'No more than it's ever been.'

Generally he avoided thinking too closely of the final days of the handover. He doubted anyone at this stage could seriously intend him harm, but in the fervour of the moment he could not guess what hidden feuds and hatreds might surface; what emotions might shake the hand that held the revolver and cause it to mis-aim. He had a deep mistrust of men who felt more passionately than he and knew that on that day he would be surrounded by them.

'But they're getting what they want, surely,' Lydia said.

She had spoken with a bitterness that made him say, 'Look, you know I'd send you back too, if I could, just to play safe.'

'I wouldn't go,' she said. 'Until you go, I'd never go.'

'It's out of the question in any case.' They both knew that she would have her necessary part to play in fragile straw and chiffon. The costume had been bought in London before they knew of Ponticelli. In it she must attend to the lady of the ruler of the Northern Province and make her unspoken statement of the confident and civilian nature of Morgan's own regime. 'But there's no need to take risks with Flo.'

'No,' she said quickly. 'She must go. I'm sure she'll understand. I could ask Daisy. She has the room and God knows she needs the money. When shall I say? The first week of June?' She was silent for a moment. Then she said, 'It's just telling Flo. She so counts on being with us, on having somewhere. She thinks we'll go back home, buy a house. It's why she's such a child sometimes. She's never had all that. I sometimes think she's fearful of finding she's grown up before she does.'

She had begun to cry as suddenly and soundlessly as she had in front of Roland Routh. She wiped angrily at the tears with the back of her hand as if to disown them, while Morgan watched, appalled at what he must ask of her.

To make amends, he said, 'I'll tell her. I'll take

her out to the escarpment, to see the view. This afternoon, if you like. I've been meaning to do that.'

He could see her relief. 'Would you really? Tell her
it can't be helped. Well, it can't, I know, but it would
come better from you.'

'Right,' he said. 'You stay behind and have a rest
before tonight.' They were to dine with the United
Nations Commissioner, a man he liked.

'But you . . .'

'I'll be fine,' he said. 'I'll take a siesta now.'

The languorous word seemed out of place. He
closed the door of the bedroom behind him and lay
down on the bed. Before he had had time to kick off
his shoes, he had fallen heavily asleep.

Lydia rang to have the tray removed and gave
instructions for the jeep to be brought to the front
door at five. Then she took off her frock, opened the
bathroom door and tossed it on the marble floor for
old Gidea to find and wash again. She slipped into her
dressing-gown, loosened her hair, laid out her meticu-
lous game of patience, lit a cigarette and began to move
the cards this way and that.

If it comes out, she told herself, the shot will not
be fired. But however carefully she put the black five
on the red six, in her overactive mind the Archduke's
plumed hat, snatched from some old newsreel, tumbled
in the gutter. She would die to save him. If it comes
out he'll get a job. One that's good enough for him. If
it comes out Flo will be happy. She shuffled these fierce
longings to and fro. To none of them would she after

all dedicate this particular hand, which looked unpromising.

Promptly at four fifty-seven Haile drove the jeep up the drive and parked it by the villa steps. He sprang out, snatched off the leather sheaths that cased the miniature flagstaffs on each mudguard, and stirred their little pennants into life with his forefinger.

At five o'clock Harry Morgan, wearing a linen suit and a soft felt hat, jogged briskly down the villa steps with his binoculars swinging against his chest. Behind him came Flo in a cotton frock, headscarf, ankle socks and freshly whitened tennis shoes. Lydia, in her dressing-gown, watched and waved from the upstairs balcony.

'I'll drive,' Morgan said. He climbed in behind the wheel and reached across his big warm hand to help Flo in. When she was settled Haile swung into the back seat. Morgan braked at the sentry box to take aboard one of the Aderran policemen, who climbed in beside Haile with his automatic rifle laid carefully across his knees. 'All set?' Morgan asked. A moment later they were speeding up the Corso, past the whitewashed tree-trunks and the strolling crowds. The pennants on the mudguards flicked like tongues.

As soon as the outing had been put to her, Flo had supposed it to be a strategy of Lydia's to ensure that she and Harry talk direct to one another. Their silent exchanges had always been their happiest ones, though by their very nature Lydia was unaware of that. Now the shy pride that Flo might have felt that all this had been set in motion to please her was burdened by the need to please and entertain him.

Morgan had began to talk steadily of altitudes and watersheds. She turned her face obediently towards him, struggling to retain facts that had no meaning for her, thrown back in memory to other such occasions.

Once it had snowed. He had stood in the passage of a house they had rented in the Lake District, spinning a worn tennis-ball into the air between his thumb and forefinger. It seemed to fall as if magnetized into his other hand which gave loosely at the wrist to receive it, continued the downward sweep, then spun it back again. Somewhere behind them in the house, Lydia had said, 'Why don't you take her out and play with her in the snow?' He had been new in Flo's life then. All the time it took to force the buttons through the stiff buttonholes of her new coat, her eyes had been held by those slow hypnotic movements. He had said he would teach her how to catch a ball. He spoke with such confidence that it seemed that all her troubles in the playground at the day-school she attended then might be over by the end of the afternoon.

Outside in the snow, with the same exaggerated grace, he had tossed the ball to her. It struck her before she even saw it come. He laughed good-naturedly. She failed to catch it the next time and the next. He didn't laugh now. He showed her, not at all unkindly, how to cup her hands in front of her. She sealed them together as he said and squinted across the glaring surface of the snow, while he pitched the ball slowly and with such precision that it came to rest in her obedient cup. She felt hot with relief as she felt it there. 'Well done!' he said. 'That's it. You've got it. Now.' He threw it harder and a little to the left. Flo, standing very still with her hands together, waiting for the miracle to recur, failed again to catch it. 'Are you cold?' he asked her kindly. She nodded. They went in. She remembered Lydia saying, 'So soon?'

Now, as he talked eagerly of the formation of the Rift Valley, she felt the same tightening of her throat and stomach. She fixed her eyes upon his full shaved lips and set herself to catch these words from which she must form the questions that would keep him talking. The place itself glided distractingly past his shoulder.

Beyond the airport the town came abruptly to its end. They drove past the string of little villas with their pistachio shutters and oleander trees; then on past sparse groves of eucalyptus growing out of stony ground. The traffic on the Corso had been left behind. The jeep gathered speed. She saw the smile of joy on Harry Morgan's face as he set himself to overtake a lorry. It swerved suddenly, to avoid something by the side of the road. Morgan blared on his horn. The crowd of faces that stared out under its canvas cover jeered. Fists were shaken. Haile and the guard leant out of their respective sides to shout abuse and threats. The lorry swerved back again to reveal the same stacks of blackened branches that Flo had glimpsed on the day of her arrival.

Now the wood lurched steadily closer until she could make out the small troop of people who carried it, hurrying as if to some pressing appointment in the town. They were wrapped in dark rags, hardly distinguishable from their burdens, and bent double so that their faces stared down at the road and their backs formed a level platform on which were stacked the great pyres, higher than themselves had they been able to stand upright. Morgan gave a short grunt of recognition and raised his hand in greeting.

The wood-carriers, clinging to the ropes that bound them to their burdens, were unable to respond, but twisted their bowed heads to watch him pass without slackening their brisk trot. Flo saw their grinning faces, black, wizened, toothless. They were women. Inside their rags empty breasts flapped. Their grotesque cheerfulness, their uninterrupted haste made them seem the vanguard of some dark mass come to overwhelm the thriving town.

'What are they?' Her voice seemed shrill and accusing. Pity that anyone should live so, and a shameful fear that there could never be enough to divide her from them, had snatched away the nervous pleasure in the afternoon.

Morgan who had turned half-towards her looked away again, she thought with distaste. 'Wood's scarce in the town,' he said. 'They bring it up from the valley. You'll see what it's like when we get there. Quite a climb.'

'But they're old,' she said. 'Old women.'

The irrelevance of the remark irritated him. 'Not a bit of it,' he said. 'They're relatively young. They couldn't do it otherwise.' She would not believe that. She had seen them. They could not be young. They were out of sight now, but she could not rid herself of the horror of them.

Morgan leant forward, looking for the turning on the featureless roadside and humming with anticipation. A moment later, with a twist of his broad capable wrists, he turned the jeep abruptly off the road. It bumped over rough ground. Ahead of them a row of peaks was sharply visible, rose-coloured in the late afternoon light. 'You see those?' he said to Flo. 'They're on the far side of the valley.'

He drove the jeep a few yards further before saying, 'This will do. Out we get.' He propelled Flo over the stony ground with his fist in the small of her back; then walked ahead as if he could not bear to be delayed. 'Come over here, Flo,' he called back to her. 'Take a look at this.'

Flo followed him to the very point where the mountain suddenly split and fell away, down among the debris of its own cliffs and boulders; a sheer drop impossible to contemplate. Across the deep rift more fissured cliffs rose as far as they could see in both direc-tions, a wilderness of glowing rock.

Morgan turned to watch, almost wistfully, her expression, as she saw for the first time this thing he loved. 'Well, what do you think of it?

'I think it's very beautiful,' she said, but the words fell, inadequate, into the huge space around them. He had moved forward again, closer to the edge than she

had dared, and now stared downward through his binoculars. 'Come over here,' he said, 'and take a look
through these. They're good ones.' He handed her the
binoculars and lifted the strap carefully over her headscarf, so that the silk rasped with a tiny thunder against
her ears. 'Don't drop them,' he said, and laughed.

They were heavy. She tried to fit them to her
narrow face and turned them this way and that. A blur
of unfocused pink slid back and forth before her eyes.
He laughed again, with his odd mixture of amusement
and contempt, and came to stand behind her, steadying
her hands in his, directing the binoculars downward.
His close presence was rare and dear to her. She wanted
only not to disappoint him.

'Do you see the road? It's the same one we came
on further on.'

'Yes.' But even with his guidance she had no clear
view of it. 'I think I see better without them.'

'As you wish.' He lifted them over her head and
stood apart. He was proud of these binoculars, an excellent pair taken from the neck of a long-dead German
officer in a burnt-out tank outside Mersa Matruh. Still
his own neck prickled slightly when he put them on.
He used them now to scan the distant mountain face
for any glimpse of movement; the glint of glass or metal
that might betray someone, less idly, watching him.

Flo watched with her naked eye the road as it
continued on without them. It looped back and forth
down the face of the mountain as if dropped there from
a great height, ready-made and still pliant, to lie as it

had fallen. She traced its course down the deep cleft until it vanished in the cloud of mist that choked the lower reaches of the valley. From that white mass the blackened troop of wood-carriers must have emerged.

'It goes right down to the coast,' Morgan told her without lowering his glasses. He tilted them downward now to trace the twisting of the road with the same serious attention. 'It wasn't safe a few months back, but it's open now. No incidents. Not for months.' She could hear the quiet pride in his voice. He had accomplished this and relished a new person to whom to tell it, but she could not respond as he would want her to. The distorted bodies of the women, and a more obscure sense that she would always fail him, lodged like twin splinters in her mind, and could not be dislodged. The women had trotted up out of that mist, from some invisible place below the tree line, back and forth across all that astonishing beauty. And all the time they had seen nothing but their own worn feet beating a relent-less progress over the unchanging surface of the road. In a child's importunate voice she said to him, 'Can they stand up straight when they go home again?'

'What on earth are you talking about?' Morgan said harshly. He was as startled as if some third person, quite unnoticed by him, had suddenly spoken.

'The women who carried the wood.'

'What have they got to do with it?'

'Can't you make it stop?'

'Why?' he said. 'It's their living. They'd starve if they were stopped.'

'You could help them.'

With a bitterness he did not intend, he said, 'Is that what you imagine I'm here to do? Make people's lives better for them?'

'Well. Aren't you?'

'Good God, no! If anything, I'm here to stop them killing one another!'

Both of them had raised their voices, shockingly, in all that surrounding silence. Now Morgan laid his finger to his lips and glanced briefly to where the two Aderrans squatted in the shadow of the jeep. They sat back to back, Haile staring out across the mountains and the policeman watching the road.

Neither had stirred, nor looked towards them with any interest. Still Morgan felt remorse that he had allowed himself to be rattled and had spoken almost violently to the girl.

Flo too understood that he had wished to give her something. In return, she had spoilt his pleasure, betrayed his shy affection. He would turn back. They would drive home. Lydia would look up and see his face and say, 'So soon?'

Now, steadying his voice to its normal pace, Morgan said quietly, 'Has Lydia told you about Haile? He owns land down there. Several villages. He's a big man in his world and a patriot. He only drives the jeep because the engine fascinates him. He'll stop up all night just to strip down the engine and put it back again. Just for the hell of it.'

He called out, 'Ya, Haile!' The man sprang to his feet and came running towards him. 'Your village?' Morgan asked him in Italian. The driver stabbed the air repeatedly with his finger, delighted to establish the place's exact whereabouts. Morgan opened his map. The driver bent his grizzled head and followed the blunt finger with bright excited eyes. They agreed between them where the place must be. '*Permesso?*' Haile asked, looking directly at Morgan and beaming at him.

'Go right ahead,' Morgan said in English. He too was smiling. The driver took the map and ran back to spread it carefully on the bonnet of the jeep and study it intently. The policeman never moved or shifted his attention from the road.

'Come over here,' Morgan said to Flo. He lowered himself on to a fallen log, his legs stretched out, his thick ankles in their hand-knitted socks crossed easily in front of him.

Flo came to sit beside him, decorously hooking the skirt of her frock over her knees.

'We'll watch the sunset, shall we?' Morgan said. It would be easier to talk like this, looking outward at the great view, rather than trying to face each other.

'God, it's peaceful,' he continued, with every semblance of enjoyment. She thought he had forgiven her. Now he said carefully, 'Your mother and I have been talking. We – well actually I – think it might be a good idea to send you home a little before the end here.' He glanced quickly at her and, seeing her small troubled features half-blinkered by the headscarf, hurried on. 'You won't be the only one. We'll be sending back as many as we can. People who aren't needed at the very end.'

'What does Lydia say?' the girl asked.

'She's all in favour of it,' Morgan said. 'She wants you to stay with Daisy. You'd like that, wouldn't you? Just till we get back, Then we'll fix you up with a job somewhere. Something that would interest you.'

Intolerably, she turned to look at him and said, 'Why can't I stay here with you?'

He dared not stress the dangers lest he frighten her, but said instead, 'Can you see that it's frightfully important to me that nothing should go wrong at the end? To spoil it all. That we move out in some sort of style and the fewer people there are about, the fewer things are likely to go wrong? Can you see the sense in that?'

She nodded dumbly and was silent, turning her face away to watch the strange alteration of the light. Then when he supposed the matter over and done with she said, 'When do you want me to go away?'

'A few weeks before the end. A fortnight, say. That would bring us to the first week in June.'

'Oh,' she said. The word came out as a sigh of relief. He saw her face relax and understood that June, which tormented him with its close approach, was indistinct to her; part of some distant period of time with which her mind need not concern itself.

'Is that all right, then?'

She nodded. Her odd outburst earlier and the painful crumpling of her face when he first spoke, made the matter too precarious to pursue. He decided to make no mention of his and Lydia's protracted stay in Africa. Nothing might come of it in any case. He had done his bit, broached the subject, prepared the ground. Her mother might take over from there. He turned entirely to the view.

Before them the mist rose steadily out of the valley. In the distance peak after peak glowed red, reflecting colour out on to the surface of the cloud. Then, while they watched in silence, a rising moon cast its cool light over that landscape still coloured by the sun, until, like some effect of theatre, the rocks which had seemed so solid became ethereal things of light and smoke and all the red gave way.

'Mustn't let it get dark on us,' Morgan said, getting suddenly to his feet. Haile and the policeman followed suit. They left in haste, awed by what they had seen, but glad perhaps to turn back from the edge towards the lighted town.

Chapter Nine

IN THOSE DAYS things moved in circles: the dancers gyrating round and round the walls of rooms; the inwards spiralling of gramophone records; the ceaseless scything of the minute-hands round and round the faces of wristwatches and clocks. It was possible to see the dance, the music and the time being spent and still hold to the illusion that everything that vanished might return, that there were always second chances. The same dance tune would start again, the same partners rise to circle the room. The needle could be set back on the record's shiny rim; the hours and the days of the week return, bringing the same diversions.

Two Saturdays after Roland Routh had made his brusque departure, Lydia heard his voice in the hall, enquiring of the major-domo whether she were in. He had come early again. At least half an hour before the others were expected. He was in the room, hurrying towards her as if he would shake hands, but he did not attempt to nor did she reach out to him. She did not think him small on this occasion. Everything about him struck her as fine and concentrated. Even the shadow of his beard was dense, like pepper pressed into the fine pale skin; all of him compacted around the central energy that moved in pursuit of its own will.

'I haven't heard,' she said immediately, before even offering him a drink. 'I put it to Harry just as you asked, but I haven't heard anything more.'

'Hasn't he told you? It's all gone through. You don't mind my coming, do you? I wanted to say thank you.'

'It matters to you, doesn't it,' she said, offering him a cigarette.

'Yes, it does. A great deal.'

Hassan, without being asked, produced a whisky. 'Is that what you want?' she said.

'Yes, actually it is. You don't mind, do you?'

'Have you been away again?'

'No. Look, I'm sorry. I've been busy. I only heard a day or two ago. I came as quickly as I could. To say thank you.'

'I didn't mean that. I only . . .'

They had lapsed into an awkwardness. Now she said as if to any tongue-tied young man, 'Did you act at Oxford? Geoffrey said that you were up.'

'I've always acted.'

'And then? After Oxford?'

'I told you, I went out to Italy.'

'You didn't tell me about the thesis.'

'Oh,' he said. 'Didn't I? I'm not sure I want to.' He dug his fingers suddenly into his thick hair. The sound of Rudi Sondheimer's record established Flo's presence in the ballroom. Almost Lydia hoped the girl would come and put a stop to this. She had only to rise, cross the floor, open the doors and call to her, but for the moment she did not. Instead she went over to the major-domo's sideboard and helped herself to ice. I've gone too far, she thought. Presumed on something that was never there.

When she sat down again she found he was looking at her, smiling both sadly and appealingly. 'If you really want to know, it was a mess,' he said. 'It all went dreadfully wrong. They were Catholics. Cousins of my mother's. There was a daughter. I didn't finish the thesis. Didn't get the degree. That's why I came out here.' He was looking at her helplessly. 'I'm very fluent in Italian.'

It shocked her that she laughed and that he laughed too, quietly and comfortably. She did not care to know exactly what his crime had been. Nor could she account for the unfamiliar intimacy that had settled in the room. He must have been absurdly young, she thought, offering him a peanut to show her readiness not to think badly of him. The young must be forgiven. But only once, her cautious numerical mind told her. The young must be forgiven only once.

They sipped their drinks without speaking for a moment, but the silence did not unnerve her now. He had come because he wanted to. He had chosen to talk to her in the way he did. She could see from his stillness in the chair that he was not yet prepared to go, and might wish to talk more about himself.

'And your father?' she asked carefully. 'You don't mention him.'

Without shifting his eyes he said, 'He went mad, I think. She never talks of it. I was four then. They carried him out in a blue wicker chair. I saw them. They brought it back again and put it back in the bathroom. I always hated it.' He paused and added, 'He never came back.'

'I'm so sorry.'

'Why should you be? It was a long time ago. He died, I think. Later. She didn't talk about it. But yes, of course, he's dead by now. He must be.'

'Weren't you curious?'

'Oh, I like secrets.'

'Was there only you?'

'Me and her.'

'She must miss you.'

'Yes. I think she does. I'm not going back though.'

When she kept silent, he said quietly, 'How could you understand?'

Rather than attempt to answer him, she said, 'Where will you go? When this is over?'

'I'm not sure yet. Paris possibly. I've an opening there. Interpreting. That's just temporary though.' He added, 'I have perfect French as well.'

The bleak tale and his painful detachment from it seemed to settle in the quiet room. The foolish tunes ground on in the background. There seemed nothing whatever to say.

After a moment he continued, 'That's why everything seems to matter so at the moment. Not to fail at anything. Even the play. Can you understand that?'

She nodded.

He had finished his drink. She could see by the way that he set down the glass that he intended to go. As he rose he smiled at her and said, 'You're doing me good, you know. Letting me come here.' There was no telling from the way he pitched his voice how sincerely he might mean this.

'Oh,' she said with a little laugh, 'the perils of believing that!' Outside she heard a car approach. From the ballroom, she heard Flo's record reach its final chorus. She imagined him writing to his mother to say that he had been taken up at the villa and it was doing him good. She imagined he had written something similar from Rome and perhaps from Paris too.

'No, seriously,' he said, looking directly at her. 'You are.'

He left, just as the others came. She heard him make his apologies to the Sondheimers in the hall. Only then did she remember Flo and realize that he had made no mention of his promise to include her somehow in the play. It was too late to run after him. Gerda Sondheimer was in the room saying, 'Have we interrupted something? Have we frightened him away?' And she could say, 'Oh, you don't know how glad I am to see you,' and find that it was partly true.

Later that afternoon the major-domo knocked at the door of the upstairs sitting-room. He was carrying a

Ann Schlee

- 116 -

white envelope on his tray. 'For the Signorina,' he said, gravely, and handed it to Flo.

'Well?' Lydia asked. She was careful not to look up from her cards. 'What does it say?'

'It's from Roland Routh,' the girl told her. 'He wants me to help with the play – with the props.' She was so still in her chair that it seemed an enchanter's hand had cast her there and left her powerless to rise or speak further.

'And will you?' Lydia persisted.

'Did you tell him to ask me?'

'Of course not,' Lydia told her, frowning at the three of hearts as if there were anything she could do with it other than place it after the two.

'Yes. I will,' the girl said.

She spoke with such intensity that her mother was bound to look up. Flo was steadily regarding her. What does she see? Lydia asked herself. What am I doing? For she had lied to her child without mercy and quite unnecessarily. Now she was equally appalled to think that Flo should believe or disbelieve her. She said quickly, 'It means a lot to him. The play. He's rather on his own here, I think. Rather lonely and unhappy. He needs standing up for.' Then when Flo said nothing, she hurried on. 'You'll have to watch your step there, with the other people. Not get too involved, Flo. They could be anybody. Not necessarily the sort we ask to the villa. I don't know any of them.'

'But you want me to go, don't you?' the girl asked earnestly.

'Oh yes, of course I do.'

'Besides,' she said with her unflinching gaze, 'you do know Roland Routh.'

All through the day of that first rehearsal Flo had felt her mother's excitement absorb and diminish her own. After lunch, as they drank coffee in the upstairs sitting-room, Lydia had talked of the Christmas, infinitely long ago in Kenya, when the young district commissioners had come in to the town after months in their out-stations and quarrelled as to who should dance with her. They had put on a play. She had been the leading lady and Geoffrey Wheeler, of all people, had played the hero. 'Oh, it was an absurd play, but Flo darling, you're to have *Hamlet*! A real play! A marvellous play!'

Suddenly she remembered that somewhere among the contents of the ammunition boxes was her blue leatherbound edition of Shakespeare's Tragedies. She ran across the room and rang the bell. She would find it now, immediately, and give it to Flo. All these months that the ammunition boxes had sat reproachfully in the corner of the room, she had felt herself quite unable to open them. Only now she thought to ask: of what had she been afraid? That after this lapse of time her treasures would be revealed as tawdry? That seeing them again would cast too searching a light on the past and the future? But the books would be safe. The books would be the same. She need only open the box with the books.

When Amde came to the door, she pointed to the boxes and mimed that he should heft each one. The heaviest would be the books. They discovered that the metal hasps that bound the wooden box at either end were secured by a single nail. Amde hurried off and returned with a claw-hammer. With Lydia directing him he proceeded to prise free the nails, lower the hasps, pull off the lid. Immediately Lydia began to lift them out, all the old familiar books, and lay them in little stacks, searching for the blue binding. Flo came to kneel beside her and peer eagerly into the box.

'It's here,' her mother cried in triumph, blowing along the edges of the little volume and clapping the pages together to rid it of dust. Then she opened it at the dedication. 'To Lydia Franklyn – the prize for English Literature – 1931.' Back it all came. Miss Richardson pounding out Schubert's '*Marche Militaire*' on the gymnasium piano while she went up and made her curtsy. Her father home from Kenya. Her special white dress. The pride of it. All that, she had meant to give to Flo. Now all she had to offer was the book.

She handed it shyly to her daughter, saying, 'Keep it. It's for you.' The girl opened it quickly to *Hamlet*. 'Have you never read it?' Lydia said, craning over the page to read it herself. 'Oh, what a treat in store for you!'

'We did it with Miss Blakely,' Flo said, with less enthusiasm than Lydia could have wished, but she could see that the girl was very pleased with her gift.

'Should you go back to school?' she said impulsively.

Then seeing Flo's quick frown, she hurried on, 'Or to college. Girls do now, study something. I always wanted to.'

'No,' Flo said emphatically.

'Are you sure? Harry wouldn't mind. He's so generous.'

'It's too late,' Flo said. 'I don't want to go back now.'

'We must think,' her mother went on. 'What you are to do in England. It's so hard to think here, but we must.'

But even as she spoke, she turned to look at her travelling-clock and cried out, 'Look at the time. You'll be late. You must wash off all that dust before you go.'

She had insisted that she accompany Flo to the theatre by car, although, in fact, it was only a few minutes' walk away. Now she sat forward in the back seat of the Chevrolet, holding the handgrip and peering out into the street as if their destination might somehow manage to elude them.

The theatre was an ornate building, facing on to the Corso. In its heyday, in the Italian era, it had been used exclusively for opera. At what stage in a diva's career an engagement in the opera-house in Aderra might become acceptable makes painful speculation. Still, by all accounts the audiences that had come night after night during the extended season had been large and noisily appreciative. The Duke and Duchess had regularly graced their box and, looking through their opera-glasses before the curtain rose, would have found nothing scanted in the way of crimson plush and gilded curves.

Now for most of the year it was kept locked. At Christmas the incumbent British regiment put on a pantomime. In the summer the amateur theatrical society put on its annual production. For those two weeks out of the year the box office was opened and the house lights switched on. The British Community would assemble in the foyer in evening frocks and dinner-jackets, to find themselves dispirited, even before they entered the auditorium, by the grime and shabbiness of the place. Those who had been before carried cushions of their own rather than risk too close contact with the seats. As they waited for the show to begin, the odour of dust and of the hectic life cycles of mice seeped out to them from the very fabric of the place. Behind the scenes it was stifling.

The British audience, too, were loyal in their applause, often rowdy. But even with a full turnout there were scarcely enough of them to fill the stalls. It was noticed that the empty balconies threw back an unfortunate echo. During Flo's time in Aderra, the place was at its best in its half-wakened state, during the weeks of rehearsal. Then, with only the stage lit, the limits of the auditorium remained obscured. The stage lights reflecting faintly on the swollen shapes and the occasional gleam of gilding suggested a setting, vast and opulent, in which any ambition might be accomplished, any fantasy realized.

Within minutes the Chevrolet had stopped in a

side-street opposite the bare flank of the old building.
A door was propped open on to the street and just
behind it they could see a soldier in his khaki drill
sawing up a plank of wood propped on two trestles.
While Flo waited for Haile to come to open the car
door for her, Lydia said, 'You will be all right, won't
you?'

'Yes, of course I will.' The door was open. She must
get out. 'Where do I go?' she asked her mother.

'He'll know,' Lydia said, gesturing at the soldier with
a cigarette she had just lighted.

Flo crossed the street without looking back and
heard the big car draw away behind her. The soldier
had not noticed it, nor looked up from his sawing. He
was startled when she spoke. To hide the fact, he said
brusquely, 'Expecting you, are they?'

'Mr Routh is.'

'Is he now? Well, best go up then. Not that he's
here, of course, but Jamie is.' He stood back, raising the
saw elaborately above his head and watching her closely
as she passed him. She was glad when the stairs turned
and he could no longer see her. It was difficult to see
at all. She groped her way upward, breathing in the
dense air of the place until the flight ended and she
came out into the wings. Above and beyond, the theatre
stretched away into the dark. Directly in front was an
expanse of lighted stage.

It was bare except for a table. A man had propped
himself against it with his head thrown back and a
walking-stick between his knees. His hands were

stretched in front of him, one on top of the other, to grasp its knob. For a moment she did not recognize him as Jamie Renfrew whom Bridie had her thing about. She had only seen him at a distance or in photographs standing stiffly in his evening blues. The stick, the shirtsleeves immaculately folded up above his elbows, the silk spotted scarf tucked into his open collar, transformed him into someone jauntily in charge.

She could not bring herself to walk out on to the stage, but stood watching and wondered if he were acting out some silent part or if he merely waited there. A floorboard creaked under her foot. He looked in her direction, frowning into the darkness and calling out, 'Who is it then? Who's there?'

When she stepped forward the animation left his face. 'Yes?' he said. He gave no indication of whether he recognized her or not.

'I've come to do the props,' she said. 'Roland said I might.'

'Oh, damn him,' Renfrew said. 'He had no business. Broad,' he shouted, hurrying past her to the head of the stairs; then, after a clatter of footsteps, 'Did bloody Rolly say anything about props to you?' Their voices sank from hearing. She waited, staring out with wonder into the great void of the auditorium. 'Look,' Renfrew said when he came back. 'I don't know what he said to you, but there isn't really anything to do. Broad sees to most things. Perhaps there'll be a prop or two later on. But not yet.'

With an awkward insistence, she said, 'But I will

come. I should get to know the play. He did write to
me and say I might.'

Again she watched his absence of response. 'You'd
best get somewhere to sit then. There's a chair somewhere.' He took up his waiting pose again at centre
stage. Flo looked about until she found a wooden chair.
She placed it carefully in the shadow of the wings. She
sat there with her mother's school prize open on her
knees, intent as if this were some new lesson to be
learned, some new examination to be passed.

The actors were arriving, pushing past her or
coming out from the opposite wings and walking boldly
out to stand around the table. As the stage lights struck
their faces, some of them revealed themselves, as do the
indistinct figures in dreams. There was Mrs Bynge who
sometimes sat with Wendy Waller at the club dances
and gossiped behind her fan. There was her husband,
the Major. There were two young corporals from the
regimental office who sometimes made up Mrs Bynge's
parties, but spent most of the evening in each other's
company at the bar. She had seen none of them except
in evening dress. Now their daytime clothes, which
might have been their costumes, suggested a studied
laxity. Their voices too had changed. Mrs Bynge, whom
she had only heard to speak in careful imitation of
Wendy Waller, now spoke loudly and revealed a deep
and reckless laugh, unheard at the club. The Major,
whom she had never heard to speak at all, greeted
everyone in a fine rich voice, like the actors in the films

they had been shown at school, about the younger Pitt and Horatio, Lord Nelson.

Next a young woman came hurrying up through the auditorium, calling out before Flo had really seen her, 'God, but I'm sorry. I've had such a foul day. A real soddy.' Everyone turned to watch her make her entrance. She was small. She needed her hands to help her scramble up the steep steps on to the stage. 'I'm in a foul mood,' she told them, crossing to the table with her anxious running step. Her red sweater was pulled tightly over small sharp breasts. She stood there, at once provocative and wary, while they crowded around her. They called her Avril. Flo recognized her as the woman who had danced so elaborately at the club with Roland Routh.

Jamie Renfrew offered her a cigarette. 'No you don't,' Avril said. She rummaged in her handbag for her own, but she allowed Jamie Renfrew to strike his lighter and hold it out to her. Then she bent her head and cupped her hands over his as if they were both standing in a gale. She threw back her head and, lifting the cigarette away, pushed out her lower lip to let a cloud of smoke escape. 'God, that's better,' she said, as if that breath had contained all the bad business of the day. They all stood about watching her. 'Don't say I'm not the last!' she said. 'Don't say Rolly hasn't made it yet! I don't believe it!'

They had to wait another five minutes before Routh came on to the stage from the wings opposite Flo's vantage point. He hurried on, shaking off his jacket, tugging his tie from under his collar, cramming it into his pocket. With his other hand he scraped his hair upright with his fingers, as if he must destroy some office self before their very eyes. The vague sense Flo had carried of his features asserted itself now with a blunt physical sensation. 'I'm so terribly sorry,' he said, going right up to Renfrew. 'I simply couldn't help it.'

'You could always try,' Renfrew told him.

But Routh ignored him. 'Shall we get on then?' he said, as if it were he who was in charge and he who had been kept waiting. He moved out on to the stage. The rehearsal might begin.

The words they spoke immediately came back to Flo and with them the classroom and the desk she had sat at, with sunlight intensified by the window-pane, burning against her neck and shoulder. It was the second scene of the play. The Major was Claudius and Mrs Bynge Gertrude. Renfrew was Laertes and an older man, unknown to her, Polonius. The two corporals were Rosencrantz and Gildenstern. Routh, as she had known, was Hamlet. The others still spoke woodenly and held up their scripts in front of their faces, but Routh when he finally spoke appeared to have his part word-perfect. It did not occur to her that he might have acted it before. His voice broke out into the darkened auditorium, high and intense, as if it came from some intimate portion of his very being. It made him seem exposed as the others were not. She sensed his separation from them. When he went forward on the stage, she caught a mocking glance exchanged between Jamie

Renfrew and one of the corporals. She remembered then that he had not been liked at school, and a fierce protective pain went through her.

When they had worked to the end of the long scene, Renfrew called out, 'That will do for now,' and shortly afterwards Mrs Bynge appeared carrying a tray of tea things. Routh was left standing a few feet from Flo but quite unaware that she was there. His face was pale and dazed. She could see he was unable to switch back, as the others had instantly, to his normal self.

Now he will notice me, Flo thought. But he did not. He went slowly to the table. She watched Renfrew speak to him and nod in her direction. She could not see his face then. He finished his mug of tea before he came over to her and said, 'Look, this must be most awfully boring for you. You don't have to come, you know. Certainly not every time.'

She felt a tightening of determination in her and heard it in her voice when she said to him, 'I want to come.' He was smiling at her with his altered face. 'Won't you have some tea then?' But Renfrew was calling, 'Come on, come on, then. Next scene.'

She went back to her chair. She had extracted from Lydia permission that she might make her own way home as long as she was back at the villa promptly at seven thirty. She looked constantly at her watch, tilting her wrist in the dark to make out the angle of the tiny luminous hands. At exactly seven thirty she got up and crossed to the staircase, taking elaborate care not to tread on the creaking floorboard. The street door was open. Outside, surprisingly, was the last of the daylight. The same soldier leant against the open door, smoking a cigarette. 'Off already,' he said pleasantly enough. 'Not going for a drink then?'

'Will you tell him I had to go?' Flo said.

'Tell who?'

'Lieutenant Renfrew,' she said, 'or Mr Routh.'

'You Rolly's girlfriend then?' He seemed amused.

'I just know him,' Flo said.

He watched her through the smoke he blew steadily between compressed lips. 'Well, he's a dark horse,' he said, and laughed. 'You never know with our Rolly.'

'Is that what you call him?'

'It's what I call him here.' She noticed the tension along his shining cheekbones. 'It's all first names here. Jamie Renfrew makes a thing of that. Boys together. Anywhere else he'd have me on a charge.' He winked at her, the first of many winks.

'Well,' her mother said when she came home, 'what did you do? Who did you talk to?'

It was difficult to answer that. Nor did Flo attempt to. Even during the short walk through the darkening streets the theatre had established itself in her mind. The bright stage, the haunted grandeur of the auditorium, the secretive regions of passages and dressing-rooms from which the actors in their altered states emerged, all formed a world complete and separate from the world of the villa. Instinct told her to allow her mother no foothold in it.

When Lydia persisted, 'They do want you to come again, don't they?' she said, 'Yes,' not because she supposed it true, but because she knew it was entirely necessary to her that she return there.

Chapter Ten

THE WEEKS continued on their circuit between
Monday and Monday. Flo had lost all sense of the
passage of time. Neither the climate nor the clockwork
decorum of the villa varied in the least from day to day.
The sun at that altitude was robbed of its equatorial
heat. Air kept to the temperature of blood. The dense
stretch of flowers between the steps of the villa and the
sentry boxes bloomed without remission. The meals
replenished themselves. The frock which she left crumpled on her bedroom floor appeared washed and pressed
and hanging in her cupboard by noon on the following
day.

What changes did occur were neither abrupt nor
violent. For instance, at some point the Wallers had
ceased to ask her to come with them to the Friday
dance. No incident had marked this change. Simply
there had been a week when the arrangement was not
made. Instead Richie South and Simon Philpotts called
for her in a taxi and the evening took its usual course.
It made little difference to her. Glancing across the
clubroom she noticed now that Jamie Renfrew was a

regular member of the Wallers' party. Sometimes Bridie's rapt face circled past her, pressed against his red, scrubbed neck and neatly barbered hair. Once she noticed her make-up had smeared all over Jamie Renfrew's collar and wondered if he would be angry as so often he was at the theatre. Once Bridie opened her eyes and smiled at her, so, whatever had caused the invitations to cease, Flo knew she had given no offence. She was relieved by that. Apart from the fear that she might have done, it did not trouble her that the frail intimacy had foundered. She had no more sense of knowing Bridie less than she had of knowing Richie South and Simon Philpotts more.

That things must develop one way or another, that the series of rehearsals, for instance, must culminate in a performance, she did not allow herself even to consider. Most especially she kept from her waking mind any thought of Harry Morgan's warning that this enchanted place would not always contain her; that at a given moment she would be cast back to a life of chill rooms in other people's houses. Instinct told her that if she kept out of sight, did what Lydia wanted of her, caused no trouble, kept quiet, said thank you, things might work out as she wanted them to. It had been so in the past. Meanwhile, only the immediate sequences of the days were safe to dwell on and these were all-important in that they threw up to her and snatched away again the precious Mondays at the theatre.

Another Tuesday, a Wednesday, a Thursday and a Friday had been lived through. It was Saturday. Freed from the ritual of buying the photographs, Flo sat in the ballroom listening to Rudi Sondheimer's record. None of the dance-bands in the town knew the music yet, nor did it ever come over her mother's wireless set. It was a part of this room and this time of day. She could hear the sound of voices, but sat quite still waiting for the record to play itself out. She thought, Roland Routh is in this house. When the music stops I will walk through that door. I will see him. The great shining room stretched around her. Outside the open windows warm rain fell. She could put no limit on such happiness.

She stood in the doorway watching them, but they did not notice her. He was leaning forward in his chair. Lydia leant back in hers. They were speaking of Flo. She did not suppose it would be otherwise. 'How does Flo get on?' her mother was asking him.

'She's very watchful,' Roland Routh said. His back was to her but she could hear by his voice that he was smiling when he said, 'You don't send her there to spy on us?'

Lydia was smiling too as she looked up and saw Flo standing there. 'Oh, you startled me!' she said.

He turned when Flo came into the room. The sudden assault of his face, forgotten since last Monday, left her speechless. Car doors were slamming. The major-domo had flung open the front door. The others, Geoffrey Wheeler, the Sondheimers, Harry Morgan, had arrived together and were talking in the hall. She should not stare so, the mother thought distractedly.

Oh, it will repel him. Why doesn't she say something?

When everyone had gone, she said, 'You mustn't creep about like that. What if you overheard something? Besides, you shouldn't stare so. What will he think?'

'He didn't see me.'

'That's not the point. You should talk to people, not stare at them.' She had taken another cigarette from the box and was flicking irritably at it with a lighter as she spoke. Harry had gone ahead into the dining-room. In a moment she must put it out and follow him. Flo watched her with a sense of helplessness. Already in her mother's eyes she had failed with Roland Routh. She remembered the quiet in the room in the moment before she entered it, the ease, and underneath that a pleasurable tension. There had been nothing to say. She had been thinking, In an hour he will go away. Then there would be the rest of Saturday, then Sunday, before it would be Monday again.

On Monday at five, she set out through the recently wetted streets. It was strange to walk alone. She felt her unsupported height, the narrow passage that her presence cut through the warm evening air. Nothing that she passed laid any claim to her. No one recognized her. She was weightless with excitement, fleshless, restored to her invisible childhood self.

Sergeant Broad, on whose cheerful briskness everyone relied, had found her a table and a stool and positioned them in the wings so that she might see an angle of the stage and hear everything that went on. She had found at the villa an unused notebook with OHMS stamped on the cover. She spread it open on the table and placed a sharpened pencil beside it. Later, when the empty pages seemed to draw attention to her use-lessness, she kept it shut and hidden on her lap, but continued to bring it week by week in case props were mentioned and she should have occasion to write a list. That no one noticed her made her feel bold. She might do what she liked, be whom she chose, watch without caution. She shifted her chair and table right to the very line where the shadowy wings made a boundary with the lighted stage.

From this vantage she watched the almost visible moment when, as the actors arrived and breathed in the different air of the theatre, they shed their daytime selves and adopted another more congenial role. They made their entrances, singly or in pairs: Jamie Renfrew and Sergeant Broad, a little later the Major, whom they all called Blotto, and his wife, Mrs Bynge, carrying a zip-up canvas bag. He had an air of cheerfulness in great adversity. 'Bearing up?' he'd say each week to Jamie Renfrew.

'Bearing up. And you?'

'Bearing up.'

He never paused but made his way backstage where he had a dressing-room. 'Relaxing his throat!' Lennie Broad told her. He tipped his elbow and gave one of his winks. Before the troupe's removal to the theatre, they had rehearsed together for several weeks in the ballroom at the club. It seemed that in that short time, before Flo knew them, they had become intimate with one another. Secrets were generally known, but never spoken. Jokes had been established. Rules had been set up and learnt too well to be explained. It had been so at the school. Arriving two terms after the other girls, she had missed whole lessons on reading music, the third conjugation, quadrilateral equations. Her footing from the start had been on ice. Too frightened to ask, she had plunged with no certainty down the confused tracks of learning. Now, although she did not understand, she winked shyly back at Lennie Broad and set herself to watch and learn as best she could.

Mrs Blotto had hurried behind the scenes to make tea. There was always a delay until everyone else arrived. The two corporals moved apart and practised duelling with invisible rapiers. The noisy plumbing of the theatre sounded.

More people had arrived. The woman called Avril and Jamie Renfrew sat side by side on the table. He was hearing her lines. Flo watched as she swung one bare leg so that the sandal shook loose. Then, just as it was about to fall, she caught it on her toe and shook it back on to her foot. Their shoulders almost touched. She would have thought they were in love, only Avril Sawley was married to a pilot. One Monday a man had sat in the auditorium, just beyond the reach of the stage lights, so that she could only just make out the outline of his head and shoulders. The red spot of a lighted cigarette curved slowly up and down. 'Who's that?' she had asked Lennie.

'Him? He's Avril's husband. He flies your Dad sometimes.' He had seemed surprised that she did not know that. For Bridie's sake she was relieved. To be absolutely sure she said, 'I thought Jamie had a thing about Avril.' Broad had thrown back his head at that and laughed. She had not asked him why.

Mrs Blotto appeared with the tray of tea things.

'Tea, Flo?'

She shook her head, although she knew it was odd of her not to join them. Sometimes, when they talked together around the table and laughed, she knew by the direction of their eyes that they talked of her. Then, as if she had swallowed an alien substance, she felt every part of her stiffen and swell. Some ugliness in her, some difference she could not control seemed to glare out at them from her dark corner. In the school she had been defenceless against such moments. It was different here. These people, she was sure, meant her no real harm, bore no ill will. The absurdity of her wasted afternoons, her inability to come forward and speak as they spoke, easily to one another, were nothing to them. Nor did she need their liking. Only she needed to be able to come again. When Mrs Blotto called out a moment later, 'Come on then, Flo. No idling. Give us a hand with the washing-up,' she felt grateful to her. It was easy then to move to the table, ask people whether they had finished, and even laugh when they laughed. It became her regular task to set the tray and wash the mugs in a square cracked sink behind the scenes. The smell from the drain was sweet and sickening, like the smell of rotten fruit.

They were waiting for Roland Routh. Monday after Monday he arrived late, although often one of the others would mention that he had been seen drinking coffee on the pavement of a particular café on the Corso. They spoke of him with awe. He had been writing something, reading a report, struggling to finish some piece of office work so that his mind might be free of it before he joined them. His job was more exacting than any of theirs. They all accepted that. Always he apologized, 'God, but I'm sorry. I really am.' But to Flo in her dark corner it seemed he apologized for more than his lateness; as if he came late in order to apologize; as if he thought they might not accept him at all unless they could be angry with him. Just as Avril Sawley needed to tell everyone how unhappy and disagreeable she had been until the moment that she came among them. Just as Jamie Renfrew needed to play at being in love with Avril with her husband the unseen audience at the back of the stalls, and Mrs Blotto needed to remind them by her manipulation of the tea things that she had played in the West End once and that she and the Major remembered this company before Roland Routh and Jamie Renfrew and the lot of them had come to Aderra.

But for all that, they could not have done without Routh. Nothing was the same once he arrived. The energy, the irritation with himself that had driven him through the tired evening streets brought a necessary tension among them. Their chatter died away. He hurried forward, always with some prepared joke or some ridiculous story he had read in the Italian newspaper. It cost him an effort. He amused them, Flo knew, to keep his own interest alive and to test their precarious acceptance of him. It was a relief when he put his mug back on the tray and said, as if it were the last thing that he wanted, 'Well, let's get back to it.' She might cease to fear for him then and listen as his voice, high and intense, broke freely into the darkened auditorium and spoke the words that were never heard in normal talk.

Flo spent less time with Lydia now. Often she pleaded tiredness in the afternoons and lay down on her bed, but though she would have liked to sleep to make the time go faster, she never did. She lay on her stomach committing whole passages of the play to memory. She never read the other tragedies in the volume, nor did she ask Lydia to prise open the ammunition box again to let her browse among the other books. The one play sufficed as did the single record.

Outside, rain splashed incessantly on the marble balcony. Through the open door came the vibrant smell of slackened dust. Her lips moved in silent rapid conversation. She spoke Roland Routh's words as well as hers in an endless monologue. He told her he wanted her to act Ophelia's part, instead of Avril Sawley. They went out on the stage. Both parts, her part and his, flowed from her until they seemed to pass without restraint between his lips and hers.

He danced with her in the ballroom. She wore the pink dress she had not been allowed, cut low and strapless. He held her close with his cheek against her cheek, repeating in her ear all the words he had ever spoken to her. She threw back her head as they danced. He kissed her neck. He kissed her breasts through the stiff pink tulle.

At teatime when the major-domo rang his gong she went quickly to the mirror to brush her hair. It bewildered her to see her face entirely unchanged by what had passed behind it.

Although within a week or two she knew whole sections of the script by heart, the play as a whole remained as confused in her mind as when she had studied it with Miss Blakely. The scenes were practised according to who was available for rehearsal rather than in their correct order. When she sat at her desk her restricted line of vision cut diagonally across the stage. She could only see the actors when they crossed it. She made no effort to distinguish the characters from the people who played them. All that mattered was her presence there, her secrecy, her access to those words of passionate intensity. At night she lay awake while the unnerving moonlight lit the wide balcony outside. She examined each minute occurrence in the theatre, telling herself repeatedly the story of her evening there. None of it she told to Lydia.

She sat in the upstairs sitting-room. The radio was on. Lydia played cards and talked as she had always done. Flo scarcely heard her. It seemed that her mother mouthed on the farther side of a glass window. She remembered watching for her with her face against the cold, lead-smelling panes of the flat in London. Now it was she that had access to a crowded, lighted, outer world while Lydia, grown remote and isolated, waited for her. The sense of power that this gave was hateful to her, but it was precious too.

It was Wednesday. It was Thursday. It was Friday. It was Saturday. It was Sunday. The unchanging circuit of the week continued. It seemed to Flo that the days went more quickly now. Something, like rapid footsteps following in the street, hurried them forward. Everything had become enlarged, intensified. To wake on Monday morning was to become instantly aware of the room, the noise of the servants, the whole intended progress of the day. She felt as if she had mastered some new movement, skating, riding, diving, the things that other children did with ease.

The play was progressing. No one was allowed to carry their script on to the stage now. They had stopped rehearsing the first act and moved on to the second, even the third. Sergeant Broad had finished the carpentry for an ingenious throne, which could be turned one way to make a bed and another to make a tomb. Now to the theatre's residue of odours were added the fumes of lead paint which he had liberated from the regimental stores.

'What do you think of that then, Flo?' he asked her when she arrived.

'It's very nice,' she said.

'I thought you might say that. It is though, isn't it? I like a job well done. Don't you?'

'Yes.' If anybody there was her friend, except of course for Roland Routh, it was Lennie Broad. She did not like him. A frightened, calculating eye watched out from somewhere in him, but he could be counted on always to be pleasant, always to treat her just as he did everyone else. Better than some. She knew he liked her, because of his winks and laughs at the expense of all the others. That made her cautious of him too. Now he winked at her and said, 'You're needed backstage. Queen Gertie's a bit off colour.'

Behind the stage there was a warren of small dressing-rooms. By now most of the cast had laid claim to one or another of these and often when they were not needed on the stage retired to these private places. There they would mutter over their lines, smoke a cigarette, stare at themselves in the mirror, or simply keep out of one another's way. Because of the airlessness of the place the doors were always left ajar. Their special smells fought bravely with the theatre's grand odour of decay. Avril's smelt of scent. She had offered Flo some once in return for finding her mislaid script. 'Oh, come on,' she said. 'It's good stuff. Ray gets it for me. Duty free. From someone in Khartoum.'

Major Blotto's smelt of spirits and very slightly of sweat. His wife's, which was separate from his, smelt of talcum powder.

Flo had learned to hurry past with her eyes averted. Otherwise she received narrow glimpses of scenes which bore no relation to what went on in the wings and on the stage. Once she had seen Avril Sawley with her face buried in her hands, shaking as if she wept; and once Jamie Renfrew bracing his arms against the wall, entrapping one of the corporals, so that they stared fixedly at one another. Are they having a fight? she thought. But their expressions, although strange, had not seemed angry. In the dressing-room beyond, Major Blotto, with a glass in his hand, stared into his mirror with an angry dignity. Only his wife's room was entirely predictable and held no fears.

Now she tapped on Mrs Blotto's open door. 'Oh, come in, dear,' Mrs Blotto said without surprise.

Flo kept awkwardly where she was. 'Lennie says you don't feel well.'

'Come in,' Mrs Blotto repeated, this time in an urgent undertone. She nodded to her to shut the door before she said, 'Blotto's had one of his turns.' She lowered the pale pink cardigan she wore and displayed her plump upper arm turned livid with a recent bruise. 'Look what the old sod's done,' she said dispassionately. 'I can tell you, Flo, I'd half a mind to stay home tonight, but we can't miss a rehearsal, can we?' She reached out to give the girl's hand a squeeze. 'Even though he

probably won't get to my bit. It wouldn't be pro-
fessional.'

'Can I help?'

'That's very sweet of you, dear. I like a little time
to myself before the show begins.' She began carefully to
readjust the cardigan.

'Shall I go away then?' Flo asked.

'Oh no, dear,' Mrs Blotto said, patting a chair beside
her. 'You're no trouble.'

Flo obediently sat down. She was drawn in by Mrs
Blotto's kindness, even though something in the stale
sweet smell of the talcum powder repelled her. She sat
and watched her as she arranged the collection of jars
and brushes on her dressing-table. 'You wouldn't think
it now, but when I was on the stage before the war
they used to cast me as quite the glamour girl. Then
I'd do myself up to the nines and sit and look at that
person until I felt exactly like her. You should try it,
Flo,' she said, turning to consider the girl for a moment.
'Here, watch me.' She began to rub foundation cream
into her cheeks and throat with swift deft movements
which were also curiously sensual, like expert caresses
bestowed on someone else who arched back her neck
and shoulders to receive them. Then, leaning towards
the glass, she began to stroke on rouge and eyeshadow.
Finally with a tiny brush she outlined generous pouting
lips and filled them in with gleaming red. She lit a
cigarette, sucked at it, lifted it clear of her face and
regarded herself with approval. 'Well, Flo,' she said,
'what do you think?'

Flo smiled. 'It's nice.'

'It wouldn't do at the club, would it. But then if some of the old crowd could see me there they'd say, "That's never old Moira." A stuck-up bitch they'd think that Mrs Bynge, wouldn't they, Flo?' she laughed. Flo thought how much nicer she seemed here than at the club. She thought of asking her why the Wallers no longer included her but then thought better of it.

'I was a dancer really,' Moira Bynge went on. 'And I've never let my figure go, not like some of my age, which I wouldn't reveal even to you, Flo. If I say it myself, I have the bust of a girl.' She twisted herself about for Flo to admire. 'And absolutely unsupported.'

Now with the same slow enjoyment she began to remove the make-up she had just applied. 'Poor Blotto. He sings you know. But not with this lot. Not with bloody Rolly telling us what we should and should not do. There now,' she said as she rose to see to the tea, 'we've had quite a conversation, haven't we? You're not the little mouse they say you are, not by a long chalk.'

The next Monday Flo knocked again at the door and closed it after her as a sign of the confidentiality of this new friendship. Although it must be weeks before a dress rehearsal could even be considered, there was beginning to be concern over what everyone should wear. Mrs Blotto had brought two evening frocks, one a royal blue taffeta and the other a pale green georgette.

They hung side by side in their drycleaner's cellophane bags.

'Well, Flo, which is it to be? The blue or the green?'

'They're both very pretty,' Flo said guardedly.

'Come, Flo, you can do better than that!' But before Flo needed to commit herself Mrs Bynge went on, 'For the bedroom scene, of course, I'll wear my Balenciaga negligé.' She gave the 'my' a splendid emphasis by pronouncing it 'may' so that the whole rhyming phrase seemed taken from the music-halls. 'It hasn't had an adventure for a good few years, I can tell you.' And she winked at Flo.

Flo winked back.

In the passage Routh's irritable voice said, 'It just won't do. You're a virgin, for God's sake.'

'Am I?' said Avril Sawley.

'Well, at least you could try to look like one.'

A door slammed. Mrs Blotto raised an eyebrow. A minute later there was a knock on the door and the same voice said, 'Is Flo in there?'

'Come,' said Mrs Blotto grandly.

He was agitated. He didn't even speak to her, but said hurriedly to Flo, 'You have a white dress, don't you? Didn't you wear it once?'

'Yes.'

'Look, would you mind awfully lending it to Avril?' He had remembered now to smile at her.

'Yes,' she said. 'If you want me to.'

'It won't get messed about,' he said. 'It's only for the play scene. It's most awfully good of you.'

'You're too good,' Mrs Blotto said when he was gone. 'You'd do anything for anybody. Nobody will respect you for that, Flo. Really they won't.' As she spoke she was folding up the soiled tea towels with sharp vindictive tugs. 'You should play that part in your own dress. You're much more suited to it than that Avril.' She sounded almost angry now, although it would have been hard to say at whom. 'You wouldn't go mad though,' she said, regarding Flo with the pile of soiled tea towels in her hand. 'You're made of sterner stuff. You might want to go mad, but you wouldn't. I can tell. I always can. You shouldn't have to give her the time of day let alone your frock, or him either, but there it is.'

'Don't you like him?' Flo asked carefully.

Mrs Blotto stopped to consider this. 'He's not the sort of person one does like. Too cocky by half,' she said. 'Although I dare say there's some as go for that sort of thing.' Seeing the expression on Flo's face she added, 'He can act. I'll give him that. I've seen worse Hamlets on the London stage.'

'People don't understand him very well,' Flo said.

'Oh?' said Mrs Blotto, watching her. 'Is that what it is?'

It was time to make tea and then once the rehearsal began to gather up the mugs and wash them. Usually she hurried through this task to get back to the wings, but tonight she felt less eager to be watching them. She washed each mug carefully and dried it on the clean tea towel Moira Bynge had brought from home. When she had finished she took the damp tea towel back to add it to the others. The light was on. The surface of the table was still littered with make-up. There was the cold cream pot with finger-marks gouged in it, the velvet pad caked with face-powder, the hairbrush tangled with Moira Bynge's wiry blonde hair. She thought for a moment of sitting in front of the mirror and putting on the lipstick and the rouge as she had been invited to. She would sit there looking at herself as Moira did until she became someone else. Only the knowledge of the moment when she would have to leave the little room, the fear of someone looking in through the open door prevented her.

It was peaceful here with all the dressing-rooms empty. She turned out the light and sat for a moment where she was. In the silence the theatre seemed to swell around her, and then to fill with a hardly perceptible rustle which might have been the chewing of myriad tiny jaws. She listened attentively in the dark. Only the faintest murmur of voices reached her from the stage where the grand drama played itself out, regardless of her absence. Perhaps hearing has no limits. Perhaps had she sat long enough and concentrated hard enough it might have reached beyond the musty confines of the theatre to where, under the pale street lights and in the shadowed ravines outside the town, a grander drama still was being rehearsed, passionate, deadly, beyond the comprehension of them all.

Instead, in the darkened dressing-room, at the centre of it all, she thought, without alarm, I am in love with

Roland Routh. It had been so for some time, but only when she had framed the words did she find herself caught up in something so perfect, so complete, that nothing else, even the presence of Roland Routh himself, was necessary.

Chapter Eleven

A LMOST IN SPITE of herself, as the weeks went by, Flo was drawn in among 'the theatricals'. It had been discovered that she could sew, a thing she had supposed that everyone could do. This small talent was greeted with amazement by the cast, many of whom were bachelors. They began to bring her buttons to sew on, small tears to mend, shyly at first, then as they saw how eager she was to have a task, with an amused sense that they did her a kindness. Occasionally when a new scene was embarked upon she was asked to hear lines, particularly by Major Blotto and by one of the corporals who was slow to learn.

'Job for you,' Lennie Broad called out on the fifth, or perhaps it was the sixth week, 'Avril in difficulties.' Usually Flo was among the first to come, but that week she was late. The rehearsal had begun. From behind Broad she could hear angry voices on the stage, Jamie Renfrew's and Roland Routh's.

'Bloody calm down and get on with it,' Renfrew was shouting. She did not want to hear or look for fear that if there was a quarrel Routh might not win. She went around the back of the stage to Avril Sawley's dressing-room, walking noisily as she approached. The door was open. Avril was waiting in her slip. 'Would you mind?' she said, smiling tensely at Flo. 'Only the bloody strap's broken. I'll take it off.'

'That's all right,' Flo said. She brought her school mending-bag each week now and, sitting down, concentrated on threading a needle rather than watch Avril Sawley climb out of her slip. While Flo sewed, Avril sat at her dressing-table in only her bra and pants. She stared into the mirror, licked her finger and dabbed repeatedly at an eyebrow, quite regardless of the open door and the people who went past and grinned at her in the glass.

Now she turned restlessly to watch Flo. 'God, you're clever,' she said. 'Who taught you to do that? Go to a convent, did you?' She seemed really interested in knowing, but just at that moment Roland Routh shouted in the corridor outside, 'What are we waiting for?'

'Look,' Avril said, 'it needn't be perfect. Just get it done, will you?' Flo finished the stitches clumsily and handed her the slip. Already she was struggling into it and as her head emerged she said, 'Help me with the dress, will you?' When it was on she kissed Flo suddenly on the cheek and said, 'Look, I'm sorry I snapped. Bad day. He's in a foul mood.' She pulled a face in the direction of the door. 'I'm all nerves.' She had begun to grope about the surface of the dressing-table for her pack of cigarettes. She held them out to Flo. Flo shook her head.

'Look,' Avril said, smiling directly at her. 'I'm really sorry. Forgive? Help yourself to scent, Flo. Really.' She turned and ran out of the room. Flo stayed for a moment. She took the scent-bottle off the table and tipped it quickly against one wrist and then the other. Then she dabbed the pulses on her forehead and behind her ears. She thought of her blood beating behind the heated smell and sending it out into the theatre. She opened the jars of make-up one by one. Then very slowly and deliberately she began to rub it on her face and blot at it with a tissue, watching the eyes grow dark and sad, the cheek bones sharpen and the lips declare themselves. It was not her face now. It was something she had stolen from Avril Sawley. She did not intend to part with it, but went out boldly to her table in the wings.

Lennie Broad came and stood beside her in the dark. 'You smell nice,' he said, but even though he stood very close to her, he didn't see her face. He was looking past her on to the stage with an expression both puzzled and shrewd. 'What do you think, Flo?' he said after a moment. 'Fireworks?' Already her glance had hurried past him to where Routh sat propped against the table with his shoulders hunched inside his jacket, his hands in his pockets. He was sweating. His face shone in the lights. Why doesn't he take his jacket off? She often spoke to herself about him in this fussy, anxious way. He was saying, 'Damn it all, you're meant to be in love with me!'

Avril said, 'I'm doing my best.'

'You could have fooled me,' Routh said. 'God,' he shouted suddenly at Renfrew, 'this just isn't working!'

'You chose the bloody play,' Renfrew said. 'No one else wanted it. You're the only one who complains. You can bloody put up with it.'

'All I'm saying is that it doesn't make sense if she acts as if she were in the bloody nunnery already. How am I expected to play to that?'

'That's your problem,' Renfrew said unpleasantly. 'Play it how you bloody please. Only get on with it.'

'All right,' he said. 'All right. I will.'

Avril had taken advantage of the break to run quickly to the table where she had left her cigarette. Now with it in her hand she said, 'Try being more virile. That might help.'

'Hear, hear,' Renfrew said.

Routh swung round to her as if Renfrew did not exist and shouted at her, 'It's a play. It doesn't matter what the hell I am. In the play you're meant to be in love with me.'

She had grown entirely calm. She stood up and blew out a mouthful of smoke before she said, 'Perhaps I only wanted to be queen. Perhaps I never gave a damn for you.'

'Oh, for God's sake,' he said. 'This is ridiculous. Can't we get on?'

She took her time carefully to dab out the newly

lighted cigarette and left it propped against the rim of the ashtray on the table. They began again:

'. . . Good my lord,

How does your honour for this many a day?'

'I humbly thank you. Well, well, well.'

But his bad temper had established itself as tangibly as if it were another actor on the stage that waited its cue. A few lines further on he shouted without warning, 'God, give her a bit of heart, can't you? She can't be totally dead from the neck down.'

'That isn't fair,' she said in a low uncertain voice. 'You know how difficult it is. I can't go on.'

Sergeant Broad made a soft explosive sound between his lips and muttered, 'He's blown it now.'

Avril had run off the stage with her hands thrown up to cover her face.

'Oh God, I'm sorry,' Routh said to everybody else, but the words came as just another outburst of anger. He went and stood in the far corner of the stage with his back to them all.

'You've gone and done it now,' Renfrew called after him. All of them, Flo included, had turned to look anxiously out into the auditorium, but there was no sign of Avril Sawley's husband.

'I'll go to her,' Mrs Blotto said, but before she could reach the wings Avril came running back again, saying, 'Right. Where were we?' as if nothing had happened.

'I can't,' Routh said, almost as if it surprised him. 'Can't you do some scene that I'm not in?'

'Oh, it's me,' Avril said. She had retrieved her

cigarette from the ashtray and held it shakily while Renfrew lit it for her. She drew on it and then used it in a wild gesture. 'There's something wrong with me tonight.'

Another scene was chosen. They began again. But all the words sounded absurd now. At seven promptly Renfrew said, 'Next Monday then.' Routh walked noisily off the stage. The others stood about uncertainly as if they expected him to reappear, as Avril Sawley had. When after a moment he did not, Jamie Renfrew called out, 'Drink?'

'Oh, please!' Avril said and, looking about her, 'Anybody else?'

'Drink, Lennie?' Renfrew called.

'I'll lock up,' Broad shouted back to him. 'What about you, Flo?'

She shook her head.

'Going after him, are you?' She knew without looking at him that he winked at her. 'Don't be long,' he said. 'I shouldn't want to lock you in.'

When they had all gone down the stairs into the street she went behind the stage. She felt again the size and emptiness of the place. She knew which room was Routh's. His was the one door that was never open. Nor if it had been would she have ever looked inside, fearful of seeing more than he might willingly reveal. She knocked. 'Who's there?' he said. Immediately, without answering, she opened the door and stood leaning against the doorpost.

He was sitting at a makeshift dressing-table with his

face set in no particular direction and fearfully emptied.

'They've all gone. Lennie's locking up.'

'Right,' he said. 'I'll be along.'

She knew by the pressure of the door-frame against her spine that she had not moved. He had turned to look at himself and, seeing her in the glass, watched her for a moment before he said with an odd laugh, 'What are you doing?'

She ran off then without a word, to Moira Bynge's dressing-room. There she spread cold cream on her face and rubbed off every trace of paint. She worked clumsily and hastily, fearful that she would meet him again in the passage. Only a single light was left burning on the stage. From somewhere Lennie Broad's voice called out, 'That you, Flo?'

'Yes,' she said. 'I'm going now.' How ordinary her voice had sounded, but coming out into the darkening street she was overwhelmed with a feeling of foolishness and loss.

It was Tuesday. It was Wednesday. It was Thursday. It was Friday. It was Saturday. The Sondheimers, the Harringtons and Geoffrey came but Roland Routh did not. Flo played her record in the ballroom. They talked without animation of the forthcoming election in Britain.

'What if they get in again?' Nell Harrington said. 'There won't be anything left of England by the time we get back there. Nothing that I recognize.'

'Perhaps we shouldn't go back,' her husband said gloomily.

'Perhaps we should all go back and recolonize England,' Wheeler suggested. He had hoped they would laugh, but no one did.

To cover up the pause, Lydia said suddenly in front of everyone, 'We're not going back. Not right away. We're going down to South Africa. We might even stay there. Retire there. People do.'

'You must not,' Gerda Sondheimer said vehemently. 'You must go home. You will make one move too many. Perhaps already you have made it. You will become a refugee like me. Even in your own country you will be a refugee.'

The remark broke up the little party which had been less cheerful than it usually was. Lydia stood in the open doorway watching the shining cars curve down the drive. She was glad Routh had not been there. He would ring perhaps, give his apologies, suggest he come another day. The cool breath of the rain made her shiver. I should ask them to light a fire tonight, she thought.

Behind her in the house the phone was ringing. It would be Routh apologizing. 'You take it, will you?' she called to Flo. She would not be hurried by him. She stood there waving until the cars were out of sight beyond the sentry boxes. When she came back into the drawing-room the receiver was back in place. 'Who was it?' she asked Flo, lighting a cigarette.

'Roland Routh. He's sorry he couldn't come.'

'I should have spoken to him,' Lydia said, flapping the smoke dismissively from in front of her face. 'He knew it didn't matter.'

But Flo was still speaking slowly, as if trying out unfamiliar words. 'It was for me. He's asked me out.'

'When?' her mother asked.

'Friday. Did you ask him to?'

'No. Of course not.' She had rallied her voice and now said firmly, 'Well, that's nice, isn't it?'

'Yes,' Flo said so uncertainly that her mother felt bound to ask, 'You did say you'd go?'

'Oh yes,' Flo told her.

Chapter Twelve

Wof the villa on Friday evening, Lydia asked him
in for a drink. Flo, knowing that she would and suppos-
ing that he would accept, had not put on her coat
although she had been ready for the past hour.

'I'm most frightfully sorry,' he said, 'but there's a
taxi waiting.' She felt stricken at the expense she was
causing him and went at once to fetch her coat from
where she had left it waiting in the hall. She hoped he
might follow and help her into it, but he stayed for a
moment talking to her mother and it was Amde, standing on tiptoe, who settled it on to her shoulders. Then
Routh came after her and taking her by the arm hurried
her down the steps to where the taxi-driver was
holding open the back door of his cab. 'It's odd how
they always smell of horses,' he said as they drove off.
'Some collective memory of hackney cabs, do you
suppose?'

She laughed because he had, and sat forward on
the seat, very conscious of herself, looking out of the
window. 'Where are we going?'

'The Sawleys. They've asked us for a drink there first. Then we'll go on somewhere after that.'

'With them?'

'You don't mind, do you?' he said quickly. 'They're quite nice and I didn't want to get it wrong in any way. I got so up against her for a time. She's quite sweet really. I've only met him once. I couldn't very well get out of it.' He said all this so carelessly that she realized he must go out every night with one group of people or another. The specialness of the evening was already diminished.

'Oh, come,' he said, and reached out to touch her arm very briefly. 'They won't bite you.' She smiled and turned back to the window, feeling still the astonishment of that touch in its precise place, just above her left elbow.

He leant back against the leather upholstery with his arm flung out along the back of the seat. 'God, it's good here,' he said, 'when the day's over and you can be yourself again. Most of it's so damnably formal. How do you bear it?'

She was too happy to answer him. She thought, If I sit back, I'll lean against his arm. He knows that and he doesn't mind. 'Where do they live?' she asked him.

'We're here. Just round this corner.' He too sat forward, withdrew his arm, tapped on the glass, reached for his wallet. She climbed out into the street and moved a little way away so as not to see how much he had spent. 'Thank you,' she said, but he had not heard her. He had her by the arm again and pushed her slightly ahead of him into the bleak entrance of a block of flats. 'It's at the top,' he said as they rode shakily upward. 'It's a nice flat. You'll like it.'

She sensed his agitation. They were late perhaps. When the lift lurched to a halt he hurried out of it ahead of her to ring a doorbell on the far side of the landing. As they waited in silence, heels came tapping towards them on a bare floor and Avril Sawley, in a bright red dress, flung open the door. 'Oh good,' she said, ignoring Routh. 'It's Flo. You've not met Raymond, have you?' A tall thin man had come less eagerly along the passage and nodded at them.

'It's very kind of you to ask me,' Flo said.

'Why not?' Avril Sawley said. 'Any friend of Rolly's . . .' She tilted her head to one side and for the first time smiled at him.

The four of them filed down a narrow passage which led into a sitting-room. It was crowded with the same lumpish style of furniture that graced the villa, but more attempts had been made to make the room seem homely. A stuffed leather hassock, with a train of camels stitched on its sides in different coloured leathers, was set before the largest armchair. Two ebony elephants with flattened brows had been given no books to support, but stood on the mantelshelf on either side of a framed photograph of the Sawleys as bride and groom. It was odd to have it there, as if something were in doubt and needed affirmation. An awkwardness had settled on the room as the Sawleys moved about mixing drinks. Flo wondered if it had been there before she and

Roland Routh arrived, or whether they had brought it with them. 'It's a very nice flat,' she said, remembering that he had told her it was.

'*Really?*' Raymond Sawley said with a ghastly politeness. 'Do you *really* think so?' He gave a snort of laughter.

'Pay no attention to him,' Avril said, handing Flo her drink, but she was struck dumb with shame. She looked at Routh. He seemed not to have heard. He stared down primly into the glass he had been given, raised it, and said, 'Well, cheers.' When Avril sat down he began at once to talk to her about the play.

Flo sat between them, turning her head from one to the other, hoping that by doing so she might appear to be a part of their conversation, and not be obliged to talk to Raymond Sawley. He lay back in his chair with his long legs stretched out in front of him, a thin, balding man who did not want to be there. When he got up to fill his glass it was with a sudden jolt, as if at someone else's bidding. His wife watched him. 'Ray's sick to death of talk about the play,' she said and winked at Flo as if he were a private joke they shared.

'Already?' Routh said in his direction. 'It will be worse before we're through.'

'Don't I know it,' Sawley said, pouring whisky into his own glass, and then, as an afterthought, gestured with the bottle towards the others. No one wanted any.

'Well, that's not very nice,' his wife said, never taking her eyes from him as he went back to his chair.

'Isn't it?' he said in the same mincing tone with which he'd answered Flo. 'Isn't it really?'

'Oh, pay no attention to him,' Avril said again. Her dull fair hair hung very smooth and very straight. As she spoke she held her narrow face cocked over one shoulder so that one lock of hair hung directly down. The other she caught repeatedly around her finger, twisted it and tucked it behind her ear. The gesture gave her an earnestness as she said to Flo, 'You should come on for a drink after the rehearsals, shouldn't she, Rolly? They're a nice bunch. You'd like it.'

'Do you always call him Rolly?' Flo asked her.

'People do,' Routh said. Then, lowering his voice very seriously to Flo, 'I'm not really called that.'

'Sorr-ee,' said Avril. Then she jumped up and said, 'Well, come on. Shall we go?' She looked past Routh deliberately and watched her husband with her head on one side. 'The Primavera then?'

'It's up to you,' he said.

'Right then,' said Routh, getting to his feet.

'Keys?' she said to Sawley, holding out her hand to him.

'I'll drive,' he said.

No one else was in the restaurant when they arrived. 'Nice,' Avril said. 'We've got it to ourselves.' They were shown to a table by the empty dance floor. Immediately an ill-shaven trio in the corner slid their drinks under their gilt chairs and began to play. When the waiter took their orders Routh said to him, 'Ask them if they'd play "Autumn Leaves", would you?' They watched him deliver the message on his way back to the kitchen. A moment later the tune they were playing slipped imperceptibly into the opening bars of Routh's request. He began to hum, leaning back in his chair and looking pleased.

'Who's "Autumn Leaves" then?' Avril asked him, tilting her head. He did not answer for a moment, but stayed leaning back in his chair smiling at her. Then he said, 'I just like the words.'

She began to sing them in a pure reedy voice, sitting bolt upright with her hands clasped in front of her on the edge of the table.

> *The autumn leaves drift by my window,*
> *The autumn leaves of red and gold.*
> *I see your lips, the summer kisses,*
> *The sunburnt hands I used to hold.*

She kept that position even when she had finished. When her husband thumped the table and said, 'Bravo,' it seemed that something had been crushed, but she smiled and bowed to him as if she did not mind at all.

'Thank you,' Routh said when he was quiet. She smiled and bowed again quite as if it were all the same to her.

'Dance?' Routh said to Flo. She realized when she moved how tensely she had been sitting. She walked ahead of him out on to the cramped dance floor. Even in the short time they had been there a number of other tables had been filled and other couples danced slowly past them cheek to cheek. Roland Routh held Flo at arms' length. When they had safely reached the far side of the dance floor he said, 'You're not enjoying this, are you?'

'*This,*' she said. 'Oh yes.'

For a moment he held her close with his scented cheek against her hair. Then he held her off again and said, 'The evening. The Sawleys. It was a mistake. It isn't fair to you.'

'I like her,' Flo said. 'I really do. She's very nice.' For a moment she feared he would imitate her as Raymond Sawley might have done, but he said seriously, 'I'm glad you do. Yes, I can't imagine you not liking her. Most people seem to.'

'She's very pretty.'

'Yes, I suppose she is.'

He held her close again. She felt his attention shift to the music. It was as if by holding her so, by dancing so, he had obliterated her altogether. She thought, This is happening. This is now. But there seemed no way that she could seize upon that fact and retain it. When they circled past the table she shut her eyes so as not to see the Sawleys. The music paused. They stood where they were, waiting to hear if it would start again. 'Did you like that?' he asked her.

'Yes, I did.'

'Will you come out with me again?'

'Yes,' she said. 'I will.'

As soon as they sat down the waiter brought their dinner. The Italian couples with their clasped hands raised above their heads pressed against one another as if locked in trance-like combat while the music propelled them round and round. Flo thought, When the plates are cleared away he'll dance with me again. But as soon as the waiter had withdrawn he rose and smiled at Avril Sawley, who stood without a word and walked ahead of him, turning her little body in the bright red dress and lifting up her arms to dance with him.

'Shall we sit this one out?' Raymond Sawley said.

'Yes,' Flo said. She found it hurt her that he did not wish to dance with her even though she did not want at all to dance with him.

She sat with her elbows on the table and her chin propped against her hands, wishing that she might shut her eyes again, but of course she must not.

'Enjoying yourself?' Raymond Sawley asked.

'Oh yes.'

'Good. That's good.'

She thought of asking him if he were, but knew that he was not either.

'Roland says you fly planes.'

'I do. That's absolutely right.'

'Is it difficult?' she said. 'In the mountains?'

'Look,' he said, leaning slowly towards her, 'nothing's difficult in an aeroplane. Did you know that?'

She did not contradict him and for a moment it seemed that he might lapse into a final heavy silence. Then he said, 'The cockpit's the only safe place there is. When I'm there nothing comes near me. Nothing touches me there. It's all right. I do what I want.' He gestured wearily to the waiter for another drink. When it came and he had had a swallow of it, he said to Flo, 'The things you see up there are beautiful, like visions.' He was watching her to see if she believed him. 'I tried to tell Avril about it once. She bought me a box of kiddies' paints and told me to paint it. But what's the use? I can't paint for Christ's sake. It didn't look the same. God, nothing like. She kept on saying, "It's good, Ray, it's really good." But it was nothing. I shut up about it after that.'

He didn't look at Flo when he was talking, but stared down into his glass or out across the dance floor at his wife, lifting his chin slightly to follow the red dress as Roland Routh steered her to the opposite side of the room, lowering his glance as they came past the table. They danced a little apart, staring fixedly across each other's shoulder, not exchanging a word, although when the music stopped and they walked back together, Routh lowered his head and said something that made her laugh.

'Not dancing?' she said brightly when they reached the table. 'Shame.'

'We were talking,' Raymond Sawley said. She looked quickly then at Flo with an enquiring tilt of her head, as if to say, All right then? Flo smiled at her.

'Shall we go on then?'

'It's up to you,' her husband said.

'Well, it's not as if there's all that choice.'

'The Mocambo?' Sawley said. 'Or the Mocambo? Or the Mocambo?'

Flo watched Routh make his way over to a group of waiters by the kitchen door. A bill was produced. He took out his wallet and paid it.

'What about you, Flo?' Avril Sawley was saying. 'Do you like the Mocambo?'

'I don't know. I haven't been.'

'You haven't lived,' Raymond Sawley told her.

Although the nightclub was only a few streets away it was decided that they should take the car. A short flight of steps led downward from the pavement into a room lit only by naked red bulbs. The music was amplified and incessant, the tables crammed together, the dancers so restricted in their movements by the crush that the scene had a heated despairing quality. Roland Routh pushed in through the crowd and beckoned them after him to a table in the corner. Drinks were ordered. She danced with him again, pressed against his cheek, feeling an intolerable sadness. Almost at once the music stopped and he guided her back to the table. When it struck up again Raymond Sawley got to his feet and, bowing grotesquely to Flo, said, 'Well, shall we?'

Without preamble he held her closely to him and began to steer her between the other dancers. It seemed that the music would never stop. Tune after tune dragged its inappropriate words through her mind. He never released his hold. He never spoke. She felt the absence of his spirit as solidly as the indifferent pressure of his body. She watched over his shoulder for the other two but could not see them. When finally the little orchestra played a flourish and lowered their instruments Raymond Sawley led her back to the table holding tightly to her hand.

Routh and Avril were sitting there watching her approach. She wondered if they had danced at all; if they had talked and broken off what they were saying to one another, or whether conversation had died between them as they watched the other dancers. Does she mind that he danced with me that way, Flo wondered, that he holds my hand? But Avril didn't seem to mind.

'Has he crippled you for life?' she said.

'No. Not at all.'

'You're lucky then.'

She danced with Roland Routh and then again with Raymond Sawley. With Routh. With Sawley. Then quite suddenly Avril announced that she was tired and wanted to go home. They climbed up to the street.

'Don't worry about us. We'll take a taxi,' Routh said. Three taxis were drawn up by the door. Already the driver of the first held the back door invitingly open.

'I'll give you a lift.'

'Don't be so tactless, Ray,' his wife said, linking her arm through his. 'Perhaps they want to go in a taxi.' She left him for a moment to kiss Flo lightly on the cheek and after her, Roland. Then she took her husband by his arm again and steered him round in the direction of their car, turning only once to wave at them.

They sat side by side in the taxi. He said, 'We'll do that again, shall we?'

'I'd like to.' She would have liked to say that next time she hoped they need not bring the Sawleys, but she knew better than to set conditions. Nothing could be risked. Without the promise of a next time, she knew that something black and impenetrable would fall immediately in front of her.

At the villa Routh told the cab to wait and, hanging his arm across Flo's shoulder, walked with her to the top of the steps. The odour of night-scented stock was heavy in the air. He kept his arm around her while she fumbled in her handbag for the key that Lydia had given her. 'Thank you,' she said, without looking up at him. 'I had a lovely time.'

'Dear Flo.' He laughed quietly as he said it, but not at all unkindly, and kissed her on the cheek as swiftly and as lightly as Avril Sawley had done.

Chapter Thirteen

A S SOON AS she heard the taxi on the drive Lydia switched off the bedside lamp and feigned sleep. She heard Flo enter, climb the stairs and reach the safety of her room. At breakfast they exchanged only the most formal questions and answers about the evening before. Yes, it had been a nice time. Yes, they had gone out to dinner. Yes, the Primavera. Yes, they had danced.

For all that day and the next Lydia watched her daughter in quick glances so that the girl's face seemed to flash continuously before her, always with the same guarded look; always with the head held upwards at such an angle that it seemed she might be struggling to contain the overspill of tears. Oh, she cannot have been made unhappy by him, the mother thought, not so soon. I should never have encouraged this. She is still a child. But even as the thought formed she noticed how Flo had altered since she had been in Aderra and the good food of the villa had replaced the grim diet of the post-war boarding-school. She had put on a little weight which became her. Her hair had thickened and the sun had coaxed out its meagre tinge of red. Her skin had cleared under its touching sheen of dampness, so that from moment to moment the colour in her rounded cheeks came and went. Her eyes, Granny Franklyn's hazel eyes, had always been her finest feature.

It is, after all, the year of her life, her mother thought. Just as I intended it to be.

Yet just as her child's skin had achieved this near transparency, the girl's mind had become obscure to her. My mind is her mind, she had said, or wanted to say, to Gerda Sondheimer at that dinner party when she had introduced Roland Routh to the villa and Flo to the world of Aderra. It had seemed true then. Now she wondered if it had been; if she had ever really known Flo. Suddenly it seemed as if all that time ago, when Flo had been small enough still to fit into the good tweed coat with the matching bonnet, she had let slip her hand in the crowded street, far, far too soon.

Sunday. Monday. Flo went to the theatre and came back punctually at seven thirty. To ask what Lydia wished to ask: was he there? Did he say anything to you about the other night? Will he ask you out again? seemed cruelly intrusive. But of course he had not or surely Flo would have said something. Even of that she was no longer sure. In frightened moments it seemed that from this time forward the girl's occulted mind might harbour any deviation from the mother's rectitude without her knowing it.

Tuesday. Wednesday. Thursday. Friday. The major-domo's chromium-plated tray came and went with its usual freight of invitations: from the American Consul, from the United Nations Commissioner, from the committee of the Circolo Italiano. Back on to the tray went Lydia's replies, carefully written under the dark blue engraved letterhead, the tiny lion rampant and the prancing unicorn, *Dieu et mon Droit*. 'Mr and Mrs Morgan and Miss Wharton wish to thank . . . They accept with great pleasure.'

Repeatedly the phone rang: Gerda asking them to tea; Nigel Harrington asking Lydia to give away the prizes at the infant school; Wendy Waller asking Flo to Bridie's eighteenth-birthday party at the club. And would she bring her young man? Either young man. Both if possible. It wouldn't clash with a rehearsal. Jamie Renfrew had promised that. Yes. Yes. Yes. Thank you. Thank you. Thank you. But nothing came from Roland Routh. After all, it was, as she had always known, impossible that Flo could hold his interest. And after all, in a way that she could not acount for, she was relieved.

Then as she watched her daughter's vacant face, her heart contracted with pity, not only at the disappointment Flo must feel, but at her own unsparing knowledge of it. They were both suspended between his ringing and his not ringing, between his asking her to go out with him again and the shame of a rejection too cruel to bear.

She went upstairs, but she dared not lay out her cards when she could form no clear wish for the future. And as she could not, might not some unacknowledged longing of her own reach out to move the hand she

laid upon the outcome of things? Oh, I am afraid of
Roland Routh, she thought.

It was Saturday. Perhaps with a subconscious closing
of the ranks as the handover approached, Lydia had
established her Saturday gatherings on an almost weekly
basis. She had never issued Routh a formal invitation.
Protocol decreed that invitations from the villa could
not be refused and from the start she had wanted him
to want to come. Sometimes, over the past months,
Routh had come early and stayed. Sometimes he left as
the others arrived. Sometimes he didn't come at all and
this, though it disappointed her, gave an added charm
to his unannounced appearances and held, she had
come to realize, no particular threat to his future visits.

Now though, as the morning wore on, she felt a
growing apprehension that his treat for Flo, the evening
on the town, had been the conclusion of something
rather than a beginning; a saying goodbye and thank
you for being done good at the villa.

She waited in the sitting-room with *Time* magazine
open on her knee so that she might seem to be interrupted in reading it. She heard his voice in the hall, his
rapid footstep on the marble. He had come. She felt
her smile to be uncontrollable. This happiness, she told
herself, was for Flo, who would come to the door at
any minute and see him there and know that he had
still wished to come.

He sat opposite her. Without asking now, Hassan
poured his whisky and soda. 'Just a short one,' he said.
'I can only stay a minute.' She felt a surge of annoyance

at him that he must keep up this pretence of having more urgent matters at hand.

'Flo enjoyed herself the other night,' she said.

'Oh good.' He rose abruptly and faced the muffled window with his back to the rest of the room. The major-domo had entered without a sound and moved about transferring glass ashtrays and little beaten silver bowls of peanuts from his tray to the occasional tables. How quickly the room had darkened. In the silence she heard the onset of the rain. The others would get wet. Her excited eye continued to observe Routh while she signalled to the major-domo, no, not now, not the glasses yet.

Routh stood motionless until the servant left the room. Then slowly, with his back still towards her, he raised his hands behind his head and stretched them upward, fingers interlocked, until he stood lazily extended. She watched this slow unfurling with a close attention. Its apparent carelessness, its charm, seemed to impose an intimacy upon the room that she was not prepared for. Why doesn't Flo come? she thought.

Still staring at the window he said, 'I must ask you, am I approved of?'

'As what?'

'Well, as me,' he said, turning to smile at her. He lowered his arms in front of him in a gesture that the slightest pause would have turned into a supplication. She had put a cigarette between her lips and now flicked irritably at a lighter before she said, 'By me? You know you are.'

'By H.E. too, if possible.'

'Well, he never says. He says you're good at your job.' She remembered Harry's grudging tone as he had said that, and lest any of that tone had seeped into her own words, she added quickly, 'That's his highest praise, you know.'

'Only I wonder sometimes if he's not quite sure of me. If I'm quite welcome here. If I have intruded. Gone further than you meant me to.'

'That's all wrong. You know that.'

'Only I seem to get up against people without at all meaning to. I should hate that to happen with you.'

'Whatever is the matter?' she asked him firmly.

He gave her one quick searching look and came to sit opposite her again. 'Oh, it's all too absurd. It's Clive Waller.'

So sure had she been that he wished to talk to her about Flo that she almost laughed. 'Is it the play again?'

'No. No,' he said wearily. 'It's just that he's written to some fossil friend of his at Oxford and dug up the fact that I was sent down. I should have told you, I suppose. It just didn't seem important. I'm telling you now before they do.'

She was silent for a moment during which she was aware he never took his eyes from her face. She wished he would tell her why this had happened, but realized he did not intend to. Finally she said, 'Does it affect anything here?'

'Of course not. It was nothing. Oh, it's all so incredibly stupid.'

'Forget it, then. It doesn't matter.' At the same time her accurate mind recorded that he had told her he was writing a thesis in Rome, and that in doing so he must have lied to her.

'But it does matter, more than anything just now. Look, I'm being a bore. I just wanted you to tell me if I'm in the way.' He smiled bleakly at her, 'Preferably a week or two before I am.'

'You're never a bore,' she said. 'Of course we want you here.' The words seemed both inadequate and rash, but he must know her sympathy was sincere enough, must hear it in her tone, see it in her face. With a mixture of desolation and relief she heard the crushing of the gravel as the cars drew up. He had heard it too and rose quickly, 'I'll slip out through the ballroom, if I may. I really can't face them all at the moment.'

'You'll come again, won't you,' she said. 'Please come again.' It was the thing she had intended never to say to him and he had gone in haste without giving her an answer.

It was Sunday. It was Monday. When Lydia came down to tea, she found Flo wearing Signora Ponticelli's turquoise linen dress. She said pleasantly, 'You're not going to wear that to the theatre, are you? Won't it get terribly dirty?'

'I'm going out afterwards.'

She paused for a moment. Then she said, 'With Roland?'

'With everyone,' the girl said quickly. 'After the rehearsal.'

'You might have said.'

'I only knew this afternoon. You were upstairs.'

'He came? Roland came here?' For the phone had not rung.

'He sent a note.'

Could she be lying? the mother thought. Could she hope that by going dressed like that the others would feel obliged to include her in their evening plans? Oh, she would be hurt! The rawness of such hurt inflicted itself even now upon her own ageing body which no longer had the resilience to bear it. How do we survive being young? she thought. She said, 'Are you *sure* that he asked you?'

'Yes, of course I'm sure.' She spoke as if the truth of this had been long ago embedded in the substance of their lives. But still the mother went on questioning. 'When did it come? Did the major-domo bring it in? Just now?'

'Yes.'

'And you're sure?'

'Yes,' the girl said desperately, 'yes.'

Flo watched her mother. Regardless of the uncleared tea things, Lydia had moved to the sideboard, poured herself a tot of whisky and taken a sip of it. She seemed a different person whose movements were harsh and on the very edge of self-control. She's like this, Flo thought, when no one's here. Her mother's waist, she noticed now, had thickened and overhung her belt. The two buttons just above it gaped and showed the slip beneath. 'I'm going now,' she said, and felt surprised to find herself, almost without her own volition, standing in the hall with Hassan smiling and bowing as he opened the door and ushered her out into the garden and the open street.

When she had gone, Lydia stayed standing by the window. Her mind continued to play out the fruitless argument that Flo's departure had prevented. The whisky burnt her mouth. She put the empty glass back on the sideboard and looked at her watch. Harry was late. They were due for drinks at the United Nations Commissioner's at six thirty. She must bathe and change to leave the bathroom free for him when he returned.

But once upstairs she stayed dressed as she was and resumed the game of patience she had laid out before tea, as if by persisting in the afternoon's activities she might set back the clock. For now it was on Harry's lateness that her vague misgivings concentrated. He would have rung, she told herself, if anything were really wrong. Nevertheless her new-found sense of desolation spread inside her.

And what of Flo? she thought with a terror so sudden and profound that surely in a moment she would trace its source away from the real world into some foolish nightmare she had forgotten on waking. Flo is Flo, she told herself, and will come to no harm. But she needed Harry Morgan's voice outside her head to say, Flo can look after herself. She's a sensible girl. What can have delayed him? she thought. Has something gone wrong? Then, don't be absurd. Then, what if this time I am not absurd, but having a genuine premonition?

She heard the car. She heard Harry speak to the major-domo. She swept up the lines of cards with impunity for she had set them out without naming to herself the particular disaster she intended to avert. She heard the heavy clip of his shoes on the marble stairs. Then he stood just inside the door looking at her. Something's happened, she thought. She said, 'You're late. I didn't wait tea. Would you like some now? Would you like a drink?'

But she could not deflect him from what he had to tell her. He would not come into the room nor sit down until he had. 'The very devil of a thing's come up,' he said. 'They want me back in London.'

'When?'

'I'll go tomorrow morning.'

'But that's so soon! I thought it wasn't for another month at least.'

'They've put it forward,' he said, coming into the room now.

'What a time for you to have to go!'

'Can't be for more than a week or two. Clive can cope for that long.'

'He'll be insufferable!' she said. It enabled them both to laugh.

'Look, I'm most awfully sorry about this.'

'It's just the surprise. You'd have had to go in any case.'

'That's true.' Still he would not sit down. He walked

quickly into his dressing-room where she could hear him rapidly opening and shutting the drawers of his wardrobe. He seemed to have escaped her; to be already walking in his dark coat in the cold streets that smelt of burning coal, and retained still the high seriousness of the war; to be climbing the steps to those magnificent offices; to be feeling the particular blend of apprehension and well-being she knew those places always gave him.

'Where's your good coat?' she said, going after him. 'At your club? Will you stay there?'

'They've booked me in. Clive phoned through.'

'Your dark suit's there too,' she said. 'You couldn't possibly need your tailcoat, could you?'

'Good heavens no.' He went on searching through the drawer without telling her what he was looking for. 'I'd better take my dinner-jacket, just in case.'

'But your black socks are so thin,' she said in a kind of wail, thinking of his exposure to the cold and other things, unnamed as yet, when she was not there to protect him.

'I'll buy some wool ones if I need them,' he said. 'I don't suppose I shall.'

When he turned around she had gone back into the sitting-room. He realized he had spoken abruptly and followed her, saying the thing that had only just occurred to him. 'You'll be all right?'

'Of course.'

'You won't worry.'

'I always worry.' She smiled at him. 'You know I hate your flying.'

'Being here alone, I mean. Surely Gerda could come to stay.' When she was silent he went on, 'Flo's here. You'll like some time with her alone.'

'Why? Should I worry?' she said as if the last words had not been spoken. 'Might anything go wrong? Is something the matter? Is that why they've sent for you?'

'No, no,' he said.

'I'll miss you,' she said suddenly and reached out her arms for him. The spontaneity of the gesture moved them both. She caught him in a tight constricting hold, only to move quickly from him when there was a knock at the door. Hassan appeared with two tumblerfuls of whisky on a tray.

'I ordered them as I came in,' Harry said with the little laugh he used to dispel emotion. When Hassan had gone they found a shyness had come between them. To counteract it, she said, 'If it weren't for Flo I could have come with you. We could have stayed at the Basil Street Hotel.' It was where they had spent their wedding night. He looked at her ruefully and said, 'That would have been nice.'

'Wouldn't it?' Perhaps because it was impossible, she was able to smile at him fully and regretfully. 'We're going out tonight. Did you remember?'

'Oh God,' he said. 'Where to?'

'The UN. Couldn't we duck out? It's only drinks. They'd understand.'

'No,' he said. 'The less that's made of this the better.

There's no need for anyone to know it's anything other than we'd arranged.' He had turned away from her as he spoke and gone out into the corridor. Presently she heard the running of bath water. When he came back he was in his dressing-gown with his wet hair springing up in curls about his head and a towel draped sportingly about his neck. 'Is Flo coming with us tonight?' he said.

'No. She's out.'

'Not Routh again?'

'Well, the theatre,' Lydia said. She spoke rapidly, anxious that nothing of their near quarrel should be apparent in her voice. 'They all go on somewhere afterwards. I think she feels left out. I said she could go.'

'Was that wise?'

'I don't see why not.'

He had begun to rub at his hair with the towel. Now he looked out from under it to say, 'She doesn't care for him, does she? For Routh, I mean.'

'No. Of course not. Well, if she does it's only a crush. It will pass.'

'Perhaps we oughtn't to encourage it.'

'It?' she said, as if she did not understand him. 'Surely there's no harm in encouraging *him* a little. Look, I know about his being sent down. He's been quite open about it. He seems to feel that Clive has some sort of spite against him.'

Morgan suddenly let out his monosyllable of laughter, but said nothing. She hurried on. 'He's young. He's different from the others. He seems to feel everyone's down on him at the moment. I'd like to help him.'

'He's amusing enough. It's just that we seem to see rather a lot of him.'

'Only on Saturdays – occasionally. I think it steadies him to come.'

He made a sceptical sound in his throat and went into his dressing-room. From there he called out to her, 'While I'm away it might be better to limit it to Saturdays, or even cut it out altogether. I don't suppose Flo would miss going to the theatre for a week or two. It might be best.'

When he came back Lydia said, 'Something has come up, hasn't it?'

He settled heavily into one of the armchairs. 'Oh, it will blow over. It's just that there's been something in the English newspapers.' He spoke distantly, with an edge of distaste in his voice as one might on reading an unpleasant episode from someone else's private life.

'What about?' she said.

'Well, about the regime here. About the summary executions. Apparently they're expecting questions in the House.'

'But you're quite within your rights. They agreed to all that.'

'Yes, of course. But you know how things can be made to appear. It's unfortunate just now. But of course they don't think of that. It's their election they're concerned about.'

'Who could have written it?'

'Some journalist,' he said dismissively.

'Knowing not the first thing about it! People are always pious at a distance.'

'That's the damnable thing,' he told her. 'Whoever it was informed him knew all about it.'

She looked at him. 'You think it's Roland, don't you?'

'He swears it was nothing to do with him. I'll have to take his word for it.'

He lied to me about the thesis in Rome, Lydia thought. She said, 'Why didn't you warn me?'

'They only settled it today. They phoned through this afternoon. They want me home right away.'

'Not to reprimand you?' she said indignantly.

He made a wry face. 'To brief them first hand. It's best that way.'

It was time to go. They dressed hurriedly. The Lancia was waiting at the door. Later, when it returned them to the villa, he ordered Colomboroli to be ready by ten to take him to the airport. 'The motor-cycle escort?' Colomboroli asked him. 'No,' Morgan said. 'No need for that.' They sat at dinner. Without guests, without even Flo, the gleaming table imposed an unnatural distance between them. Across it they exchanged those portions of conversation from the cocktail party which were suitable to share with the servants, if indeed they understood a word that was being said. While they drank coffee, Morgan briefed the major-domo as to when he should be called in the

morning and what it was necessary to pack. The old
man bowed impassively and asked no questions.

They retired early. Flo had still not returned. Harry
fell instantly and heavily asleep. Lydia sat up in bed
reading a detective novel. As soon as she heard the taxi's
wheels in the drive she switched out the light and lay
down in darkness listening as the tyres skidded to a halt.
There was a brief pause before she heard the taxi's doors
open and slam shut, another pause, too brief for any
but the briefest of kisses, if it had come to that. The
doors slammed again: once when Routh resumed his
seat and once when the driver did. A moment later the
taxi had gone and she heard Flo's cautious footstep on
the stairs.

By ten o'clock on the following morning, the
Lancia with its bulging mudguards and goggle headlights
was drawn up by the front steps of the villa. Colomboroli stood to attention by the bonnet while Amde and
Hassan lifted two thickly labelled suitcases into the boot.
Harry Morgan appeared at the door, taking his dispatch-
case and his mackintosh from the major-domo and at
the same time shaking him by the hand, in farewell.
Colomboroli snatched open the rear door, arched out
his chest and jerked his hand to his brow in a quivering
salute. Lydia and Flo climbed into the car. Then Morgan
stooped double followed them. Colomboroli slid into
the driver's seat, released the brake and engaged gear all
in one perfected movement. The great car set off
smoothly over the gravel drive with the little Union
Jacks darting like tongues in the morning breeze.

The commercial airline had no flight until Thursday. An RAF Auster waited on the tarmac to fly Harry Morgan on the first leg of his journey, to Khartoum. Only a very small group had gathered to see him off: the Wallers, the Colonel of the regiment, Geoffrey Wheeler. He shook hands formally with each and each of them called 'Happy landings' or 'Good luck to you' as he walked away. Before he was hoisted clumsily into the tiny plane, he turned to wave to them. Then he was out of sight. A mechanic spun the propeller into motion and darted back. The plane moved forward, teetering on its wheels. It gathered speed and flew off parallel to the ground; then sank from sight into the boiling cloud at the edge of the escarpment.

Returned to the safety of the car Lydia briefly wept for him. A moment later she blotted her eyes roughly with her handkerchief and lit a cigarette. 'Now watch this,' she said to Flo, waving the smoke impatiently from before her face. Beside the bonnet of the car, Colomboroli furled each flag tightly with his forefinger and enclosed it in its leather sheath. At precisely the same moment the Wallers' driver released identical flags on the mudguards of their Cadillac. Then he drove off, with the Wallers erect in the back seat, leaving Colomboroli to follow in his dust.

Lydia and Flo sat side by side, as they had done on the day of Flo's arrival. Once more they drove past the concrete buildings with their shutters, the whitewashed oleanders and peeling eucalyptus. Once more they overtook the khaki-hooded lorries with grinning faces in the rear. Then, aghast at one another's unfamiliarity, they had talked. Now, with months of shared living between them, with specific things that needed to be asked and answers urgently wanting to be known, they said nothing. When Lydia could bear it no longer, she seized Flo's hands and shook them slightly as if by doing so she might dislodge the sad expression that had settled on the girl's face. 'I'm glad you're here,' she said almost shyly. 'I miss him so when he's away. But we'll enjoy ourselves. We'll go to Ponticelli's, shall we, and order something new?'

To her surprise Flo held tightly to her and said, 'Oh yes, please. I should like that.'

Something in the girl's tone, and her own need to distract her mind from following Harry Morgan's downward flight through the mountains, made Lydia reach out immediately to tap on the glass partition between themselves and Colomboroli. The driver, without taking his eyes from the road ahead, crooked his arm backward, slid open the panel, and leaned his ear towards the gap. '*A la casa della Signora Ponticelli,*' Lydia said gaily. '*Pronto, per favore!*'

They watched him smile and nod approvingly in the driving-mirror. The Lancia's ignominious progress down the Corso had been averted. He turned sharply to the right and made his way through the backstreets to Ponticelli's flat.

Chapter Fourteen

THE SIGNORA looked at them aghast, thinking that by some dreadful oversight she had forgotten an appointment. 'No, no, you must forgive us,' Lydia said, seizing both the woman's hands. 'We have come suddenly, just because we wanted to.'

It was fate, the signora told her, beaming now. Only yesterday a consignment of new fabrics had come from Italy. The boy had been putting them on the shelves all yesterday afternoon. They would be the first to see them. She ran ahead up the dark stairs with her loose-heeled sandals slapping against her feet. '*Ecco!*' she cried. Piled on the counter were several bolts of dark shot taffeta.

'For London in the winter!' Lydia cried. 'There, that's the one for Flo!' She pointed to an olive green that matched Flo's eyes. The signora rolled it out along the counter top and crushed the thin crisp silk together in her hand. Gold sprang out along the crests of the wrinkles. Recklessly, without enquiring the price, without pausing to think what occasion the London winter might provide, Lydia ordered fifteen yards. For herself she chose a beautiful metallic brown. It was so nearly perfect. But they all agreed it needed something more to set it off. 'I know! I know!' the signora cried. She pattered across the floor to a chest of drawers and began to sort through carefully folded tissue-paper packets. '*Ecco!*' she cried again and held out to them a remnant of black Venetian velvet. They stroked it reverently with their fingertips. It was as soft and as dense as mole's fur. The signora crossed the room and laid it on the taffeta. 'For the hem,' she said. Now it was perfect. It was a remnant, she told them, from an opera-cloak made for the Duchess before the war. All that time she had kept it. 'It could not be for anyone, you understand,' she said gravely. 'But for you, yes.' She would not charge for it. Such things can only be a gift.

And there were woollens. 'It would be madness not to stock up before we go back,' Lydia whispered while the signora ran to the stairs and called down to the boy to bring the woollens up at once. Without any difficulty they chose an open Prince of Wales check for Flo and a fine brown worsted for Lydia; two tailored coats and skirts for less than something off the peg in London! 'You can travel back in that,' Lydia said. 'It will seem cold even in summer, coming straight from here.'

'But that is months away,' the signora cried. 'She is young. She must live for the present too!'

Instantly Lydia remembered throwing open the doors to the ballroom on that first morning and crying out, 'We'll have a dance!' Some vague discomfort was associated with that moment which she would not

contemplate just now. 'A dance frock,' she said decidedly. 'A dance frock for your birthday.'

The signora regarded the girl. 'She has changed,'
she said approvingly. 'She is ready for the tulle now!'
She reached down a bolt of a soft *café au lait* colour and
held it to Flo's cheek.

'That's it! That's it!' Lydia cried. 'Look what it does
for you!' Flo turned for the first time to study herself
in the glass. The net fell like a blurred extension of her
own pale skin; an unspecific nakedness on which
her face, with all its imperfections, sat exposed. But in
the excitement of the moment they could all believe
in the signora's transforming magic. The tulle was
ordered too; the patterns chosen from the signora's stack
of Italian magazines.

They sat in the back of the Lancia, dazed and exhil-
arated by the beauty of the fabrics and the grandeur of
Lydia's extravagance. But as soon as they entered the
villa they felt the muted reality of Harry Morgan's
absence. Their wild well-being receded. They had
returned only with the memory of their purchases.
There was nothing to open after lunch; to try on; to
discuss possible alterations to. They sat at either end of
the polished table while the major-domo stooped over
them with a platter of fish. They ordered coffee in the
upstairs sitting-room and climbed the stairs.

I should speak to her about the theatre now, Lydia
thought, while she is happy. But already she knew that
the propitious moment had passed. She laid out the
cards that would ensure Harry's safe arrival in England,

but with the girl's disturbing presence in the room she could not give the game the attention it deserved. They drank their coffee. The afternoon stretched ahead of them and the evening, void of Harry Morgan's charged presence. Yet just when the old intimacy might have been re-established, Lydia felt, as she had in the car, that all likely subjects of conversation had become forbidden. Again awkwardness grew between them, until she was reminded of the frightening moment in the game of cards when, without warning, gaps appear after all the kings. There is no movement permitted then; nothing to do but to sweep up the cards and start again. By an unspoken agreement they spent the afternoon apart and retired early to bed.

It was not until five on the following afternoon that Clive Waller rang to say that he had just spoken with Harry on the phone. He had arrived safely in London.

'Is everything all right?' she asked. Then realizing that perhaps she should not know what might be wrong, she added quickly, 'Does he feel the cold?'

In his measured voice, Colonel Waller told her that he had failed to ask that, but had checked on the weather in London. It had been raining. 'He has his mackintosh,' Lydia assured him. He had sent his love. A letter was in the post, but there was no knowing exactly how long he might be. 'Coping all right?' Waller said before he hung up. 'Good for you. You'll call Wendy, won't you, if there's anything you need.'

In the upstairs sitting-room Lydia abandoned her latest game of patience. Harry had arrived safely. There were at least two weeks before he must fly again. What troubles he might have had no reality until he brought them home to her. She would not allow herself to worry. She tapped the pack of cards together and shut them away into a drawer. For a moment she was aghast at the feeling of feckless contentment that swept over her. Oh, it is not Harry, she assured herself. It is the job, the endless pressure of the job. For that fortnight the duty to be constantly pleasant to people would be lifted from her. The world of Aderra would recede, while the outer world, the world with Harry in it, existed once more.

She was filled with resolution and suddenly able to look ahead. She wrote affectionately to Daisy Mayhew, asking her if she would accept Flo as a paying guest. It would be for a month at the most by which time, in all likelihood, she and Harry would have returned to England. If not, if a worthy job were secured, they would send for Flo to join them. She switched on the radio and twiddled the dials to try to find a better tuning. She blew on the dust, even rubbed at the more substantial tubes with an old toothbrush, but stopped at once for fear she damage it and snap her only fragile link with Harry, England and the future.

In the morning Lydia woke to find herself stretched across the double bed, filled with some bright expectancy which must have carried over from a dream, for what might she expect? Then she remembered that it was Monday and she could no longer shirk the task of telling Flo she could not go to the rehearsal. At breakfast with the servants waiting on them, she said nothing. When the cook was shown in she ordered sandwiches for two to be served in the upstairs sitting-room instead of dinner.

Already Flo had disappeared to play her record on the ballroom gramophone. There was no need to tackle her until the sequence of tunes had reached its end. The small noises of the servants' activities were distant in the house. Sunlight penetrated the net curtains without a sound. Gerda rang to ask her how she was. Geoffrey rang to ask the same. She urged both of them to come on Saturday as usual even though there was no chance of Harry being back by then. The feeling that other people found her brave under adversity filled her with an energy for which there was no outlet. She must do something.

In Harry's last posting in Khartoum, she had devoted hours of each day to gardening, nurturing hot bright patches of zinnia, canna and petunia. Her first task after breakfast had been to gather a bunch of flowers for the dinner table. It had seemed a kindness there to bring them in to spend their last hours out of the ferocity of the sun. Here, where even these gentle tasks were taken from her, she had shown no interest in the dense flower-beds that stretched between the sentry boxes and the villa. Now she would seek out the gardener and make up for her neglect. From the shelf in her wardrobe she took down a coarse straw hat which she had bought on first arrival but never worn and ventured down the front steps.

The gardener was on his knees scratching at the soil with a rusty knife. He scrambled to his feet and stood at rigid attention with his eyes averted as if he hoped to pass unnoticed among his plants. She greeted him in his own language. It was the extent of her knowledge of it. Then in her halting Italian she told him how beautiful his garden was. He received her praise with a little nod of pleasure and continued to stare obliquely at the ground. She beckoned him to follow her as she made her way along the crowded paths, stooping to touch this bloom or that, enquiring the name of some plant that seemed to flourish in the shade and might therefore be useful in some unknown garden that awaited her in England. A moment later she made a sound of pure pleasure and bent to smell a clump of green-white nicotiana, the exact shade of those that had grown outside the dining-room at Frant Road. She turned to the old man and, abandoning language altogether, told him by the level of her hand that she had known these flowers as a child. He smiled at her delightedly.

She had come intending to cut flowers for the sitting-room but found that, in her present mood, she had lost the will to curtail or lay claim to any of this abundance which was in no sense hers. She was sweating slightly. The gardener's shy pleasure in her interest had become a weight she could no longer sustain. She thanked him and turned back towards the house. The major-domo was standing at the top of the steps in an attitude of ease that made him unfamiliar. He had been watching her. He too was smiling; with recollection perhaps of some early morning ritual when the Italian Duchess had walked in her garden pointing imperiously to this bloom or that, and the unwrinkled major-domo, with his basket on his arm, had received the cut flowers and carried them into the villa.

I do not even know his name, she thought. It was the next thing she would do, to ask his name. She began to hurry through the tall plants towards him. But at that moment a flick of alien colour caught her eye. The nose of the Wallers' Cadillac, with its flags flying, had protruded between the sentry boxes and crept up the drive. For a moment she was tempted to freeze among the plants, as the gardener had done, and hope to go unnoticed. Instead she waved gaily with her hat as the car deposited Wendy Waller at the villa steps and bore her husband on to his office.

'I was just passing,' Wendy Waller said improbably, when Lydia came up to her. 'I thought to myself, I'll just pop in and see how Lydia's getting on.' Only the faintest nervousness underlay the quelling brightness of her tone, but that was enough to touch Lydia with remorse. She had come, presumably at Clive's insistence, knowing herself to be unwelcome. Chastened by her servants' perfect manners, Lydia said, 'Oh, how kind you are!' and took her arm, so that they climbed companionably up to the front door.

'Where's Flo?' the visitor asked as she settled herself beneath the monkeys.

Lydia gestured towards the sound of the gramophone.

'You should have brought Bridie. I'm sure they want to be friends. It's just that things get so busy here.'

Too firmly for comfort, Wendy Waller said, 'I thought we'd have a talk, just the two of us.'

The major-domo, without being told, had carried in a tray of coffee and biscuits with childish shapes stencilled in pastel icing. His rare smile lingered. He's pleased, Lydia thought. This is what I'm meant to do; to entertain the other English wives to coffee in the morning. Wendy Waller raised her cup and said, 'To H.E., then.'

'How extraordinary to think that he's in London,' Lydia said and gave an involuntary shiver with her shoulders.

'You must worry.'

It was said with a sickroom sympathy that goaded Lydia into saying, 'For Harry? Why never!' Then in a perfect imitation of her visitor's tone she added, 'Of course, it puts a fearful weight on Clive.'

'It's the least he can do.'

'Well, Harry knows how lucky he is to have him.' There was a pause. The major-domo appeared briefly at the door carrying a letter on a tray. Even at that distance she thought she recognized Routh's assured black hand. He would be too delicate to come in Harry's absence. He had written instead. She would phone him; invite him over for a drink; talk to him; explain the sudden ban on Flo's activities coming so soon after her expression of trust in him. She gestured to the major-domo to leave it on her desk.

'Actually, Clive and I thought you might be brooding.' She reached a swift pat of her hand to Lydia. 'I'll tell him not, shall I?' she said, as if at that moment they had both agreed to be very brave about a secret illness.

What has she come about? Lydia thought. The meaningless touch, as any touch must, had drawn them into a semblance of closeness. It had at the same time reminded Lydia of the curious smell that haunted Wendy Waller, the faintest blend of TCP and untanned shoe leather.

Now, though the major-domo had withdrawn, Wendy Waller kept her voice low. 'I've often wanted to ask you. What do you *tell* Flo?'

'About what?'

'You know what I mean. The facts. The birds and the bees. I don't know what you call it.'

'Well, she knows, of course,' Lydia said. 'I can't say it's something we discuss.'

'Don't you? Oh, Bridie and I have great talks.' There was something avid in her eye. 'Only sometimes I wonder if she takes it in. There are such dangers in a place like this, when of course nothing must *happen* until we get back to England.'

This is intolerable, Lydia thought. Barnyard talk. Soon she'll tell me the details of her periods. But she continued to smile and nod sympathetically. Now she glanced at her watch and wondered if she might decently ring for a drink. It was far too early.

'Am I keeping you?' Wendy Waller asked sharply, but made no move to go.

'Of course not.' Quickly she refilled their cups. The final chorus ground out on the gramophone. Perhaps Flo would come and put a stop to this, but a moment later the orchestra struck up the overture once again. She sat there, sipping her coffee, refusing to give the slightest indication of wanting to know what it was that Wendy Waller had come determinedly to tell her.

Now, snapping a biscuit, she began again. 'I hear that Flo's been out with Rolly Routh . . . and the Sawleys?'

Lydia had, until that moment, known nothing of the Sawleys and could not immediately place them. 'Yes,' she said. 'They've been dancing once or twice after rehearsals.' She was aware of the slight inaccuracy of this even as she spoke it. Something intolerable in the woman's look made her add, 'There's nothing in it, you know. It isn't at all serious.'

'Don't please think me interfering. It was Clive really – just at this time. He thought you might not know.'

'I know enough of Roland Routh,' she said, 'to know that I can trust him. Harry thinks well of him.' But she knew that Harry did not, that Clive might know better than she what Harry really thought, that without a doubt Wendy Waller knew everything that Clive knew.

'Well, that's all there is to it. If Harry approves . . . the last thing he would want me to do would be to worry you just now.' She had begun to grope for her handbag which had slipped into the crease of the chair.

Now, abandoning it, she leant impulsively forward and said, 'Oh, you'll think me the most dreadful poke-nose, but are you certain he's not taking advantage of her? It's just that he's so much older and he does have something of a reputation.'

'I am absolutely certain,' Lydia said.

'Of course, he cuts such a dash here, with all the *angst* and Bolshie politics. But back in England . . .' The hand threatened to reach out again, but this time, instead, it fastened on the handbag. She rose to go. 'My dear, you must know that they can seem God's gift to women out here and too uncouth to bear when one gets back to London. That's what I tell Bridie. That's why I tell her that she must be so very very careful.'

As they walked out into the hall she lowered her voice still further: 'You know, of course, that Jamie Renfrew is very keen. He's so attractive and you know he's very well connected and seems so absolutely serious, but still you never know. And with Harry's position here what happens to Flo is just that bit more significant – while we're here at least – than what may happen to my poor Bridie.'

'Oh, she is a dreadful woman,' Lydia said to Flo, who had appeared the moment that Wendy Waller left.

'What did she want?'

Lydia bent her head over her lighter and said indistinctly past her cigarette, 'Her spies had told her you were out with Roland. She thought I didn't know.'

'What did you say?'

'I said it wasn't serious. You won't let it be, will you? You'll keep it light?'

'Light?' the girl said with her puzzled look. Her evenings out with Roland Routh, their air of tired intimacy, their close-held silences and glancing kisses had from the start seemed tense but scarcely light.

Her tone made Lydia say the more vigorously, 'It's quite absurd. What is it? Twice? Three times? Four times? And you weren't even alone, she tells me. The Sawleys! You might have told me about them. I felt an awful fool not knowing. She says that Bridie tells her everything.'

'Perhaps Bridie has nothing to tell,'

Her mother gave a snort of laughter as she blew out smoke. 'Only you might have said something. Who are they anyway?'

'She's in the play.'

'And they're . . . nice . . . people?'

The girl considered this. Then she said, 'They're friends of Roland's.'

'Then I'm sure they are.'

'Yes.' But Lydia thought there was little conviction in it.

In her agitation she had forgotten Routh's note. Now, she hurried to the desk at the far end of the room in order to retrieve it. Over her shoulder, she said indignantly, 'She calls him Rolly! I hope *you* don't call him that. He's hardly a Rolly.' Through the open door Flo watched her search among the papers on the table. 'There was a note here. Did you see it?'

'It was for me.'

'Was it from Roland?' Lydia said slowly. 'What did he want?'

'He wants me to go out with him tonight.'

Lydia walked slowly back across the room. Hassan had come to clear away the coffee things. She waited until he had gone before she said, 'I should have said this days ago. It's just that Harry's not too keen on your going out so much on your own.'

'On my own?' the girl repeated as if she had grasped immediately that it was Routh that Harry had objected to.

'When we are not with you. He wanted me to ask you, would you mind awfully giving up the theatre for a week or two – and all this dancing. Not the club. That's harmless enough. It's just this going out.'

The girl was looking seriously at her. The fear in her expression, its defencelessness made Lydia break off and say, 'Oh Flo, my darling, it's probably just till he comes back. You know how it is out here. How we can't entirely choose what we do. I know it's absurd to think, but in the very smallest way we represent the Royal Family just as Harry does the King and just as any breath of scandal in their lives would be unthinkable . . .' The girl's attentive regard made the words seem tawdry. 'I mean, I know that I can trust you, but if you are seen in the town, in places where other people might behave badly – these Sawleys, for instance. What do we know of them? Oh, you've no idea how much could be made of it.'

'But I must go,' Flo said.

Something hopeless in her tone made Lydia look more sharply at her. 'What do you mean, you *must*?'

'I always go to rehearsals. I've promised that I would.'

'Well, surely you don't do so much that they can't manage without you for a week or two.'

'I have to go,' the girl repeated as if it were a lesson she were fearful of forgetting.

'And going out dancing, surely he doesn't tell you that you must do that?'

'But I must go.'

'Oh Flo, Flo, he could take someone else. For two weeks . . .'

'No,' she said. 'It wouldn't be the same. They wouldn't like it if it were anyone but me.'

'They?' Lydia said sharply. 'Who is this they?'

'Well, everyone.'

'You are not making sense.'

'It doesn't matter,' the girl said. 'Don't you see it doesn't matter.'

'What doesn't matter?'

'I don't matter. It's what he wants.'

'That's a terrible thing to say.'

'But it's true!' the girl said. 'It's true!'

Such talk was intolerable and must be stopped. 'At least,' Lydia said, 'promise me that you'll tell him this is the last time you'll go out until Harry comes back. I can't explain, but it's important. He'll understand.' Then, realizing that Roland Routh would understand

her motives all too well, she added, 'I'll ring him. I'll
say you're tired,' for now it seemed that suddenly the
girl looked tired to death. 'I'll say I'm keeping you at
home for a while. Look, if you're worried about it we'll
have him over for a drink. We'll have these Sawleys if
you like them. Then no one's feelings need be hurt.
Shall I ring him?'

Because the girl said nothing, her insistence that her
own will was of no account seemed still to echo in the
room. 'Surely it's not too much to ask,' Lydia said
angrily. 'After all . . .' So nearly had she said, After all
Harry has done for you . . ., but she would not be
drawn down that track which suddenly she realized
might lead to regions she would not at any price enter.
'After all,' she said, 'it's not as if you knew Roland well.
It's not as if your heart were involved.'

But Flo had stood up and left the room with a
strange authority that might at any moment have dis-
solved in tears.

She did not appear when the major-domo rang the
gong for lunch. Lydia told him the signorina was not
well and endured his kindly concern like a penance
exacted for the lie. As she ate her solitary meal she
resolved to do the thing she had meant never to do, to
telephone Roland Routh and ask him to call in to see
her during the afternoon.

The office closed at four. She gave him half an hour
to get home. She had to look up his number in the
station list. She dialled holding it open in the same hand
that held the receiver and must in her agitation have

misdialled. An Englishwoman's voice abruptly answered, 'Yes?' Fearful suddenly that her own voice might be recognized, she put down the receiver without a word and dared not ring again lest she make the same mistake.

Flo did not appear again until six o'clock. She was wearing her turquoise linen dress and simply said, 'I'm going now.'

'You know what you must say to him. That you can't go out again. Not until Harry gets back.'

'Yes,' the girl said. 'Yes. I said I would.' As soon as she had gone Lydia rang the bell and told the major-domo to bring a whisky and soda. When he brought it she said, 'You may bring my supper on a tray up here. For one only. And another whisky.'

She turned on the radio. While she laid out the cards that would ensure Flo's safe passage through the streets, she listened to the dance tunes requested by British soldiers serving on the Rhine; each with its freight of secret sentiment which women in Hudders-field and Bridlington would thrill to. At seven the major-domo tapped at the door and carried in the supper tray. On it was a small vase of green nicotiana. 'Oh, thank you,' she said. The particular kindness had brought tears to her eyes. The old man smiled and backed through the door with a series of dismissive nods, as if to say that it was nothing, nothing.

When he had gone she drank the second whisky and wept for a time out of this recurring sense that something had been allowed to slip; the thing that she had meant to give to Flo; the thing, whatever it might be, that had been fought for; the thing that made Harry Morgan's job both justifiable and good; that as a child, she had had. She bent over the little bunch of flowers as intently as if it might be situated there. Perhaps it was. Perhaps this piercing sense of something real and lost was nothing but the memory of some single afternoon in the safety of the garden in Frant Road. She must remind herself that Flo had had that too. Somewhere in the ammunition boxes was the photograph to prove it, of Flo standing in that garden, shouting, surely out of joy, with her hands clasped around her throat to feel the sound.

That was gone. The house had been sold to pay the debts incurred during Granny Franklyn's final illness; the garden divided into plots for bungalows in that winter before she knew that she could count on Harry Morgan. 'I let it go,' she cried out loud to the bleak room.

And Flo, too, she had let go, turning from her as she sat, pale-faced, in the school train, thinking, I cannot grieve. She is in safe hands. I cannot live her life as well as mine. It isn't fair to Harry. What did I do to her? she thought now, for she had known quite well that the headmistress was mad.

And now, with only the weakest resistance, she had let Flo slip out into the restless town with Roland Routh of whom she knew nothing. She had shirked the task which Wendy Waller had not shirked, the mother's task of telling her daughter the hard facts of lust.

But it was you who wanted this, cried the silent inquisitors whom Harry had left behind him. Not that. Not that, she cried back silently. They would ask next, what was it then that you did want? And what had been in her mind when she flung open the ballroom doors and declared with such conviction, 'I have found just the young man for you'? What friendship of what nature, sufficiently delicate and unresolved, to contain both Flo's innocence and Roland Routh's undoubted lack of it? It is I who am mad, she thought.

She rang for a third whisky and, carrying the glass in one hand and her travelling-clock in the other, set them on her bedside table before she undressed for what remained of the night.

Chapter Fifteen

THE NOTE FROM Routh had explained a change of plan. It was Raymond Sawley's birthday. Avril would not be coming to the theatre because she was having a party, but all the cast was invited to come on to the Sawleys' flat, later in the evening.

When the rehearsal was finally over everyone went down into the street to call for taxis. As the second one drew up Routh suddenly remembered that he had left his jacket in his dressing-room. Lennie Broad handed him the keys through the taxi window.

'Don't wait,' Routh said. 'I'll lock up. Flo and I will come on afterwards.'

She turned away rather than see Broad wink. The taxi drove off. She waited in the street until Routh reappeared and took her arm in a proprietorial grip to hasten her along. Still it astonished her to be touched by him so casually.

'You don't mind, do you, if we eat something first?' he asked. 'I just felt I had to get away from them.'

She looked down at her feet when she said, 'I'd like that,' for fear that he might see how much she would.

They walked the short way to the Primavera. It was
early still. They were put at a table for four, in a corner
where a piece of green-painted lattice supported a sickly
ivy plant. Routh left her and hurried across the empty
dance floor to the bar to order omelettes. He leant
casually on the counter. He was talking to the waiters
in Italian. He made them laugh. She sat watching him
and knowing that the others would not come. The
empty places at the table seemed to reproach her for
feeling so much happiness. He came back carrying a
glass of wine for her and a whisky for himself.

The orchestra was just arriving one by one. They
smiled and nodded at them before setting down their
instruments on the dais and going over to the bar themselves. Routh said, 'God, it's good to be alone.' She
wondered if this aloneness in any way included her.
She wanted to ask if they need always go everywhere
with the Sawleys, but that would be to assume there
would be other times, which she had promised Lydia
there would not be. Instead she said, 'We don't need to
go at all if you don't want to.'

'She's gone to so much trouble,' Routh said wearily.
'She doesn't have much of a life with him, you know.
We have to go.' He had finished his drink already and
now watched Flo sip hers.

After a moment he said, 'This going out the way
we do. If you don't like it we'll stop it now.'

'I told you before, I do like it.'

'You don't though, do you?'

'I like you,' she said so quietly that she could not

be sure he had heard. He gave a sigh, of exasperation perhaps, and said, 'I didn't think really. I thought you'd like it simply to get out from time to time.'

'I can't come any more,' Flo said. 'She won't let me.'

'Who won't? Not Lydia?' His face had taken on the emptied look she had glimpsed once in the theatre. Slowly it filled with a bitterness she could not comprehend. Nor could she comprehend the childish petulance with which he said, 'She promised me. She said . . .'

'It's just for now. Just till Harry comes back.'

'Why?'

'She didn't say.'

'She must have said.'

'It was something to do with Harry.'

'And what was it to do with Harry?' He spoke loudly now, as if to an imbecile. She looked quickly to see if anyone had noticed, but the waiters had withdrawn to the kitchen and the musicians, just assembled on the dais, seemed absorbed in desultory tuning. She stammered slightly as she said, 'I don't know what it was. I wasn't there.'

'But you must have asked her.'

'No,' she said, 'I didn't.'

'Didn't you care? Didn't you care what she might think of me?'

'It wouldn't make any difference,' she said.

He rose abruptly and went over to the bar. She heard him tell them to hurry with the omelettes. He came back with another drink and emptied it in silence.

Then he said, as if the answer scarcely interested him, 'What would you do, if I asked you out again?'

'She wanted me to promise not to.'

'Did you?'

'Only that I'd tell you. Nothing else.'

'Then you'll come out with us if I ask you to?'

'I don't know,' she said, because even while they spoke she had thought how impossible it would be to escape the defences of the villa if no one wanted her to; because the word 'us' had struck her to the heart.

The waiter had come with the omelettes. Routh pushed his moodily away. Flo began to cut hers into smaller and smaller pieces.

'Well, that's that then,' he said. 'Come on, we're going. You don't really want to eat that.'

Outside he stepped into the road to flag down a taxi and climbed in after her, giving the address of Avril Sawley's flat. As soon as the taxi door was closed she began to cry. 'Oh God,' he said. 'Don't do that.' He arched his back to reach a handkerchief from his trouser pocket. She took it dumbly and hid her face in it. Its warmth, its close human smell made her cry the more.

She felt the seat give slightly as he moved closer to her. He put his arm around her shoulders and with the other hand took back the handkerchief and began carefully to dry her face. His hand was trembling slightly. 'Is that better?'

'Yes.'

He stayed with his face so close to hers that she could feel his warm spiritous breath come and go against

her cheek, against the corner of her mouth. He waited
there for her to turn towards him, but she stayed gripped
by stillness. 'You're supposed to want this,' he said with
a low untroubled laugh. When she kept her face averted,
he sighed and moved away. She did turn then, oppressed
with the fear that she might have offended him still
further. He had hunched himself back into the corner
of the cab where he watched her by the erratic light
that flashed in from the street. 'Aren't you even curious?'

'What would be the point?' she said. 'It wouldn't
mean anything.'

'It would mean that I like you; that I'd like to have
a pleasant evening; that I'm grateful to you.'

She smiled at him uncertainly. 'Oh, come now,' he
said. 'It's not that bad.' He reached out his hand to her
and she held it as tightly and insensitively as a child
might. 'You'll get over it,' he said and laughed again.

The taxi had drawn up outside the block of flats.
As she stood waiting in the warm street for him to pay
the driver, the sound of a party, well advanced, came
down to them from the open windows three storeys
up.

The door to the flat was open, and people, far more
than were in the cast, crowded the hall and spilt out
on to the landing. Without pausing in their shouted
conversation, they lifted drinks above their heads and
pressed against the walls to let the newcomers pass. The
din of voices fought against a loud-pitched gramophone. In the dining-room couples danced, pressed
together in the semi-darkness. 'You'd better have

another drink,' Routh said, 'or this will be unbearable.'
He disappeared and came back carrying a glass of cloudy
fluid with a slice of cucumber floating on the top.
'Drink it down,' he said. 'It's all there is.' They leant
side by side against the wall in the crowded lounge. She
sipped the drink obediently. There was nothing left to
say that could be spoken loud enough to hear.

Avril, wearing a red silk frock, pushed her way
towards them and shouted, 'What kept you? Have you
eaten? There's food in the kitchen.' She went away
again.

'We'd better dance,' Routh said. They went into
the darkened room and danced. She watched the other
couples. There, among the unfamiliar faces, was Mrs
Blotto and her Major, dancing at arms' length with
chins raised, at twice the speed of everyone else. Avril
and Jamie Renfrew went past, talking and talking, with
only an inch or two between their mouths. She pressed
her cheek, her narrow chest, her entire body hard
against Roland Routh's. She felt leaden in his arms.
The floor was oddly pliant. When the music stopped,
he said, 'You get something to eat. I'll have to dance
with Avril.' Even here it was so. He put his hands on
her shoulders and pushed her out into the corridor. She
turned around and he had gone.

In the kitchen food had been set out on the table
but only a few cubes of cheese, speared on to toothpicks,
were left stranded on the grease-stained paper doilies.
Lennie Broad was standing there, saying something she
did not catch. He took her hand and pulled her along

the corridor to the dining-room. There he danced, holding her a little way away, sweating with concentration at his own elaborate footwork. The record changed. She danced with Major Blotto, a few stately absent-minded rounds. Then, almost with relief at the familiarity of his thin, tense arms, she danced with Raymond Sawley. On and on, round and round. He sang to her as they danced, words too indistinct to struggle after. A little way away from them Avril Sawley danced and talked with Jamie Renfrew. Once when they passed close to them Sawley reached out and pushed Renfrew roughly on the shoulder.

'What the hell?' Renfrew said.

'Oh, give over, Ray,' his wife said pleasantly. 'Change partners?' She winked at Flo as if to say, I'm doing you a favour really, and putting her arms around her husband made him dance away. Renfrew looked at Flo and said, 'God, that man makes me sick.' She thought that he would dance with her but he turned on his heel and went away.

Roland Routh appeared with another glass of Pimm's and handed it to her saying, 'I'll be right back,' but he did not return. She drank it in quick sips for want of anything else to do. Avril Sawley appeared at the door and shouted, 'Anyone for bacon and eggs?'

Flo leant against the wall in the lounge. Mrs Blotto sang. 'Daddy wouldn't buy me a bow-wow . . .' 'Show us your garter,' someone shouted and she made a simpering face and lifted her skirt just high enough to show the suspender catch at the top of her nylon stocking.

There were jeers and whistles which seemed to please
her. The Major sang, 'Pale hands I loved beside the
Shalimar . . .' while Mrs Blotto played. The music from
the dining-room fought with the singing on and on.
People sat on the floor or leant against the wall. Jamie
Renfrew leant beside Flo, but didn't seem to notice that
she was there. Slowly and carefully he tapped the ash
of his cigarette on to the central parting of one of the
two young corporals, who sat on the floor in front of
him. The young man stared fixedly ahead, not seeming
to notice; nor did he seem to mind that Jamie Renfrew
repeatedly ran the toe of his shoe back and forth beneath
his buttocks.

Flo sat at the kitchen table. Very slowly the edges
of the room closed in and went away again. She stared
at the people in the room, one by one. A man and a
woman sat arguing, their faces twisting in rage, but
speaking so quietly that she could not hear a word they
were saying. Sergeant Broad held an egg in one hand
and broke it open with one swift vicious stroke of a
knife.

'How do I light the bloody cooker?' Broad called
out. The angry woman got up, lit a match, put it to
the hissing gas and tossed it away. Flo watched fire flare
up in the bin beside the stove. It seemed some time
before the woman screamed and Broad, swearing furi-
ously, wrapped his hands in a towel and threw the
flaming bin out of the open window, into the street
below. Briefly angry voices rose up to them, then there
were shouts of laughter and the sound of the bin being

kicked along the street. The eggs were burnt. Broad, still swearing monotonously, scraped them into a newspaper. The room was filled with an acrid, homely smell.

She went into the corridor. Without a word Roland Routh put his arm around her. He smiled, but not at her, rather at some remote diffused pleasure that had no connection with this tired, overheated place. They danced in the dining-room which was in total darkness now except for the dim light from the street below. Round and round. Angry voices came from the lounge. Roland Routh murmured in her ear, 'Oh, shut up, shut up, shut up.' Round and round. He had left her so abruptly that she staggered with dizziness and might have fallen, had her hand not reached out and found the wall. The angry voices rose and fell above the music and beneath it.

Raymond Sawley's: 'Don't be such a bloody fool. What the hell do you think you are doing?'

Jamie Renfrew's, high-pitched, unsteady: 'Keep out of it. It's none of your bloody business.'

'Oh, isn't it?' Raymond Sawley shouted. 'I'd say it was very much my business. You disgust me. Bloody well get out.'

A voice said: 'Oh God, put it down. Put it down, will you.'

And another voice, loud as a man's but sexless with terror: 'Jamie, Jamie, no!'

There was a noise like the slamming of a door. The gramophone shrieked in the room as someone tried to turn it off. A woman screamed repeatedly.

'Shut the windows,' someone shouted. 'For God's sake get him out of here.' She was in the corridor. Roland Routh was gone. The light had been switched off. People pushed past her. The front door was open and the light from the lift shaft showed them jostling to get out. There were clattering footsteps on the stairs and raised excited voices. No one had waited for the lift. She heard Avril Sawley shout, 'Ray, for God's sake, Ray.'

She went into the lounge. Avril was sitting in a chair with her head in her hands and her hair falling between her fingers. Routh was bent awkwardly over the back of the chair. As Flo came in he was saying, 'Calm down, won't you. He doesn't know a thing.' Otherwise the flat, so crowded a few minutes before, had emptied. As soon as she saw Flo, Avril jumped to her feet and held out her skirt in both hands, saying, 'Look, look, there's blood,' with such insistence that Flo came close to her and looked gravely for the minute specks scarcely visible on the red dress. 'It was Jamie Renfrew,' she said, turning to Routh now as if she wanted him to verify what she said. 'He had his revolver. Oh God, oh God, I never thought. But I got it from him. He was going to kill Ray. I know he was. Oh my God,' she said, displaying the skirt again, 'he must have shot him. He must be hurt. Look at the blood.' She sat down again abruptly and began to cry.

Routh stood kneading her shoulder with his hand. He looked at Flo as if he hated her. 'I'll have to stay till he gets back,' he said. 'I can't leave her alone to take you home. See if you can get her out of that dress.'

Avril looked wildly up at him, 'Rolly,' she said. 'For God's sake, Rolly.'

'It's all right,' he said. 'I won't go.'

'I could wash it for you,' Flo said.

Avril jumped up eagerly then and ran into the bedroom. When Flo came to the door she was pulling clumsily at the buttons. 'I can't let the servant see it,' she said. 'Oh my God. He might have killed him.' She climbed out of the dress and thrust it at Flo as if she could not bear to touch it now. But she followed her into the bathroom, telling her where the soap was and how it must be washed. She had put on Raymond Sawley's dressing-gown and stood huddling it around her, peering down at the water, asking repeatedly, 'Has it come out? Has all of it come out?'

'There's hardly any,' Flo said. It was impossible to tell whether the slight discoloration of the water was caused by blood or the running of the cloth itself. All the time she scrubbed and rinsed, she listened for the sound of Raymond Sawley's return. He would come back. Routh would call a taxi and take her home.

'I took it from him,' Avril said again. 'I went up to him and said, "Just give it to me." And he gave it to me. My God, if I hadn't had the guts to do that he'd have killed him.'

Flo wrung out the dress a final time. Immediately Avril grabbed the wet stuff of the skirt and stretched it out over the side of the bath. 'Is it clean?' she said. 'Are you sure it's clean, all of it?' There was no telling. The frock when wet was dark and shining as if it had been soaked in blood. It sickened Flo to handle it. 'Where do you want me to put it?' she asked Avril.

'In the bedroom. In the cupboard. The servant mustn't see it.'

'Won't it drip?' Flo asked.

'Oh, for God's sake give it me.' She ran into the bedroom with it and hung it on a coat-hanger in amongst the other clothes. When she had shut the door, she asked Flo querulously, 'Why isn't Ray back yet?'

Flo went out on to the balcony, more to be free of Avril's voice than in the hope that she might see Sawley drive up along the deserted street.

'Come back,' Avril Sawley said behind her. 'You make me nervous.' When Flo came reluctantly into the room, she began again, 'What got into him? He must know what would have happened if I hadn't been there.' She began to cry.

'I'm sorry,' Flo said.

'Whatever for? It's nothing to do with you!'

'That it happened. When you took such trouble with the party.'

But Avril had run into the lounge again to plead with Routh, 'It's just so lucky I was there; that I managed to keep calm. Wasn't it lucky I was there?'

They heard the whine of the lift. Avril ran out into the passage and opened the door, calling excitedly, 'Is that you, Ray?' Sawley pushed roughly past her without a word and went into the bedroom, slamming the door behind him. The cistern gushed and went still. In the lounge Avril clung to Roland Routh and repeated hysterically, 'You can't leave me with him. You can't.'

Over her shoulder Routh said to Flo, 'Just go away for a moment, won't you? In there, anywhere.'

She went into the dining-room and leant out of the open window. He called after her, 'Don't do that. Someone might see you.' He shut the door which she had left open. She sat at the table listening. A door slammed. She heard Sawley's voice angry and indistinct. Another door. Avril calling his name shrilly. She heard the lift doors. He had gone.

The door opened. 'Come on,' Routh said, 'quickly.' There was no sign of Avril. She felt immense relief, as if the Sawleys had been swept off the edge of the earth. In the lift, although Routh did not speak to her, she was alone with him. Before it stopped he took her arm, threw open the rattling gate and propelled her through. Outside in the road a taxi was waiting. When he gave the name of the villa the driver turned round to look at them in astonishment. 'Just get there, will you?' Routh said. He sat back in the corner of the cab with his head in his hands as if he had forgotten Flo's existence in the desperate need to think what to do next.

At the gates of the villa he leant forward and knocked on the glass partition. The taxi drew up to the kerb. They climbed out in the glare of the sentry boxes. 'Wait,' he told the driver. He took Flo by the arm and walked with her slowly, their heads bowed, up the gravel sweep. She seemed to see them from the house, walking so confidingly, as if they had been married for years.

Her body had begun to ache with the knowledge that she must part with him. Step by step. Perhaps he would kiss her. Perhaps he would forget.

In the shadow of the porch he said, 'What will you tell them about all this?'

She remembered the ease with which Avril Sawley had clung to him. 'Are you in love with her?' she said. She could not look at him. He made a sound like a laugh, but shorter and harsher, and said again, 'What will you tell them?'

'What do you want me to?' He was watching her. She was trying to think what it was he wanted. 'Must they know?'

'They'll have to know something.'

'Because of the gun?'

'Something like that.'

'I should say, then? Before they hear?'

'I think so. It's not what she thinks, you know. They weren't quarrelling over her. Renfrew was drunk. Ray was only trying to take it off him. It was all to do with Renfrew and someone else.'

She knew instinctively who, but said in bewilderment, 'Why?'

'Oh God,' he said, 'if you don't know, I can't explain. Some men like men. That's all.'

'But he goes out with Bridie Waller.'

'Yes,' he said wearily. 'Yes, that's true.'

'I'll say I didn't see anything. It's true. I didn't. I'll say you brought me straight home.'

'Good girl,' he said, giving her arm a squeeze. 'Don't

say any more than that.' He held her then, briefly and harshly against him, cheek against cheek as if they danced. His skin was cold and damp. She felt him trembling, but she could also feel the determined beating of his heart under the thin stuff of his jacket. He turned and walked rapidly over the gravel to the waiting taxi.

Chapter Sixteen

WHEN LYDIA woke, she found herself sitting upright against the pillows of her bed with the taste of whisky soured in her mouth and the wireless emitting empty crackling noises in the next-door room. She looked in alarm at the luminous hands of the clock. It was three in the morning. She must turn on the light, get up, see that Flo was safely back. A crazy logic gripped her that if she stayed where she was, in the dark, she might at least hope that Flo was safe until the morning proved it otherwise. She reached for the light and forced herself upright. Then, in her bare feet, ran in a desperate haste down the corridor that led to Flo's room.

The door was shut. With elaborate caution she turned the door handle and pushed it open. Flo lay on the white sheets. One arm was curved with a curious grace above her head; her lips set apart; asleep, beyond, it seemed, all reach of harm.

In the morning she breakfasted alone and warned Hassan that the signorina should not be disturbed. She watched his face, suddenly aware that he might know, better than she did, when Flo had returned. His features kept their usual impassivity; she could read nothing there. Her head throbbed. She would rather attribute that to anxiety over Flo than to the whisky. She saw the cook and ordered sandwiches again. She saw the major-domo but had no instructions for him, no summonses for Colomboroli or Haile. She went upstairs, took two aspirin and listened outside her daughter's room, but heard no sound. Behind her, in the upstairs sitting-room, the phone was ringing.

She reached for the first cigarette of the day, held it between her lips and lit it quickly with the receiver nestled on her shoulder. For a second a voice crackled out of earshot. When she adjusted the earpiece, Wendy Waller was saying, 'It's all right. I've sent the servant out. No one can hear. Is Flo all right?'

'Yes,' Lydia replied. Her voice and heart were frigid.

'Did you see her when she came in?'

'I was asleep.' She added quickly, 'I've been going to bed very early. I don't wait up.'

'But she's there. She's safe. You're sure?

Her instinct was to drop the phone and run back down the corridor to capture again the innocence of Flo's abandon on the bed, but she controlled herself to say, 'Yes, of course I'm sure.'

'Jamie Renfrew's just been on the phone to me,' Wendy said, in a voice so hushed it seemed she feared that, after all, the servant might be there in the passage with her ear pressed to the keyhole. 'He didn't feel he could ring you, of course, but he was most concerned.'

There was a pause which Lydia refused to fill.

'He's terribly responsible that way.'

Still Lydia kept silent.

'He was afraid that she might have come home in a dreadful state and given quite the wrong impression. You know what this place is like. And because he and Bridie are so very close he wanted to set us straight before we heard it from some other source. That's why he rang so early.'

Another pause. Another silence.

'My dear, you don't know, do you? There was a shooting incident.'

'No,' Lydia said. The image on the bed was vivid now, but had it breathed or moved? If she had thrown back the spotless sheet what horrors might have been revealed?

'It's all right. No one was hurt.'

'Thank God.'

But the voice persisted like a hot breath against her ear. 'It was those Sawleys. Apparently he drinks a lot and gets absurdly jealous. It was just good luck that Jamie happened to be there. Apparently he was the only one who kept his head and managed to say quite calmly, "Give me the gun," and he did.'

'What has this to do with Flo?'

'My dear, isn't it enough that she was there and saw it all? One of the reasons he rang was that he couldn't bear for her – and the villa – to be involved in anything so sordid.'

'But she, herself . . .?'

'She was *there*,' Wendy Waller said emphatically, 'with Roland Routh.'

As Lydia put down the phone she became aware of Flo standing irresolutely at the door of the room. She needed time to think and to subdue the rage she felt towards Wendy Waller, lest it leap sideways at her daughter. For how could Flo have put her in such a position?

Now, to give herself that time, she reached for her hairbrush in its chintz bag and, setting it at the edge of the table, said, 'Won't you do my hair for me? It's so long since you have.' As she spoke she groped for the hairpin that held it back and shook out the warm, red mass about her neck. Flo made no answer, nor did Lydia turn towards her. Instead she began systematically to lay out her cards. There was a pause in which it seemed the girl might speak. Then Lydia heard her move slowly across the room. From the corner of her eye she saw Flo's hand take up the brush and a moment later felt its first tentative pressure on her hair. When the final column was in line she said without raising her eyes from the hand she had dealt herself, 'I need to know about last night.' She listened to the girl's long sigh before she said, 'You weren't involved in any way, were you?'

'No.'

'Was Roland?'

'No.' But there was just sufficient hesitation in the rhythm of the brush for Lydia to add quickly, 'He did bring you home, didn't he?'

'Yes, of course he did.'

'Well, that's something, at least.' She had spotted the aces and must release them one by one. The backward tug of the hairbrush jarred her head as she laid the black five upon the red six and caused the line to go awry. As if the tiny spark of irritation that provoked had fallen on all the dry stuff of the mind, she heard her own voice speak out angrily. 'How could you? I warned you. I asked you especially. How could you do this to me?'

'To you? No one's done anything to you.'

'But you have. You've laid me open to that dreadful woman. What must she think?' Still she kept her eyes fixed on the cards.

'I did what you told me,' Flo said. 'I told him you didn't want me to go out with him again.'

'And what did he say?'

'Oh,' the girl said as if she were weary with this already. 'He asked me if I would.' She had let the brush fall heavily on to the side of the table and had moved away. Her voice seemed to come from a greater distance than the crowded room could possibly provide.

'And will you? After this?'

'If he asks me.'

'Flo, this is madness. You can see what happens. You should never have gone with those people last night.'

'Nothing happens.'

'There was a shooting incident. It's all over the

town. You were there. People know you were there. You saw it.'

'I didn't see anything.'

'But you were *there*,' Lydia said as relentlessly as Wendy Waller had to her.

'I didn't see anything.'

She's lying to me, the mother thought. And if she lied at all, what limit could there be to the deceit or to the hidden thing which made it necessary to lie? At the same time she placed the black seven securely on the red eight. 'And Roland? What was he doing?'

'It's nothing to do with him. He wasn't there. We were in another room.'

At last the mother swung around to see Flo hunched in a chair beside the door as if at any moment she might take flight. 'What other room?' And suddenly it seemed that there were no limits left to curb the length of time or distance she might go. '*What* other room?' For what was the nature of this place where Flo's indeterminate form had moved from room to room with Roland Routh, whispering, beyond her earshot, words she could not possibly imagine; though now it seemed, intolerably, as if they must whisper mockingly about herself. In her agitation she turned back and searched across the surface of the table for the red six that must go on the black seven. There was none. She took up the discard pile in her hand and began to slap cards face upward on the table, saying, 'What is there between you? What is it that you can't tell me? Why can't you be honest about it?'

Inside her head, like a demented echo, her voice went on, Why doesn't he come here any more? What does he say about me? How angry was he? But that she must not speak.

'There's nothing between us. That's why.'

'That's impossible.'

'It's true,' the girl said with contempt. 'In the sense that you mean, it's true.'

'What other sense is there?' Lydia said, twisting around to face her. 'I need to know what happened.'

It seemed by the intensity of her look, the parting of her lips, as if she would say then whatever words the mother wished to hear. Instead she said, 'You wanted me to go out with him. You told me he was right. You said he was Frant Road.' She spoke the words with such contempt that Lydia knew they could never again be used between them. But the girl's shrill voice was not done. 'You don't tell me everything.'

'I don't know what you mean.' She forced her mind to think, red six, red six. Behind her she felt Flo's tense silence and heard her slow intake of breath.

'You never tell me about Edward Wharton.'

She laid down the cards and sat there very still, very alert. 'What don't I tell you?'

'You don't tell me anything.'

'He's gone. There's nothing I can say about him. What there is is private.'

'He's as much mine as he is yours,' the girl said. 'He's more mine.'

'He didn't know you.'

'It isn't true. He did know me. He must have done. I remember him.'

'You can't possibly.'

'I do. I do. He fed the swan.'

'What swan?' the mother said in bewilderment. 'I don't remember any swan.'

'You're lying. You were there. Behind me somewhere, I know you were there.'

'I never lie.'

'You do. You do.'

They heard their voices then, the voices of two women they did not care to be, escaping into the empty house, along the marble corridors to reach the silent servants.

Lydia leant her elbows on the table, careless of the cards, and held her head in her hands, not in grief, but to contain within it the things which must be contained. For they could not afford to quarrel as other families could. What broke now would not mend. She must force her mind back to the source of this which was Wendy Waller's phone call. She began to straighten the columns she had just disordered, thinking, There are two red sixes in the pack. It must be here. And there it was, the next card on the pile. The six of hearts to place on the seven of clubs and so release the five of diamonds and the four of clubs. Her hand was trembling, but she knew that it would yield to her now. All other thoughts must be erased but Wendy Waller's phone call, and what had happened and what Harry would wish her to do. Behind her she heard Flo move across the room and braced herself, if the door handle should turn, to call her sharply back for there was more to say that must no longer be evaded.

Instead she heard the click of the switch on the wireless and the remote whisper of static. She looked at the travelling-clock. Noon. News. The outer world would rightly come and force itself between them.

But instead of the sprightly tones of 'Lillibullero', they found themselves listening to Beethoven's funeral march. They looked at one another now without expression until the music ended and a voice, frail with distinction, announced that King George VI had died.

Chapter Seventeen

LYDIA WEPT briefly. Flo could not. Even after they had turned off the solemn music, awe filled the tawdry room which seemed unable to accommodate it. Their anger had been taken too quickly from them; their own distress was still too raw to adjust to the scale of this. Flo went to her room to dress. The turquoise linen frock lay crumpled on the floor. She should wear it perhaps out of respect because it was her best, but the thought that it might hold the stale sad odour of last night's happenings made her unable to touch it. She found in her cupboard the pink and white gingham she had worn at school on Sundays and travelled in to Aderra. She put it on and went down to the drawing-room where Lydia was already seated. They smiled uncertainly at one another. Lydia reached out and briefly squeezed her hand. They sat in silence. The grand death hung over the house, confusing itself with other deaths that now could not be mentioned. From time to time the servants looked into the room and shook their heads with a deferential sympathy which Lydia felt she could not deserve. She went into Harry's study and phoned Clive Waller. 'Can you come round? There must be something that I'm meant to do but I really don't know what it is. Could you find out for me?'

'He was so kind,' she said when she came back in to Flo. 'The oddest people are at times like this. Really I should have made more effort to like them; had them over more.' The morning's phone call, everything could be set aside.

She went upstairs again and came down wearing a navy blue frock. 'It seemed wrong to put on *black* just for Clive Waller,' she said to Flo. 'Perhaps you should change.'

'Into what?'

'Oh, I don't know. Into something less . . . less . . . Well, perhaps not.'

They heard a car in the drive. A moment later Clive Waller stood in the doorway to the ballroom with a momentous expression on his face. He said, unnecessarily, 'I came as soon as I could.' The sight of him made Lydia turn away abruptly and press her handkerchief hard against her upper lip. Turning back she said, 'It's so ridiculous to take it as a personal grief, but it's so sad. It carries so much with it.'

'You must feel it,' he said, seizing her hand awkwardly in both of his. 'The war . . . all of that.'

'Yes,' she said and began again to cry.

'Harry called just now from London. That's what delayed me.'

'Oh, is he all right?' For the whole world seemed under threat.

'He's been delayed, I'm afraid. He thinks he should stay for the funeral. All his meetings have been put back in any case.'

'When's that?'

'Not for another week apparently. It takes time to lay on a thing like that. And she, poor young lady, abroad and coming home to shoulder such a burden.'

'Oh, he should be here, surely!'

'I doubt he's been given much choice in the matter. He sent his love. He says he'll write.'

'The letters take so long to come. It's hardly worth it.'

'It's hard on you,' he said.

She had sounded petulant – at such a time. Now she spoke as he would want her to. 'Is there anything we are meant to do? The flag?'

'That's been done. I noticed as I drove in. I thought you must have told them to.'

'Oh,' she said, blotting at the corners of her eyes with her handkerchief, 'the major-domo is too marvellous.' She noticed Flo had left the room without a sound and thought, How rude of her, when the Wallers have tried so hard to be kind.

'It's more a matter of what we can't do,' he was saying. 'Public appearances. All that. There's a directive at the office. Geoffrey's hunting it out. He says he'll bring it over.' When? she wanted to ask. How soon?

Mutely she handed him the cigarette box at the same time that she helped herself.

'I think best not,' he said.

'Look, won't you at least sit down a moment?'

When he had settled stiffly with his attaché case upon his knees, he said, 'What a time for Harry to be away!'

'Poor Harry!'

'It's been a wretched business, this bother in the press at home. Perhaps he didn't say. Wendy was not sure how much you knew. Oh look, the last thing either of us wanted was to worry you.'

'Not at all,' she said quickly. 'We're all upset. Of course he told me.'

'I haven't had the chance to say, but perhaps this isn't the moment.'

'Perhaps it is,' she said smiling at him. 'Perhaps at times like this it's easier to say things.'

'I just wanted you to know that we are all absolutely behind him. He's a splendid man, as just as anyone alive. It's outrageous that he should have to endure a breath of criticism for what he's done here. Believe me, every-one who's ever worked under him feels that.'

'Someone doesn't.' As surely as if she had mentioned his name, she knew that she had referred to Roland Routh and that in her present sobered mood she might suppose him capable of any treachery.

'Ah well,' Waller said bitterly, 'there's always someone.'

'Do you know?'

'We suspect. And as for Wendy and myself, we wanted you to know that we understand perfectly the position you've been put into and, speaking for myself, I think it's really rather splendid the way you've handled it, going on exactly as before until it's proved one way or the other. And if it is he who's been disloyal enough to send confidential information to the papers, all I can say is that it's a rotten way to repay your kindness to him.'

Her agitated mind had grown so still that she could hear at last what it was they had been saying to her: Harry, the Wallers in their cautious turn, and Roland Routh himself, standing there with his arms extended, asking for approval before he made sure of being seen about the town with Flo and so advertising the villa's trust in him. So that's it, she thought. Out loud she said, 'I take it we refer to Roland Routh.'

'Look, I haven't spoken out of turn, have I? Harry had warned you? We did wonder, Wendy and myself.'

She had turned aside to stub out her half-finished cigarette and now said with a little laugh, 'The one thing Harry *didn't* think to say was who knew about it and who didn't.'

'Well, only he and I officially, but you never know. Anyway, all this should simplify things.'

'Simplify?'

'Well, no parties for a bit. No going out.'

'It puts it all in proportion rather, doesn't it?' she said.

'Doesn't it just!'

'A drink?' For she must set all this apart in her mind; shut it away until she could think in private.

'No. No. I think not.'

'No, of course.' Then sensing that things had taken slightly the wrong turn, she let public solemnity back into her voice and said, 'Oh, it is so sad. A great deal more than any single death. I can't take it in.'

'Terrible,' he said, shaking his head. 'Terrible.'

He had risen to go. To her surprise she did not want him to and began to speak rapidly. 'Will it make things awfully difficult for you? I mean, how will they take it? Does it make us vulnerable in any way?'

'Are you anxious?' he said. 'Would you and Flo like to stay with us for a night or two? I'm sure Wendy . . .'

'Oh good gracious, no! We're quite safe here.'

'Well, we'll have to see how things go.'

She followed him out into the hall and at the door took his hand again and said, 'Harry saw him once. Quite close to. He was wearing make-up. Apparently they have to, to be seen. Like actors. Well, they are in a way. An awful life really. Poor, poor man.' Her eyes had filled with tears again, but already the legitimate moment for them had passed. Clive Waller's free hand twisted unhappily about the handle of his briefcase. He was embarrassed by her and wished to go. 'That reminds me,' he said. 'I'm afraid this puts paid to the play. I'll ring Renfrew. He's a decent fellow. He'll probably have realized what it means.'

That evening when Geoffrey Wheeler rang at the front door of the villa, he was holding a copy of the official directive on state mourning, printed on the occasion of the death of George V. A phone call to the embassy of the Northern Province had established that they too had nothing more recent to go on. After some discussion in the office it seemed wisest to accept the pamphlet as the letter of the law. The fact that no one but themselves would ever know whether or not they had, made rigorous adherence all the more binding.

The major-domo greeted him with an expression more sorrowful than usual and made a series of small sympathetic noises in his throat. 'Awfully sad, isn't it?' Wheeler said, gripping the old man by the hand. 'Good of you to feel it so.'

'God, he's good at it,' he said to Lydia as he kissed her cheek. 'It puts one to shame really.'

'Won't you have a drink?' she said and went quickly to the sideboard to pour one for both of them.

'Heard at all from Harry?' he asked as he sat down.

'Only through Clive.'

'He'll get back as soon as he can.'

'Oh yes. Really I seem to fall apart without him.'

'You never show it.'

'Well, that's all right, then.'

After a swallow of whisky he raised the directive on mourning. 'You won't believe this, but for the next month ladies are to wear, on evening occasions, long black frocks with white gloves extending above the elbows and, in the daytime, a small black bow pinned above the left breast. Old Clive found that last bit rather *risqué,*' he said, peering above his spectacles at Lydia. 'That's why he sent me along.'

When she laughed she feared she might be unable to stop. She put her hand immediately to her mouth in shame and wanted a moment later to cry.

'Is something wrong? Something else, I mean?'

'No,' she said. 'Not really.'

Already he was on his feet swilling the ice-cubes in his glass before he took a final swallow. To his surprise she reached out her hand to him and said, 'Don't go. Not yet.'

'There is something, isn't there?'

'It's only Flo,' she said. 'She asked me about Edward. Just before the announcement. She wanted to know about him. Anything. We nearly quarrelled. I couldn't tell her anything.'

'Well, that's understandable.' He sat slowly down again, not wanting her confidence, though at one time he had craved it. Now he found himself wishing dully for everything to stay just as it was. A still, confessional light had settled in the room as daylight faded beyond the curtains. At any moment he thought, almost with longing, the door would be flung open, the servants enter, switch on lights, replenish drinks; but there was not a sound outside the room.

Her voice had taken on a sad monotony as if she had rehearsed these words again and again in her mind. Perhaps she had, though he doubted she had had anyone to speak them out to. 'We weren't happy, you know. He was very jealous. Without any reason, of course.

Perhaps if we'd stayed in Kenya it might have worked out, but he wanted to make a go of things in England. That mattered to him. We lived in that flat in Cheltenham. He was studying to be an estate agent. He never went out. We were children really. Our parents paid for eveything.

'When Flo was born, I went home for a while and that was heaven, but I had to go back again. There was the terrible guilt of knowing one was meant to be happy. God knows I was ignorant enough of how happy I was meant to be, but I knew that I was failing. I kept pretending that I was – so blissfully happy. And of course when Flo was born it was just assumed that everything was all right between us. It was a relief in some ways that he never wanted to go out. I thought people would notice, although I don't expect they did. When the war came he enlisted straight away. I went home again. He was killed at Dunkerque, you know. I couldn't feel a thing except the awful pity of his not being loved.

'I thought no one would ever find out. But I knew he had known. There was nothing I could do about it.' She said it in the curious way that he had found people tended to hand him their lives, summarized, complete in all their awfulness as if to say, Well, there it is. What are you going to do about it?

'I'm so very sorry,' he said, because truly he was.

'Oh, don't be,' she said. 'It's over.'

He was angry at her too. She would like him less for knowing what she had told him. He would never feel as simply happy as he always had when he was with her. Already she was saying, 'I don't know why I told you that, except that Flo asked me about him and I couldn't tell her.'

'What can I do?' he said. 'Can I say something to her?'

She was staring past him as if she had seen a ghost. 'Isn't it odd,' she said, 'not to have realized it before. He was a little like Roland Routh.' She had reached out and taken his hands impulsively in hers. 'Is it possible that Flo might know that too?'

He smiled at her and said, 'Usually there's a simpler explanation for things.'

'Yes,' she said, twitching her shoulders slightly. 'Yes, of course.'

Without letting go her hands, he had risen to his feet and drawn her from her chair. 'I'll phone tomorrow,' he said. 'Just to check that everything's all right.' But of course he was telling her that he must go away. 'I'll tell the others to come on Saturday, shall I? Surely within doors we should go on as normal. It will do you good.'

Bleakly she remembered drinks on Saturdays.

He kissed her quickly. 'Harry will be back soon.'

'Oh,' she said, 'I wish it were all more extreme. I wish I had a thick black veil to hide behind; to hide the things I cannot feel.'

'I know,' he said, as if conceivably he did. 'I know.'

Chapter Eighteen

B Y THE MORNING a new visitors' book had appeared
to replace the usual one on the table in the hall.
An inkstand, an array of pens, blotting-paper and a vase
of arum lilies were set beside it. It seemed as if these
things had lain for years, in some cupboard of the
major-domo's, in readiness for just this event. From
nine o'clock the front doors of the villa were thrown
open and a stream of sympathizers filed up the steps to
sign their names: the various consuls, the Roman Catholic and Greek Orthodox bishops, the cadi, the Italian
mayor, the head of the Greek mercantile community,
the United Nations Commissioner and his staff. Mingled with them were members of the British community,
many of whom had never crossed the threshold of the
villa before and were unlikely to again. The women
wore their darkest dresses, the men black armbands and
black ties. For a time Lydia and Flo stood watching
through the glass doors of the drawing-room. Among
them, Flo recognized Mrs Blotto and her Major and
the Sawleys. Jamie Renfrew walked within a foot of
her and so did Sergeant Broad, but no sign of

recognition could pass between them with everyone so altered and subdued. Only of Roland Routh was there no sign.

The house servants stood in line beside the door, hands clasped behind their backs, heads bowed, murmuring solemnities to those who spoke to them. 'How do they know so exactly how to behave?' Lydia whispered. After the confused emotions of yesterday, she felt herself held upright by their perfect dignity, grateful that she might brace herself against these sure formalities. It seemed that every aspect of her life was covered and prescribed by Geoffrey Wheeler's directive on state mourning. There would be no rehearsals now, no dances at the club, no going out with Roland Routh or anyone else. Any social life must be held within the decorous confines of the villa. Everything was safe once more. However wrongly, it was impossible not to think that had this happened only a day sooner, much might have been averted. She glanced sideways to glimpse the girl's expression but could see nothing there distinct from the great generalized sadness that had descended on them all.

It was Friday. Again the doors of the villa were thrown open. Again the patient queue formed to sign their names in the book of condolence. Again Lydia Morgan and her daughter remained in attendance, but withheld by the glass doors of the drawing-room.

Towards mid-morning Lydia remembered that the first of their fittings with Signora Ponticelli was to have been that afternoon. Should she ring and cancel it, or would the tactful signora assume that at such a time so trivial a matter would be forgotten? Immediately she was ashamed at having not forgotten and uncertain how soon it might be suitable to arrange a new appointment. There was no one she could ask. In the end she dispatched Hassan with a small sum of money to request a half-yard of black silk and at the same time deliver a note of regret that at this sad time they could not keep their appointment.

He was back within the hour and Flo managed to fill the entire afternoon devising two black bows and attaching them to safety pins.

Still there had been no sign of Roland Routh. Glancing, that evening, through the book of condolence, Lydia failed to see his tight black hand. She would not allow herself to dwell on the significance of that. The grand event had distanced her from everything.

Only in the night did goblin thoughts torment her. It must be several weeks now since she had talked with him. That part of her that never cheated with the cards, that was incapable of putting the four of clubs anywhere but after the three, compelled her to admit she knew how many Saturdays that she had waited with the unadmitted hope of hearing his eager step outside the door and finding herself immediately drawn in to the bright compulsion of his thoughts; his week's activity; his refusal to accept as blameless the things that everyone accepted; even she missed her mistrust of him. She had missed him and the pain, now that she acknowledged it, was all the sharper that his absence at her Saturdays coincided so exactly with his evenings out with Flo. How quickly in this silent room her mind fled into its darkest void.

For what if he had only ever come there to mock the crude pretensions of the villa; worse, to draw from her some indiscreet reference to her husband's activities that might be used against him. Had they ever spoken of such things? She thought not. But the voices that beset her were not to be stilled. What if he had played on Flo's innocence to cover up his guilt; had paraded her in the town to show he had the villa's trust; what if he had dropped the pretence of enjoying his talks with her as soon as he had Flo to serve his purpose; what if all along she had bored him as Flo, in all probability, bored him now; what if, now that he was thwarted, he dropped Flo, as suddenly and ruthlessly as he had dropped her?

When daylight appeared behind the curtains, she would not, could not believe in such a thing. For what if he were innocent? How does one prove one hasn't written an anonymous letter to a newspaper a thousand miles away? That was why he had appealed to her for her sympathy and support. Again he stood before her for that second with his arms outstretched asking for trust. And she, having promised, had instantly withdrawn it and made her child reject him, cut him off from all that was trustful, kindly and secure. Poor, poor young man.

In every void, it seems, there is a deeper void. Now at the back of her closed lids the image started of her wide freckled body curved around the small, pale, clenched form of his. She swung her feet over the side of the bed and ran into the bathroom. She would not look at the face that had formed that thought, but shutting her eyes, reached blindly for the tap, turned it full on and splashed her face repeatedly with cold water. Then she rubbed it fiercely on Harry Morgan's towelling bathrobe that hung behind the door.

It was Saturday. The queue had formed again. During the morning a complicated note was delivered from Gerda saying that although the quality of their friendship was such that world events in the past could never influence it, she could not bring herself at this time to intrude upon the sorrow of the villa. The note ended, 'Next week perhaps, my dear, dear friend.' Lydia telephoned at once, to be told by the servant that the signora was out.

Geoffrey would come. She did not know about the Harringtons. She did not think that Roland Routh would come, though a moment later she told herself that perhaps it was the knowledge that he meant to come that had made him delay in signing the book of condolence. When the phone rang she hurried to it. 'Clive Waller here,' the voice said. 'I wondered if I might pop in before lunch. There are one or two things about the memorial service I'd like to clear with you.'

'Yes, how nice. Bring Wendy. Bridie even.'

She had given no instructions to the major-domo,

but at noon he closed the front door to the public and appeared in the drawing-room with Hassan in his wake, carrying a tray of clean ashtrays and small bowls filled with peanuts. Minutes later she heard the muted crackle of the gravel in the drive. There were several voices in the hall and the sound of several pairs of feet. Clive Waller and his wife advanced upon the room. He was saying, 'I hope you don't mind, Lydia, but I brought Colonel Kirkbride from the regiment and the padre as well. We've been discussing the memorial service and thought we'd come along and fill you in.' Geoffrey, caught up in their arrival, grimaced helplessly from behind their various shoulders. 'Were you expecting someone else?' Waller asked her.

'I'm sure Harry would like anyone to feel they might drop in.' It sounded evasive, deceitful even, with the major-domo's peanuts waiting visibly on the occasional tables. The Harringtons had just that minute arrived. 'Well, this is a bit of luck,' Clive Waller said to Nigel Harrington. 'It saves me phoning you this afternoon.' Everyone had sat down and murmured their requests for drinks. Clive Waller had slipped a typed paper from his briefcase and, with it, the precious directive. Already the little gathering had taken on the aspect of a meeting which Waller was determined to address.

'Well, now,' he was saying, 'is that everyone? I won't take up more than a minute of your time. I needn't say how much we all regret that Harry isn't with us on this sad occasion, but I know he'd be as gratified as I am

that everyone has rallied round and especially proud of
Lydia – how she's carried on – not easy, not easy.'

'Hear, hear,' said Wendy Waller loudly. There was a
nervous setting down of glasses lest a round of applause
might be in order, but Clive Waller continued hastily,
'My own wife too, of course, and all the ladies who
have shown such ingenuity with their needles.' He
touched his armband and went on, 'The state funeral
will be on Friday next . . .'

Lydia was not attending to him. Her ears so long
attuned to the subdued messages of the villa had heard a
new arrival and a moment later Roland Routh appeared
through the door with his jacket over his arm; the knot
of his black tie loosened; his collar button undone. He
hurried over to her, saying without any attempt to lower
his voice, 'Geoffrey said you needed cheering up. I had
no idea it was – a party.'

'Won't you sit down as you're here?' Waller said
without looking directly at him. 'We've had some discussion,' he went on to the others, 'as to whether to
take into account the difference of time – the power of
united prayer and all that . . .' He nodded to the padre.
'But in the end we thought we'd follow the standard
drill for Armistice Day. Eleven o'clock local time right
across the Empire. I've phoned the embassy at Routa
Routa and they will back us up.'

It seemed to Lydia that Routh had drawn forward
his chair with the maximum amount of noise and now
struck successive blows across Clive Waller's voice as he
dropped first his briefcase and then a book he carried

on to the marble floor beside him. 'Whisky, please,' he said to the major-domo in a stage whisper more penetrating than any speaking voice. A ripple of sound crossed the still surface of the room as if forbidden laughter had found outlet in a myriad restless movements. Lydia too would have liked to laugh, at least to smile in his direction. Instead she ignored him as if by pretending to be deaf she might hope to silence him.

Clive Waller had gone on to say that as the church room would never accommodate the number of people wishing to attend, they had decided to hold the ceremony in that portion of the cemetery set aside 'for our own men'. There was a murmur of consent. He went on to outline the way they must conduct their lives over the next three months until the period of official mourning came to a close. 'Is that all clear then?' he said at last. 'Any questions?'

Immediately, Routh raised his hand. Waller ignored him and searched slowly round the group for a response from anyone else. When none was forthcoming, he said, 'Well, Routh, what is it?'

'You say there are to be no public entertainments. What about private ones?'

'I take it you mean entertaining in our homes?'

'No,' Routh said, 'I mean going out – privately.'

'I fail to understand you?'

'To the cinema,' Routh said with the clarity reserved for foreigners or those with low intelligence, 'restaurants, nightclubs, the normal sort of thing.'

Waller moved his glance around the group, gathering up sympathy as he did. 'I hardly think there's any mention of anything like that in here,' he said tapping the faded directive. That was an end to the matter. He glanced around again as if for a more sensible question.

'So that's all right then?' Routh said. Lydia, who had now turned to look at him, found his chill glare directed straight at herself. 'If it's not mentioned in the booklet, there can be no objection to any of us going to such places?'

As if the matter were beneath his notice Waller began to put away his papers,' It's up to you,' he said. 'I don't expect the rest of us are much affected by such things. So long as you don't make an exhibition of yourself.'

'As if I would,' Routh said. His unsmiling look was still addressed towards her. Now he rose and made his way across the room. He opened the doors into the ballroom and without bothering fully to close them, disappeared inside.

'Any other business?' Waller said. Routh's rapid footsteps could be heard to make their way down the length of the marble dance floor.

'Well!' Lydia said and at the same moment Wendy Waller took it upon herself to say, 'Well!' with just the same coercive brightness. The major-domo circulated with his tray taking requests for second drinks, but the discomfort of not knowing who had been invited and who not; whether this was a meeting or a party or a wake; whether the display of bad manners they had just witnessed was of a public or a private nature, encouraged people to drink up quickly and take their leave.

'I'm sorry you were subjected to that,' Clive Waller said, as he shook Lydia's hand. 'I can't think how he came to be here in the first place.'

There was a pause which she found herself unable to fill.

'Look,' he went on, 'it's wretched for you and Flo being on your own. Shouldn't you both come with us to the service?'

Now she knew exactly what was required of her. 'Why don't we all go together in the Lancia?' she said smiling round at Wendy. 'There would be more room.'

'God, he's enjoying every moment of this,' Geoffrey whispered as she kissed him. She wished that he would stay, but only Wendy Waller lingered to press her hand, and say with a significant look in the direction of the ballroom, 'Are you all right?'

'Of course I am,' Lydia told her.

There was time to pour herself another drink before she heard Routh's footsteps approach the ballroom door. He entered without pausing, as if he had hoped to pass through without acknowledging her, but after all he could not and turned to look at her with an impatient sigh.

'I haven't seen you for weeks,' she said, as if that alone might explain the intolerable thing that had settled between them.

'No,' he said, 'though Flo has.'

She gave a little shrug and reached for a cigarette,

thinking, It must not be allowed to be like this. He said, 'Look, I obviously wasn't meant to come today. I thought Wheeler said I should. It was a mistake. I'm sorry.'

'What was that all about?'

'Oh God,' he said. 'They make me sick. I really thought you were on my side in some way.'

'What way? What side?'

'I asked you if you trusted me. You said you did.'

'I trusted you with Flo.'

'She told you, didn't she, about the other night.'

'She told me that it was nothing to do with you. She said you brought her home. That's all I need to know.'

'You are incredible.'

'You asked to be trusted. I'm trusting you.'

'All right,' he said. 'All right, all right.'

'In any case, it wasn't that that Harry cared about. It was this trouble in the office. No doubt you know about it. Everybody seems to know.'

'You think I wrote it?'

'A number of people seem to think so.'

'Well, I didn't. They just want to believe that. I might have but I didn't. I haven't had the time.'

'I believe you then.'

'Thank you.'

'All I'm asking is, for the time being, if you want to see Flo, you come to see her here.'

'I'm sure that's what you're asking, but can't you understand it isn't what I want? Not now.'

'And Flo?'

'That's her choice,' Routh said and turned and left.

When he had gone she felt tired, detached, forgetful of what had gone before. She moved through the sitting-room, through the glass doors into the ballroom, on to the dais, down the steps, past receding images of herself in the tinted mirrors. My God, she thought, it's like watching yourself grow old. Flo sat cross-legged on her sofa staring through the netted windows to the blurred clumps of flowers beyond them. Lydia sat heavily at the opposite end, but made no effort to speak. There was, she found, relief in silence. Finally Flo said, 'He asked me out again.'

'I imagined that he had. You said you'd go?'

'He seemed so angry,' the girl said. Her lips as she spoke seemed swollen as if bruised. They formed the words as if by feel, with difficulty.

'Not angry with you,' Lydia said. 'With me perhaps, with all of us, but not with you.' Again the painful lips shaped themselves to form a word. Again the mother intervened to say, 'You don't really want to go, do you?'

'No,' Flo said after a moment's silence.

'Then don't,' her mother pleaded with her. 'There's no earthly reason why you should.'

'But in any case,' the girl went on, 'I've said I'd go.'

On the morning of the funeral Lydia changed at ten into a black dress that she had worn in London to cocktail parties. From the shelf of her wardrobe she took down the small black hat and veil she had worn with it. Trying it on, her hands had set it at its true provocative angle, which she quickly corrected. The veil was coarse and gathered, not at all the sort she had spoken of to Geoffrey Wheeler. Flo wore her mother's navy blue, which, though unbecoming, was entirely suitable.

At ten forty-five a procession of black limousines drew up to the cemetery outside the town, deposited government and consular officials and their wives, and then withdrew to wait in the insubstantial shade of an avenue of eucalyptus trees. Last to arrive was the Lancia. Clive, Colonel Kirkbride and the padre mounted a wooden podium set up by the public works department on the previous day. The mourners in their dark European clothes stood in rows in front of folding wooden chairs. Behind them were the army wives.

For some minutes the regiment itself had been heard to march towards them led by the solemn music of its band. At the gates of the cemetery there was a pause followed by the opening notes of the 'Dead March' from *Saul*. The men on the podium stiffened to attention. The regimental colours, lowered so as just to clear the dust, were carried past, the two standard-bearers exactly matched in height and build. Their thick arms shook with the strain of the heavy poles carried at so awkward an angle. Dark sweat stains soaked the sleeves of their tunics and spread outward from beneath their shoulder-straps. Their set, young faces were half-obscured by the visors of their peaked caps, but still Flo recognized Simon Philpotts and Richie South pass by like recollections of a former life.

The band now played 'Abide with Me'. The strident instruments bore up the frail sum of voices, that might easily have been lost in the shining space around them. The padre read the funeral service and gave a short address about unflinching duty in times of great national peril. He spoke above the ceaseless chirring of cicadas and that subdued sobbing which occurs when many hidden rivulets of private grief can briefly be released into the main respectable stream.

Chapter Nineteen

PROMPTLY AT nine, Flo stood by the sentry boxes waiting for Roland Routh. He too was prompt as always and jumped out of the taxi before the driver could hold open the door for her. 'I wasn't sure you'd come,' he said when they were seated side by side.

'I said I'd come.'

He hugged her shoulders briefly, but didn't seem inclined to talk. Instead he sat morosely in his corner, staring out at the street. The minutes alone with him seemed to flash tangibly past the windows of the taxi and be lost. Already he was groping in his pocket for the taxi fare and had it in his hand by the time the driver drew up outside the nightclub. Until the last moment there could be the hope that the Sawleys would not be there, but from a distance she could make them out waiting under a street lamp, standing a little apart with the abandoned air of people who have waited longer than expected. Had she not known, she would have supposed them strangers whose efforts to ignore one another had become embarrassing.

Routh paid the taxi-driver as he climbed out. He

kissed Avril on the cheek and hurried past into the nightclub to secure a table. The others followed him down the dark steps and saw him beckon impatiently from the far side of the dance floor. They sat down facing one another. 'Well, here we are again!' Sawley said loudly. There was a looseness and dampness about his face. It seemed to hurt him to shift his gaze from one to the other. When no one responded he added, 'As happy as can be.'

'That's right,' Avril said, smiling at Flo. 'Long time no see.' But no one wished to be reminded of their last meeting and she seemed as tense and wretched as Routh.

Sawley was waving at a waiter. While they were ordering drinks the band struck up again. 'Do you mind?' Routh said to Sawley. He had taken Avril's arm and pulled her abruptly to her feet.

'Feel free,' Sawley said.

When they had gone Flo turned her face blankly to the dance floor. She had no desire to watch them. In any case the hellish lighting of the Mocambo drained all distinction from the dancers unless they came right to the edge of the floor. Rather she would avoid Raymond Sawley's painful eyes for as long as possible.

After a moment he said, 'Rolly thought you mightn't make it. After last time. Don't they care what happens to you?'

'Lydia doesn't,' she said without turning her head. 'She pretends to, but she doesn't really. Harry's away.'

'I know that,' Sawley said. Their drinks had come. Sawley paid the waiter and drank down half his whisky as if to quench a thirst. Then he said, 'Proud of him, are you?'

'Of whom?'

'His Excellency,' he said with a disagreeable laugh. 'What do you call him? Daddy? Sir?' He said the word in a high-pitched little girl's voice.

Flo looked directly at him and said, 'He's not mine to be proud of.'

'How's that?'

'He's my stepfather.'

'Avril never said.'

'Why should she?'

She had turned her face away from him again to stare at nothing, willing the music to stop, willing the dancers to come back to the table. 'I came in with a smile,' the orchestra played. 'I went out with a tear, while you danced, danced, danced.' Sawley had leant heavily towards her across the table. 'Why don't you bloody say anything? Don't you think? Are you stupid or something?'

'I'm not stupid.'

'Well?'

'I don't have anything to say to you. I don't like you.'

'Well, Rolly then. You're keen on him, aren't you? Everybody's keen on bloody Rolly. God almighty, what do you find to say to him?'

'We don't talk much. We understand each other.'

'I imagined you must.'

The cynicism in his voice made her say, 'He must like me. He wouldn't go on taking me out if he didn't.'

'You don't know much, do you?' Sawley said. 'You don't know what's going on. You can't be that green. No one's that green. Oh God, perhaps you are.'

'I do know,' she said. 'I do know.' As soon as she had said it, it seemed that she had always known, since the first night that she had seen them dance together in the restaurant, or before that when they had quarrelled on the stage, or even before that when Avril Sawley's red dress had wrapped itself around his trouser leg.

'Then why do you let him bloody do it to you? You're in love with him, aren't you?'

'Shut up,' she told him ferociously. 'Just shut up.'

He smiled at her. 'That's better. You're coming on. Dance?'

If they danced he would stop talking. She stood up and walked on to the dance floor. There she turned and placed one hand on his shoulder and the other in his hand without looking at him. He held her to his thin unhappy body and began to dance. His mouth was so close to her ear that the words were blurred and magnified. He said as if it really concerned him, 'Your stepfather, is he good to you?'

'Harry? Yes, he's very good.'

'You mean that?'

'Yes. I do.'

After a moment he said, 'Avril and I had a kiddy. Did Rollo tell you that? He died though.'

From the moment he had spoken about the child Flo had known he must be dead. He had begun to tremble violently as a dog will. 'She never mentions it,' he said. 'It was very hard on her that he died.'

'And on you.'

'Yes,' he said as if he lacked sufficient information about himself to be sure of that. 'Still, the hard part was not knowing what to say to her.'

'My father's dead,' Flo told him. 'In the war. He's always been dead. I didn't really know him. Lydia wants it that way. She won't talk about it.'

'I know,' he said, rocking them both. 'I know. I know. I know.'

'I haven't anything to say. There isn't anything to say. It isn't worth trying to say anything to anybody. Nobody listens. I can't make them listen. I don't know how. I don't know how to say it right to make them listen. She just goes on talking and telling me I under-stand her. They talk to each other. That's enough. They can't have any more.'

'Poor child,' he said, rocking her against him. 'Poor, poor child.'

She laid her head down upon his shoulder and began to cry. Still they danced. Sawley, though drunk, was too adept a dancer to be affected by it; Flo too swept away by grief to set up any resistance to him. Round and round they danced until the movement calmed them both and was superseded by an unexpected pleasure. When finally the music stopped he held her more closely still and said against her ear, 'Well then, Flo. You and me it seems. You and me.'

At the table he insisted on ordering another round of drinks although Avril said suddenly that she wanted to go home. 'We've only just got here,' he said. 'The night is young.' When she left her drink untouched he drank it as well as his own, 'You haven't danced with me,' he said to Avril.

'Look, Ray,' she said. 'I'm tired. Can't we please go home?'

'No,' he said.

'All right, all right we'll dance.'

'Do we have to wait for them?' Flo said to Routh when they were left alone.

'I can't leave her with him in that state,' he said, staring at the circling couples, drumming his fingers on the plastic table top, making no further attempt to speak to her.

Before the music stopped they came back to the table arm in arm. Avril said brightly, 'Ray's going to be a good boy now. We'll go, shall we?'

Outside on the pavement, in the cool air, Sawley shook his head stupidly from side to side. Then he straightened himself up and said, 'What the hell, let's go for a drive.'

Avril and Routh glanced at one another. He saw that and said, 'You think I'm drunk, don't you?'

Routh turned and walked a little way away. Avril said quickly, 'Of course you're not. Only I'm tired, Ray.'

'That's what it's called, is it?' he said to her. 'Being tired?'

'Oh don't,' she said, turning away from him. 'Just don't.'

Routh said suddenly, 'All right, we'll go for a drive then. I'll drive.'

'Like hell you will,' Sawley said.

'Don't worry,' she said quietly to Routh. 'He'll be all right. You two go on.'

'No,' Routh said.

'Shall I have Flo in front with me then?' Sawley asked him.

'No, Ray,' Avril said quickly. 'I'll ride in front with you.'

He laughed but his laughter had come apart from what was said.

'Get in,' Routh said quietly to Flo. In the back of the car he put his arm around her shoulders just as if they were driving home in a taxi on any ordinary night. She looked into the driving-mirror to see if Raymond Sawley were watching them. Sometimes the street lights lit up a portion of his face quite clearly. Sometimes his eyes seemed cut out of his face in two black holes. Roland Routh sat tensely forward. His other hand gripped Avril's shoulder so tightly that the knuckles gleamed.

'Where are we going, Ray?' Avril said. They had passed their block of flats by then. He was driving rapidly but surprisingly steadily along the road to the airport. After a moment he said, 'Let's go out and see the moonlight. Flo likes moonlight. Don't you, Flo?'

None of them said anything. They drove past the entrance to the airport. Abruptly there were no more street lights, only the jolting beams of the car lights as Sawley accelerated over the pitted surface of the road. Flo thought, Why doesn't someone put a stop to this? Why does he just sit there? She too just sat there, waiting for Roland Routh to do something; for Raymond Sawley to slow the car, to laugh, to turn round and drive it home again.

'That's enough, Ray,' Avril said, as if she were indeed tired beyond caring. But still it seemed that at any moment he might stop the car; that they might get out and admire the moonlight just as he had said and then turn round and drive back the way that they had come. Avril had begun to scream, small frightened continuous screams, while Roland Routh, like a man in a dream, kneaded her shoulder and repeated dully, 'Don't, don't, don't, don't.'

That had seemed some time before the car went off the road but it was difficult to be sure. Everything that happened seemed merely to be the memory of something that was already over. I am going to die, she thought. The words formed very slowly, just as all those confused moments seemed to happen very slowly. It will hurt but probably not for long. She was shocked though at the painless violence of the thud her body made, at the great noise of the crash, and the extent of the silence that followed it.

All that warm night the silence spread around her lit with dreams or memories that unfolded slowly, without terror. Something dragged against her cheek. Again and again. A harsh dry pressure. That's a dog's paw, Flo thought, but she knew it was not. A human voice repeated something. There was a smell of wood fires, delicious and alien. She lay on her back on the ground. The stars were very close. That's because the air is clear, she told herself. She felt entirely comfortable, looking up through branches at the stars. She was lying on dry leaves. She scraped up a handful and crushed them. Then she manoeuvred her hand to her face. It too carried an odour that delighted her and filled her with well-being. I'll sleep now, she thought, but she was loath to lose these sensations and thought she would prefer to stay exactly as she was. There was no hurry. For some time she stayed like this, still able to distance herself from a particular sound. Eventually, just before she lost consciousness, she accepted it for what it was: a man's voice sobbing.

Chapter Twenty

THAT SILENCE persisted even when Flo knew that she was in a bed in the military hospital. She did not think that it would ever go away; nor did she want it to. It was a separate thing, entirely hers.

Her mother was clinging to her hand and weeping. 'I'm perfectly all right,' she said. 'I am all right, aren't I?' she said to Harry Morgan who stood behind her mother's chair.

'Oh yes, perfectly.' His voice was so normal and reassuring that her own eyes filled with tears.

'We are a pair,' her mother said. 'We are a pair.'

But we are not, Flo thought. It was as if a part of her sat there weeping over something she could not remember. But she, herself, was quite distinct from that. She wished that they would go away and let her have her silence back again.

She was irritable with the nurse who woke her and later woke her again and forced her to sit up. She ached all over now and no position in the bed was comfortable. Later that morning Harry Morgan came into the room holding a bunch of roses ahead of him as if they must excuse his coming on his own. Immediately she said to him, 'Is Roland all right?'

'I've just been in to see him. He broke his arm. He was damn lucky to get off so lightly. I said you were all right, shaken but all right. Poor chap, he's fearfully cut up about it all.' He spoke with a mixture of pity and distaste, shaking his head slowly as if such things were quite beyond his understanding. 'It's rotten for him, of course. He seems to blame himself.'

'Why?' Flo said. 'He wasn't driving.'

'There's no question about that, I suppose? Sawley was driving?'

'Yes.'

'Well, it's a bad show,' Harry Morgan said. 'A thoroughly bad show. Your mother's most fearfully upset about it all.'

'Everybody seems to be upset.'

Her tone had startled him. 'Well, of course,' he said. 'She is your mother after all.'

'That's true,' Flo said.

'Look, you must be tired.'

'Tired?' she said as bitterly as Raymond Sawley had done.

He had risen, and stooping, took her hand and kissed her on the forehead, saying, 'Goodnight, darling. They'll let you come home tomorrow.'

'Ray's dead,' she said. 'Isn't he?'

'Sawley? Yes. Look. I'm sorry. I should have broken it to you more carefully.'

'Has she gone away?'

'Yes,' he said. 'They flew her out this morning. She's been rather badly hurt.'

She gave a little sigh of relief as if she had been holding her breath and now released it.

'I'm glad she's gone.'

As if he must convert her words into some more acceptable meaning, he said, 'It was for the best. She had people in England. Poor girl, what an awful thing for her – for all of you, of course – but for her especially.'

'He wouldn't mind being dead.'

He had retreated to the door and was fingering its handle behind his back. Now he quickly crossed the room again and said, 'Why do you say that? I shouldn't ask you perhaps, but there's bound to be an inquest. He couldn't have done it intentionally, could he? Surely not.'

'He was drunk,' Flo said.

He made a scolding noise with his tongue and retreated towards the door, shaking his head as he had when he came in. As if she would still detain him she said politely, 'Did you have a nice time in England?'

'Yes, thank you,' he said. 'It went very well.'

In the morning he came again. She was helped into a wheelchair and wheeled down a corridor, looking quickly through the open doors in search of Roland Routh. Light was dazzling on the white sheets. The place had an air of morning haste and optimism. She could not believe it still contained his grieving body. Over her head Harry spoke briefly to the nurse.

The Chevrolet was waiting. Haile held open the

door, shaking his head and clicking his tongue in dismay. 'I am all right,' she told him. She would not let him help her into the car. She sat stiffly, knowing that as soon as they reached the villa the refuge of her silence would be taken finally from her.

'Is Lydia feeling better?' she said at last.

'She will be when she gets you back again.'

'I don't think I can bear all that,' Flo said. They were driving past the roadblock at the entrance to the army camp. Harry returned the sentry's salute absently. His mind she knew had reverted to that unseen structure of order and event around which his days were built.

'Are you late for the office?' she asked him.

'Only a little.'

She said, 'Perhaps I shouldn't have come home so soon.'

'What do you mean?' She could hear in his concern the impatient fear that his sacrifice of time had been wasted, the day's plan thrown awry. 'Don't you feel well?'

'I don't know what I feel,' she said. 'I can't remember.'

He was looking at her helplessly. 'Do you want to go back then?'

'No,' she said 'of course I don't.' She had turned her head away from him like a fretful patient's on a pillow. She stared out, hating the unchanging season of the place, hating the heartless way it went about its business. She caught sight then of the bobbing stacks of sticks on the road ahead and began to rock her forehead to and fro against the glass.

Morgan instinctively bent forward to salute them and they raised their heads and grinned at him. She had let out a cry. 'Is it your head?' Morgan said sharply.

'No,' she said. 'No.' She thought, It must stop. The car must not glide forward. 'It's wrong. It's wrong.'

He said, 'I don't know what you mean.'

'But you do, you do,' she said. Then, seeing the steady look of his eyes in which concern, fear even, still just exceeded contempt, she realized, with a small sound of hopelessness, that he comprehended none of it. She said, 'Those women.'

'Oh, them,' he said, remembering her odd behaviour once before.

Haile had slowed down the car and steered it towards the kerb. His troubled eyes were held in the mirror while Morgan sat perplexed at this. Should he stop? Should he after all turn back? If they stopped the little troop would gain on them. They would be trapped there. People would stare in at the windows, knowing who he was. He pulled the dividing panel open by an inch and said, 'No. Go on,' before shutting it again.

'You should do something,' but what exactly she wished him to put right, even she could not have said. She leant back against the leather upholstery. The space in the back of the car was too small for anger. There was too little between them to sustain a quarrel. She could feel his uneasy stirring beside her. 'Look,' he began, wanting to make amends, before their arrival, 'I . . .'

She interrupted him, asking in a small frightened voice, 'Did he go over the edge?'

'Yes.'

'He was dead?'

'Oh yes – very.'

'You saw him?'

'I had to.'

'But someone was crying, a man.' It was only then that he gave a shudder of distaste. 'Routh probably. Look, Flo, I know he's a friend of yours, but he hasn't come out of this very well one way and another. Once he's rested up we're sending him out on tour. He'd have had to go next month, in any case, to see to the elections, but it will keep him out of the town until this blows over.'

She had her face turned from him.

'One thing. I don't know how much your mother may have told you, but he's quite in the clear about that other matter. I thought you'd like to know that.'

She was looking at him now without the slightest comprehension. He saw no reason to pass on the fact that a draft of the article, pre-dating its publication, had been found yesterday amongst Sawley's papers. Instead with forced cheerfulness he said, 'We'll have a week or two away ourselves. It's all arranged.'

The front wheels of the Chevrolet had touched the gravel of the drive. 'It was a rotten show,' Morgan said as if that put an end to it. 'A rotten show.' He climbed out first and turned back to give a hand to Flo. 'Steady on, won't you? Your mother's had an awful shock.' But he could see that Flo was quite composed now, sitting forward, waiting calmly to get out of the car. 'You'll be careful what you say to her?'

'I won't say anything,' Flo said.

Later that month a small procession prepared to draw away from the villa. The jeep came first driven by Haile with Harry Morgan beside him wearing his bush kit and stitched cotton hat. Behind him, his wife and step-daughter sat side by side in cotton frocks and head-scarves. They were embarking on the long journey to Routa Routa, where Morgan was to sign the treaty which would make an autonomous state federated to the Northern Province. It had been decided, all things considered, that Flo and Lydia should accompany him.

A line of military vehicles was waiting in the street outside. Two more jeeps carried a detachment of armed Aderran police. Behind them two lorries were packed with the tents and provisions needed for their journey. More armed policemen were crowded into the cab, while through the gap in the canvas cover at the back appeared the excited faces of the villa servants: the cook, the cook's boy, Hassan and Amde. The other servants, headed by the major-domo, whose safety in the Northern Province would be too much at risk, were grouped on the pavement, smiling and waving, while the travellers shouted and waved back to them.

The whole party felt that lifting of the spirit that is inseparable from the start of a journey. Even before they were completely free of the town, the streets became unfamiliar, for this was not the road that led out past the airport. It passed through less prosperous suburbs and then set out across a flat stony upland in a line so straight that it might have been laid down by the Roman ancestors of the Italian engineers who had built it.

In this vast space their movement, though they drove on steadily hour after hour, seemed negligible. By the afternoon the long journey had set up its own tedium and exhaustion. Their faces were stiff with dust, the women's hair, even under the hot silk scarves, like filaments of wire. When they climbed down from the jeep for the evening halt, their legs were drained of all sensation by the constant jarring of the unsprung seats. Yet probably all of them, in their hearts, were thoroughly relieved to be removed from Aderra.

Exactly one month after their departure the procession of jeeps and lorries drew up outside the villa once more. The weary passengers climbed down. Now that they were safely back their journey seemed a thing of wonder. For a moment longer, vast panoramas shimmered in their minds. Across them, down ravines of giddy depths, up steep escarpments to the high plateaux, the road looped intricately back and forth. Already after steaming cups of tea, to which the major-domo of his

---

own accord had added generous tots of whisky, after hot baths and clean clothes, these visions began to fade. Familiarity closed in, making no concession to the great distance they had travelled or the time they had been gone.

Only in Harry Morgan's mind there remained stark details which he had mentioned to no one. The Italians had built the road to carry their invading army; for a similar purpose, he was now convinced, it would be used again. On the Aderran side, the surface was in bad repair. At the start and finish of their journey, they had jolted over potholes and skirted around collapsed culverts. The cost of maintaining it would have swallowed his entire budget many times over. He had been quick to notice then how much work had been put into the road on the far side of the border, and recently too, by the looks of things. How long would it take them to complete the work on the Aderran side? He had no idea but imagined it to be the span of Aderra's brief autonomy. So be it. It was not in either his brief or the realms of possibility to secure the future, though in the secrecy of his heart he raged and grieved over the sure betrayal of so many hopes.

One night they had slept in a rest-house at the head of the pass leading to the plateau where Routa Routa was situated. Outside it they had found a folding card-table crowded with glasses, a soda-water syphon and several bottles of imported brandy and whisky. It was manned by the servants of the governor of this province, the potentate's second son, the man who would take control of Aderra.

At dusk a troop of horsemen rode up to the rest-house. Their leader was swathed in an Italian cavalry cape and was just old enough, Morgan reckoned, to have killed its first owner. The cloak's pale blue was still distinct in the failing light. It swept magnificently from his shoulders and spread out over the rump of his mount so that man and horse presented a single archaic form. He dismounted and introduced himself, in flawless English, as the local military commander in charge of repairs to the road.

Morgan had congratulated him on its good condition.

'The road is for the entry of the Prince to Aderra.'

Morgan regarded him steadily and said, 'The Prince will come by air.'

The young man shrugged, 'That is true, but his Rolls-Royce and the other cars must come by road.'

When they had toasted their respective rulers in an excellent Scotch whisky, the horsemen mounted and withdrew into the dusk, but not before Harry had noticed the startling modernity of the rifles slung across their saddles. The make was unknown to him. Certainly not British nor American. Later, when the others were asleep, and the risen moon gave sufficient light, he went quietly out and climbed a nearby rise. Less than half a mile away he could see the massed fires of the soldier-roadmakers. He set himself to count them as, when a child, he had set himself to count the stars, but soon gave up.

The following day the draft treaty was signed. Early on the morning of the next day they set out on the long journey back to Aderra.

Chapter Twenty-One

THE GARDEN reflected not the slightest change of season. The villa opened its empty dustless rooms. Baths were drawn. While they soaked off the journey, old Gidea trotted from room to room gathering up their soiled clothes. By evening these would be returned to drawers and wardrobes in their pristine state. Drinks were poured. A meal was served.

But as the afternoon went by they noticed some things had indeed changed. The period of mourning was over. They had seen at once that the villa's flag flew from the full height of its pole. The book of condolence had been removed, the arum lilies replaced by a more cheerful bunch of phlox and daisies. A pile of invitations was waiting neatly stacked on the major-domo's chromium tray. Among them Lydia came upon a jubilant note from Wendy Waller announcing the engagement of Bridie to Captain Renfrew. 'Is that possible?' she asked her daughter.

'It's what she wanted,' Flo said. Those two people, Bridie Waller and Jamie Renfrew, returned indistinctly to her mind as standing a long way off from one another.

It required too great an effort to draw them close together.

'Lucky Bridie then.' As their tour progressed, Lydia had relaxed the habit of watching her daughter's eyes for signs of pain. There had been so much else to see. Now she found nothing there that might not be taken for a pale reflection of Bridie's assumed happiness. Perhaps she is forgetting, she thought. The young are incredibly resilient. Later she said, 'Do you remember that we were going to have a dance? What would you think of making it an engagement party for Bridie? They did so much for you when you first came out. I felt I never repaid them.' It seemed a gracious solution to a problem that had troubled her, and Flo too, she thought, greeted the idea with relief.

'Of course,' she said. 'The ballroom. I think they'd like that.'

'I'm sure they will,' the mother said a little grimly.

On the following week the dances at the club began again. The long abstinence from parties, the knowledge that only another month or two of this life remained before the handover, meant that the first of these was particularly well attended. A sentimental attention was paid to the engaged pair. He was so very handsome in his blues and Bridie in her astonished joy had taken on a lease of prettiness. They made a more than adequate couple and suggested any promise for the future that people cared to wish upon them. There was much talk during that auspicious evening of the young Queen.

Several faces, though, were missing. Avril Sawley

was still in hospital in England. People who feared a less generous remark might escape them said that wonderful advances in healing had been made during the war. On the whole the subject was avoided. In so small a community, where the threat of violence was ever present, ever suppressed, it had been shocking for violence of any nature to break out amongst their own.

Sawley had been buried at the very edge of that section of the cemetery set aside for British subjects. There had been some demur at this. His neighbours would mostly have fallen in defence of King and country or at least of its remote concerns, while Sawley – the rumour persisted – had in a fit of drunken self-pity driven off the road deliberately. In so doing he had risked the lives of two more or less innocent people, and one entirely so. No statement was ever made about his disloyalty to the regime. It had shocked Harry that, in London, he had been advised not to investigate the matter lest the perpetrator be seen, even among the British community, to be martyr to some vague humanitarian cause. As it was poor Sawley had made a martyr of himself and might, in silence, be forgiven.

As if the edges of Flo's stay in Aderra had been turned neatly sides to middle to repair a rent, Richie South and Simon Philpotts began to call again in their shared taxi and take Flo to the club. On Saturdays Geoffrey Wheeler, the Wertheimers, and sometimes the Harringtons came again for drinks at lunchtime. Twice a week there were dinner parties at the villa and once or twice a week the Lancia drove the three of them to dine at other people's houses, or to attend receptions at the American Consulate, or the Circolo Italiano.

At all these events Flo's faint prettiness played its undemanding part. When parties convene nightly, conversation is easy to maintain. The guests need only ask one another what they have been doing during the day. She had learned the knack of that. No one suspected the degree of dislocation between the contents of her head and the activities of the people living and moving on the outer side of it. During the visit to the Northern Province there had been the comfort of thinking, I am in a strange place. Now she must be a stranger in a familiar place.

Coming unexpectedly into the monkey room she heard her mother say to Geoffrey Wheeler, 'Oh, the young are dreadfully resilient.' From the way he leapt up, from the nervous warmth of his greeting she knew they had been talking about her. When she had closed the door behind her she stood still, listening to their voices resume. It was after all herself she spied on and the information was necessary to her, but he was saying, 'My God, poor Bridie. It's she will need resilience.'

She heard her mother's astonished voice ask, 'Why?'

Wheeler lowered his voice. 'Young Jamie's been a naughty boy,' he said. 'He had to marry or leave the regiment.'

'Not Bridie?'

'No,' she heard Wheeler say, 'not Bridie by a long chalk.'

Once, Flo found herself alone in the upstairs sitting-room with the station list lying where Lydia had left it by the telephone. She quickly turned the pages to R and studied for a moment the name of Roland Routh. It was written indelibly there, but reading and re-reading it failed to make what had happened any more real to her. She turned the page to S. There at the top of the list were Flight Lieutenant and Mrs R. Sawley. Someone, Harry presumably, had neatly pencilled a line through them. Though she, Flo thought, is somewhere still alive.

The play had been abandoned. There was no time to mount another one, but something had been promised, and as the weeks went by people's thoughts returned to their enjoyment of the revue put on by the regiment a year ago. A revival was suggested and agreed upon. One or two people had inevitably been transferred, but the rest of the performers could easily be reassembled. Under the very slightest pressure they admitted to remembering their turns and even to having kept their costumes.

Richie South and Simon Philpotts still had their fathers' old tailcoats and top hats in which to sing 'We're a Couple of Swells'. It took no more than a week to brush up their rudimentary tap-dancing, their business with borrowed swagger sticks. The success of the act had depended on strong young tenors, well trained in their school choir, and of course on the remarkable similarity in their appearance.

'We're much the best,' Richie South told Flo as she sat between them during a pause in the dancing. 'She ought to come to rehearsals some day.' He spoke across her to Simon Philpotts.

'He'd be most awfully chuffed if you would,' Philpotts said to her.

'So would he,' his friend said quickly.

She did not, though the performance itself was unavoidable. There is no way to prepare the mind against smell. The mousy odour of the theatre, which caused the audience disgustedly to wave their programmes in front of their faces, had lain in wait for Flo and cruelly surprised her. Fortunately they had been the last to arrive. Their entrance had been followed immediately by the lowering of the house lights, the din of the opening number, the small thunder of applause.

The days went quickly now. All the events long planned: the elections, the counting of the ballot and the reporting of the scrutineers, the summoning of the new elected representatives to Aderra for the reading of the constitution, the reception afterwards, the constant vigilance through all of this for any hint of intimidation or corruption. All these events passed with the ease of dreams.

It was the final day that Harry Morgan had most cause to fear. All but a few officials would have left by then and a large portion of the regiment. The ceremony of handover would be performed at the new parliament building at noon. He would lower the Union Jack from the flagstaff outside the Palazzo. The plane for Khartoum would be waiting at the aerodrome. It was the getting there, the final marching of the colours through the town, that he had little taste for. Yet it must be done. They must leave proudly: the colours flying, the band playing, he and Lydia, following in the open Rolls-Royce belonging to the Prince.

That's when they'll have a go, he thought. In any case it was no occasion for Flo.

He and Lydia finalized their plans in quiet voices in the upstairs sitting-room, pausing when the servants' footsteps were heard outside the door. They both wrote wills leaving her well provided for and sent them to Harry's solicitor in Andover. It was decided that Flo should fly back a fortnight early, on the very morning after Bridie's engagement ball. A cable was sent to the Foreign Office informing Major Denbigh of the flight. Daisy Mayhew was phoned and it was confirmed that she would have Flo to stay long enough at least for Harry and Lydia to have a holiday in South Africa. Then they would send for her. After what had happened it seemed folly that they had ever supposed she could manage in England on her own.

'Should I have said anything about . . . well, you know . . . the wills?' Lydia said as she put down the phone.

'She'd only get into a flap. She's Flo's official guardian in any case. She'd see her right.'

'Oh, she'd be all right with Daisy,'

Flo was not his child, was not, he had felt lately, a child at all. 'All the same,' his wife was saying, 'I think I had better send Daisy some money just in case of emergencies. There's no need to say anything. She hasn't got a bean, you know, and she's always been so good to Flo.'

He watched her with awe as she wrote out a generous sum on a Barclays DC&O cheque and put it in an envelope. All her intricate alarms were swept away. Finally life had reached a pitch of drama, of danger even, that would suffice to hold her interest. She wore her hair tied more severely back in those days. It suited her. The afternoons she spent downstairs at her desk, casting the final household accounts for the villa. The first departures had begun. No one with whom she had had any contact left without a little note or a bunch of flowers. Some of the junior officials coming in with families from the provinces were put up overnight at the villa and dispatched to the airport in the morning in the Chevrolet.

They had entered the final phase. Geoffrey Wheeler, whose work in the office was more or less wound up, was detailed to act as ADC and help with the final spate of parties and the complicated protocol involved in welcoming the Prince. As they sat companionably making up a guest list for the reception on the night of the Prince's arrival, Lydia said suddenly, 'What about Roland Routh? Surely he deserves to be there?'

'Harry thinks not. Not to the functions at least. The Prince has sent him some splendid gong. The Order of the Vulture, something of that ilk. In any case I think you'll find Routh has no taste for the final junketings. He's going home a day or two before the end.'

'You've seen him then?'

'He's back in town. There were one or two things to clear up.'

'Of course.'

'Look, I don't know how you'd feel, but he wanted me to ask you if he might come round before he goes, just to say goodbye. He asks after Flo. He's most concerned.' When she did not immediately speak he said, 'He'll quite understand, but it would be good of you.'

'Of course,' she said, picking up her pen again and directing her attention to the list of names. 'Tell him he can come, of course.'

He could not leave it there. 'Tell me,' he said, 'only if you want to, what happened. Is Flo all right? I'm bound to ask.'

'I was simply wrong about him,' she said. 'Isn't that the hardest thing to believe about oneself?'

'That and failure,' he said comfortably. He surmised from her tone that Flo's virginity at least was still intact. 'No harm done then?'

She was looking directly at him. 'It's hard to tell. But yes, harm of some nature was done.'

Chapter Twenty-Two

IT WAS THE morning of the ball. The day before had been one of constant activity. Sergeant Broad had been co-opted to string up some of the stage lighting in the ballroom. Apparently he had done it once before for Harry Morgan's immediate predecessor. Someone had told Lydia that and, at the time, she had noted down the name.

'What a very able man that is,' she had said to Morgan over tea. She had had a separate tray carried into the ballroom where Broad was finishing his task.

'Oh,' Morgan said. 'He'll put his hand to anything.'

Afterwards she and Flo went to see what he had done. They drew the curtains and switched on the lights. A blue, a red and a green light played together on the ceiling. The effect was magical. A moonlit space without substantial walls where every movement created its replicas in further mirrored depths. 'Oh, how lovely,' Lydia cried out. When Broad had gone, she had seized Flo by the hands and whirled her round. Out of the corner of her eye she saw the crowding dancers in the mirrors whirl like sparks off a Catherine wheel.

She did not look too directly at them lest she discover the ghosts of some more brilliant ducal gathering,
the men's sleeked dark hair, the women's floating chif-
fons and rigid Marcel waves, their movements sensual
and decorous, come back to haunt her with her own
inexperience of ballrooms.

But of course, she told herself for the hundredth
time, the servants will know.

It was true. The major-domo at the very mention
of a ball had made a little gesture with his hand as if to
say, leave it all to me. The cook on being told to prepare
supper for a hundred guests had merely nodded. Ten
or one hundred, it was all the same to him. The invitations had been sent and every one of them accepted.
Yesterday a tent had appeared rigged around the tiled
veranda outside the French windows of the ballroom.
Carpets were carried down from the guest-rooms to
cover the tiles. Pots of lilies had been brought in from
the garden, braziers set in readiness against the cool
night air. Unwanted armchairs from the ballroom were
brought out here to make a delightful sitting-out place.
Oh, how can it fail? Lydia thought.

Had it been, as first intended, a dance for Flo, she
might have wavered. Any action in these last momentous days seemed representative of something more significant and to celebrate Flo would have been to
celebrate what? It had been a stroke of genius to transfer
the spotlight on to Bridie and her Captain.

So it was that on the morning of the dance there
seemed nothing left to do. Their frocks, Lydia's

glistening taffeta and Flo's *café au lait* tulle, hung on the front of the doors of their wardrobes to avoid crushing. At the final fitting Signora Ponticelli had tactfully suggested that Flo's frock be brightened by a length of printed chiffon. When Lydia had tried to pay her for it, the signora had pressed Flo's hand under its folds and said, no, it was a present.

The sash was very beautiful. Flo thought it would give her more pleasure to handle than to wear. She had saved the task of hemming it until last. Now, with all her cases packed for the following morning, she took it and her sewing-case down to the ballroom.

The smallest changes have such effect upon an empty space. The length of the great room was darkened by the impromptu tent. Its sounds were slightly muffled. The glass doors at the end were opened wide to air away the humdrum smell of polish. The flimsy curtains were sucked in and cast out again by slow currents of warm air. Between them a long shaft of morning sunlight fell and seemed to penetrate the shining surface of the floor. Flo had little taste for watching the lines of women who fell in with her and, rank after rank, progressed across the emblazoned marble floor. She laid down her sewing things on a sofa by the doors. Here she could see to make the tiny stitches the fineness of the fabric required. But first she crossed over to the gramophone. Tonight they would dance to the music of that same detachment of the regimental band that had played at the club dances. Now for the last time

she put Rudi Wertheimer's record on the turntable and
set the needle on its rim.

Lydia was in the sitting-room writing names on to
printed invitations for the reception they would give
the Prince on the night before the handover. Hearing
the music she thought, This is wrong. She is going
tomorrow. We should sit together. We should talk. She
did not for the time look up from her task but listened
for the well-known sequence of tunes to wear themselves out. Then I will go in, she thought. Then we
shall say what we have to say to one another, but before
that moment arrived she was startled by the sound of
voices in the hall. In the next moment Hassan ushered
Roland Routh into the sitting-room, withdrew and
shut the door behind him.

Routh was left standing there watching her with his
palms extended in a helpless gesture. Neither of them
could speak. He had in some way shrunk back on to
the bone. She had noticed that at some point in their
lives men do that; take up what is to be their final
form. His was of a neat, good-looking, clever man
who makes things difficult for himself and had gone
perhaps already as far as he would go. This was the
observation of an instant. In the next she found that
she was simply glad to see him. Regardless of the time
of day, she went to the sideboard and poured him a
whiskey.

'Thank you,' he said. And then, 'It was good of you
to see me.'

'Of course,' she said, sitting down so that he might.

'How's Flo?' He had heard the music and turned slightly towards the ballroom door as he spoke.

'She's all right, I think. Would you like to see her? I'll get her shall I?'

'No,' he said, with his old command. 'I'll go through, if I may, in a minute. I wanted to see you.' He took in an audible breath as if with the effort to cast his mind back to the last occasion. Then looking directly at her he said, 'I must apologize for being so dreadfully rude. I can't think what got into me.'

'Oh, it was nothing,' she said. The word trailed away to suggest the unspoken part of her thought: nothing to what came after.

'But it was,' he insisted. 'It was unforgivable. You had been very kind.'

'One has to break away sometimes,' she said, unable not to smile at him. 'Oh, especially to break away from kindness.'

'Not like that.'

Before he could speak again, she said, 'You're off, Geoffrey tells me.'

'The day after tomorrow.'

'So soon?'

'Not soon enough.'

'What next?'

'I'll look for a job.'

'You'll find one.'

'Oh yes,' he said. 'My mother's been phoning round her contacts. She has a few interviews lined up already. She calls them lunches.'

She had risen and stood with her back to him lighting a cigarette. Now because of the self-mockery in his voice she gave a short sympathetic laugh.

He said, 'I'm going to marry Avril Sawley.'

'Oh no!' She had turned around and now hurried back to sit opposite him again. 'Oh, you can't do that. I mean it for your own sake only. You must not.'

'But I can,' he said, smiling sadly at her. 'And I must.'

'But why? You aren't at all responsible for – what happened. It was Sawley. He was drunk.' She clapped her two hands suddenly across her face and said with her voice trapped and altered by them, 'Oh, he might have killed you all. It's a miracle that he did not.'

'Did you know that she was having a child?'

'No,' she said. Her hands had fallen away and she was staring at him.

'She lost it.'

'Well surely then . . .'

'Oh no. You must see that it's all the more reason.'

'I don't understand.'

'Oh, I think you do.'

'But your whole life . . .'

'Well?' he said.

'Have you told your mother?'

'Not yet. She won't forgive me, or so I very much hope. I thought you might?'

She was quietly regarding him, thinking with awe of the life he had carved out for himself. It crossed her mind to say: you know you won't be able to see it through. The wedding, yes. That he would do, if only to break free of older tyrannies. But the long aftermath of marriage. That, he had not the resource for.

As if she had spoken, he said, 'I'm going at least to try.'

'Something like this happened in Rome, didn't it?'

'In Rome,' he said, as contritely as she could wish, 'it was the mother.'

There could be no reply to that. He said, 'I'll say goodbye then. If it's all right to speak to Flo, I'll let myself out.'

They shook hands then as formally as when they had first met and he walked from her through the glass doors into the ballroom.

At the far end Flo sat on a sofa, bent over the length of bright cloth that lay across her lap. She lifted her head at the sound of his footsteps on the dais and stared at him as he walked quickly towards her. Only when he was quite close did she bow her head and start to sew again. He lowered himself on to the floor beside her, leaning back against the sofa, thinking how charming he had always found her, intent and set apart in time. He watched the graceful movement of her wrist as she raised and lowered her needle. Then he said, 'How very pretty.'

'It's a sash,' Flo said. 'To wear tonight.'

'That will look nice.'

'How is your arm?' she asked him.

'It's all right.' He said. He stretched it out, unbuttoned the cuff and pushed up the sleeve to reveal his

defenceless inner arm to her inspection. She studied it
gravely but the white skin bore no trace of the damage
to the bone inside. 'Doesn't it seem a long time ago?'
she asked him now.

'Doesn't it? I'm going away. Did they tell you?'

'When?'

'The day after you do. I needed to come and see
that you were all right.'

'I wasn't hurt.'

'Do you remember it?'

'A little. Harry told me afterwards.'

To talk of these things, even so slightly, after months
of silence, came as a great relief. Routh leant his head
back against the soft seat of the sofa with his eyes shut.
He felt the sun on his face, the silent shining room
under the thin surface of the music, the girl's peaceful
form beside him. Now he turned his head towards her
without raising it from the cushions. 'I'm going back
to marry Avril.'

'Yes,' she said as if it were something she had already
been told. The record had come to an end. There was
a pause, a click, another pause and the brutal optimism
of the overture began again. He sprang up suddenly to
his feet and, taking the fabric carefully from her hands,
said, 'Will you dance with me?' He began to drape the
length of fabric around her shoulders. Then when he
was satisfied with the effect he put his arm around her
waist and began to dance.

He was clumsy at first, uncertain of the rhythm and
she was intractable in his arms. Then he held her closer

to him, humming the tune against her ear. 'Now,' he said and with his hand tightened on the stuff at the back of her frock he began to force her ahead of him, spinning her, then driving her forward again until he felt her lighten and yield. 'There,' he said, contentedly. 'There you are.'

Round and round they danced, up the length of the room across the top by the dais steps and down again. There was the music, the close sound of each other's breathing, the click of their shoes, the warm gusts of air against their ankles. 'Open your eyes,' he whispered once. 'You'll get dizzy if you keep them shut.' He spun her round and round as elaborately as he had danced with Avril Sawley at the club. Round and round past the mirrors while she, wide-eyed at so much borrowed happiness, watched the room grow populous with themselves. 'How lovely this is,' he said. 'I wish it didn't have to stop.' He spoke the words against her ear with a slight air of distraction, straining to catch the new tempo as each unfamiliar tune began, but to Flo each note was intimately known both in relation to the tune and its position in the record as a whole. So that minute by minute she was bound to measure the shrinking distance to the record's end and realized before he did that the final tune had come.

'I'm going now,' he said. When it had stopped and they stood still she was too dizzy to keep upright but fell against him while he steadied her. She said in a frightened voice, 'What will happen now?'

'I've told you.'

'To me?'

'Oh, you'll be all right,' he said. 'You're just at the beginning. It will all work out. You'll have a marvellous time. You'll see.' He kissed her quickly, reluctant even to say goodbye lest he be tempted out of habit to soften the words with promises to meet again. And she turned quickly from him, hearing the music stop; the familiar pause and click while the arm rose. She could at the moment think only how intolerable it would be if it were given time to settle and the tune to start again.

At nine thirty on the following morning the Lancia set out again for the airport to take Flo on the first lap of her journey home. The fact that each flight now carried someone or other home to England had not weakened the custom of coming to wave the traveller off; rather it seemed more urgent to come and touch and speak to these harbingers of their own uncertain future.

Flo stood squinting in the sun, dressed too warmly in the new coat and skirt, bewildered by the kindness of people. The dance, which everyone had said they would never forget, had continued triumphantly until four in the morning. Then, without a word of instruction from Lydia, the major-domo had appeared with a tureen of clear broth, a hundred soup-plates and a hundred spoons. It was the gracious signal that everyone should go home and leave their hosts an hour or two of sleep, and as such was immediately understood. Yet here, after so short a night, a touching number had reassembled to say goodbye. Bridie and her mother, Jamie Renfrew, Geoffrey Wheeler, the Sondheimers and the Harringtons, Richie South and Simon Philpotts. There were presents: a fine silk scarf from the Wallers, a volume of *Old Possum's Book of Practical Cats* from Geoffrey Wheeler, a bunch of violets from Richie South and Simon Philpotts which they had banded together to buy and proffered gallantly with a kiss from each on either cheek. 'Thank you,' she kept saying, 'thank you.'

Harry Morgan kissed her too and said, 'Good luck.' They all said that. Finally Lydia clung to her briefly and wept, aware of something irredeemable in this parting although in a month, it was supposed, they would meet again.

The time had come to walk with the other passengers across the glaring tarmac, to climb the gangway, to turn and wave at the little group beneath the flagstaff. Already they were separate from her and greatly diminished. And then there was the surge of power that would carry the plane clear of the escarpment, the sudden glimpse of Aderra laid out so small that a child's hand could lift the buildings and rearrange them. A moment later the plane sank into the cloud that ringed the mountain top and all was obscured again.

Chapter Twenty-Three

At Heathrow Flo found Major Denbigh waiting at the barrier.

'Ah,' he said, raising his swagger stick to her. 'There you are!'

He hurried her through customs and out to the waiting car. There they sat side by side as it moved slowly towards the city.

'Harry well?' he asked her. 'And your mother?'

'Very well, thank you.'

'It looks as if he's pulled it off,' the Major said. 'I always thought he would. Not everybody did though. It goes to show.'

'It's not quite over.'

'All over bar the shouting,' he said settling himself back into the corner of the seat to survey her. She was improved, he thought. Sharpened up in some way. 'Had a good time, did you?'

'Oh yes.'

'That's the ticket. Thought you might. What now?'

'I'm not quite sure.'

'Something will turn up,' he said comfortably.

The factories of Brentford had come into view. Like someone running out of time she asked him suddenly, 'Was the dead man in the tent my father?'

'No,' he said. 'No.' For a moment he had been bewildered by her, then a little frightened. 'Look, if I gave you that impression I'm most frightfully sorry . . .'

She had not looked at him. 'It's just that no one ever mentions him.'

'Rotten that,' he said, 'but for the best you know. Best to move on. No choice when you come right down to it.'

'No one talks about anything really, do they?'

She had turned to him. He noticed then the narrow defiance of her shoulders and was surprised to see her face entirely calm. Still waters run deep. 'What's up?' he said kindly.

'Only I knew someone who died out there,' she said. 'It's harder to forget him than the others.'

'Well,' he said, 'the living move on. You lose touch with them.'

'Not the dead though.'

The unseemly remark exposed him to thought he usually kept at bay. He was silent. Then he said decidedly, 'No more of that. There's been more than enough of that in my lifetime.' He took out his monocle and polished it fiercely with a red and white-spotted handkerchief. After a decent interval he said, 'Harry's retiring, I hear, after this little jaunt to South Africa. They'll come home, I imagine, and buy a little place in the country. You'll like that. Ride at all, do you?' he added hopefully.

They were coming into Hammersmith. It surprised her to know with such certainty that she would prefer a place like this with people's faces coming past her in a constant stream to the countryside which must always remind her of the damp restrictions of the boarding-school. She said, 'I don't know what I'm going to do.'

There was so little expression in her voice that he could not be sure exactly what meaning was attached to the words. He chose the least threatening to them both and said, 'Oh, I daresay Harry will fix something up for you. He must know a few people. Besides, you'll get married before you know what's happened to you.'

No, she thought. She felt the same unfamiliar jolt of certainty as when a moment ago she had rejected the life of a daughter in the English countryside. Again she did not contradict him. He had supposed the remark to be a compliment. He was being as kind as he was able. She merely smiled at him.

As the taxi drew up outside Daisy Mayhew's flat, Denbigh startled her by reaching out to squeeze her hand. 'I say, there's probably nothing that a chap can do to help, but if there ever were, we're friends of a kind you know. You have my office number. Here,' he said, reaching into his tunic pocket. 'Here's my home number as well. You could always ring and ask if there were something.'

He insisted on accompanying her up in the lift and hefting in and out her two suitcases, though he declined

Daisy Mayhew's offer of a cup of tea. 'Pressure of work, you know,' he said improbably. Flo watched him sink from sight. He touched his swagger stick to his visor, winked at her and called out, '*Au revoir.*'

'Oh, she shouldn't have done!' Daisy Mayhew cried when she opened the envelope containing Lydia's note and cheque. Her voice struck a perfect balance between pleasure and distress. For a moment Flo thought she might tear up the cheque, but she was not entirely surprised when instead Daisy clipped it smartly into her handbag.

'I think she's not quite sure how soon they are coming back. She didn't want me to be any sort of burden.'

'As if you could!' Daisy said.

'They're coming home quite soon I expect.'

'Well, early days, early days,' Daisy said. Still the bargain had been struck. They were immediately more at ease with one another.

In the morning Daisy went out and put a down payment on a television set. 'There will be something about Aderra on the news. You'll see. Won't that be exciting?' She had enjoyed telling the man in the shop the reason why the set must be installed by the end of the next week. 'Besides,' she said to Flo when she came back, 'you're sure to find the evenings here a little boring after all the fun you've had out there.'

On that Wednesday night the telephone rang and Daisy went to answer it. 'Flo,' she shouted, 'it's your mother! Darling? Where are you?' she continued into the receiver, 'Are you all right? Yes, Flo is right here with me.' She handed the receiver excitedly to Flo.

Far away, surrounded by the same cloud of static that had accompanied the English announcers on the wireless set, came a small excited voice, just recognizable as Lydia's. 'Flo darling, can you hear me? This is so important. We're not coming back. Did you hear that? Harry's been offered a job in Johannesburg and we're staying out here. Isn't it marvellous! You're to come out and join us in three weeks' time. Don't worry about the cost. Harry says it doesn't matter. Is that clear? Can I trust you to explain to Daisy and to phone that Major Denbigh and get him to book you a ticket? Do you have his number?'

'Yes, I do,' Flo said.

'When you know, cable through to this address. Have you got a pencil and something to write on?' There was a pencil and a notebook laid neatly by the side of the phone. She wrote down the address. 'Are you all right?' the tiny voice shouted at her. 'I've written you a letter. Goodbye, Flo darling, goodbye for now.'

'What did she say?' Daisy wanted to know. The conversation had been too one-sided to decipher.

'They're not coming back,' Flo told her. 'Harry's got a job in Johannesburg.'

'But what about you, poor Flo?'

'They want me to take a secretarial course,' Flo said without a pause. 'Right away and find digs in a hostel somewhere near by.' The words came suddenly from memories of what the other girls at school had planned to do.

The next morning Daisy went to work. Flo waited until ten thirty. Then, checking carefully that she had the latchkey Daisy had given her, she let herself out of the flat. Some superstitious fear of being overheard although Daisy was not there, and some scruple at making Daisy pay for the call she was about to make, made her head for a public phone box, which she had spotted from her bedroom window. She opened the heavy door and released the thick odour of trapped cigarette smoke that for one moment reminded her piercingly of Lydia and the upstairs sitting-room at Aderra. Nevertheless she fumbled in her handbag for her address book and, opening it at D, rang Major Denbigh's office number.

'It's Flo Wharton here,' she said. 'You told me I could ring you if I needed help.'

'Right,' he said cautiously. 'What's the problem?'

'I need somewhere to stay after next week. Lydia and Harry aren't coming back.'

'What about the Mayhew woman?'

'Oh,' Flo said, 'I just can't.' She added quickly, 'She's been very kind.

She heard his comfortable laugh on the other end of the phone. 'Going it alone, are you? Good for you.' After a pause he added, 'You've got the wherewithal for rent, I suppose.'

'In Barclays Bank DC&O, in Cockspur Street,' Flo said carefully. 'Only I don't know how to get it out.'

'Right,' he said, more cheerfully this time. 'Look here, Flo, it will take a day or two to sort things out. Universal Aunts should do the trick. A hostel for young ladies, that sort of thing. Grim as all hell, you know, but better than the status quo no doubt.'

'That sort of thing,' Flo said.

There was a moment's silence before he said, 'Why don't you have lunch with me on Friday? Then we'll pay a visit to the bank and sort out matters there. Then we'll have a shufti at any digs I've managed to line up. If there are any eyebrows raised we'll say I'm your father.' He was surprised to hear her laughter close to his ear, as loud and spontaneous as a child's. 'That's right,' he said. 'Keep your chin up. Friday then. Twelve thirty at my club. The In and Out in Piccadilly. Got that? Take a taxi. The driver will know. Oh, and Flo—'

'Yes?'

'There was a call for you at this number. Some man who said he knew you in Aderra. I didn't give him La Mayhew's number. Thought I'd better check with you. He left his if you want it. It's somewhere here.'

She didn't answer right away although she automatically extracted the pencil from the spine of her address book. Routh's face, which had eluded her since their parting in the ballroom, suddenly appeared to her mind with absolute clarity. This way and that, a series of expressions like the sheet of forty Polyphotos of Edward Wharton. For one instant those two confusing faces seemed to merge, and cause her to recognize that neither in the living nor the dead could she ever reach through to the directing mind behind. Close to her ear she heard papers rustle on Major Denbigh's desk in the Foreign Office. 'Ah, here it is,' he said. 'Pencil and paper at the ready?'

Still she was silent and now she heard his patient breathing as he waited for her. The pips went. She laid down the address book to struggle in her purse for the necessary coins and put them in the slot with fingers made clumsy by haste. Suddenly it seemed of overwhelming importance that the invisible line between her and Major Denbigh should not be cut; that if it were she should never find the courage to re-establish it. 'Are you still there?'

'Still right here.'

'I won't be needing it, thank you.'

He sounded pleased. 'Wise decision, no doubt. Till Friday then. Twelve thirty. The In and Out. I say, it will be all over in Aderra by then. Till Friday.'

'Goodbye,' she said, 'and thank you.'

Chapter Twenty-Four

A T TWELVE THIRTY on that final Friday, Harry
Morgan in top hat and tailcoat and Lydia in her
flowered chiffon and straw, stood on the steps of the
villa saying goodbye to their servants. Their futures, so
far as any ever can be, had been assured. The cook and
his two underlings, old Gidea, the laundress, Amde,
Hassan, the gardener and his boy, would stay on at the
villa and take their chances with its new owner. Haile
had refused to serve anyone from the Northern Province. Two days previously he had departed for a village
in the mountains of which he was the chief. He carried
with him Harry Morgan's parting gifts of the map and
the binoculars, which recently, to his surprise, Morgan
had found too repellent to handle. Matters were more
complicated for Colomboroli and the major-domo. The
Italian must be separated from his beloved Lancia and
the proud old car suffer demotion to second place,
after the Prince's Rolls, in the new ruler's cavalcade.
After some negotiation it was agreed that he and the
Chevrolet might be handed over to Geoffrey Wheeler,
who was staying on as British Consul in Aderra.

As for the major-domo, the best that Harry Morgan could do was to secure him a post as the *maître d'hôtel* on the coast where the first stirring of a tourist industry had begun. What little English he had learnt with Lydia's encouragement deserted him completely in those last days. It was difficult to explain to him that he had been relieved of his duties. Nor was it clear that he understood the necessity of quitting the town before the new regime arrived. In the end the problem was solved by Colomboroli who had a week's leave due to him and volunteered to spend it driving the old man to the coast in the Chevrolet before reporting back to Wheeler.

On the previous Friday therefore the major-domo in his immaculate tunic and leggings had handed over his keys to Lydia and walked for the last time down the villa steps. He moved one foot at a time and settled it carefully before he moved the next. His back was rigid. His gaze, directed straight ahead, jolted downward with each step he took. He carried nothing but a small basket in his hand. His dignity was unassailable. He was, Lydia realized through her tears, very drunk.

Colomboroli held the door of the Chevrolet open and after a moment's thought the major-domo climbed in unassisted. Overnight the flagstaffs had been unbolted from the mudguards, the holes filled in and rendered almost invisible with black paint. They drove off past the sentry boxes while Harry Morgan kept his hand raised in a half-salute and Lydia waved and waved. The major-domo neither waved nor looked back but kept his blurred gaze fixed on the road ahead.

Now a week later they too were leaving. Colomboroli had returned and for the last time unsheathed the Union Jacks on the Lancia. Side by side they were driven to the parliament building where the long-prepared formalities were completed. The document was signed. A gold pen inscribed in English and Aderran was given to Morgan to mark the occasion. Afterwards he lowered the flag without mishap and stood to attention while the Aderran flag was raised in its place. Then seated opposite the Prince and his consort in their open Rolls they set out at a snail's pace preceded by the regimental band marching with their colours for the last time through the town.

Morgan was quite removed from it by now. Nothing in his upbringing could enable him to understand the joy of the people who packed the wide pavements on either side of the street and leant forward waving and shouting as their former ruler and their new one were driven slowly past. Lydia, sitting upright at his side, was not conscious of any fear. Nevertheless she listened so acutely that hearing seemed to grow into an additional, sixth sense. Nor did she define to herself exactly what it was she listened for but knew it to be a tiny sound, a click, a rustle, a second's silence in the midst of all that clamour. All her awareness was concentrated on that one thing, the bullet, the explosion, which did not come. The rest slid past as if she watched it on a newsreel, except that the buoyant educated accents of the commentator were not there to establish this as yet another victory. Without him she must make of it what she would. On they crept down the tunnel of white shirts, black faces and wide pink interiors of mouths that chanted a single syllable again and again. The human voice loses its humanity when it limits itself to one word. It becomes a barking and a baying, a terrible, exhilarating sound. She had never learnt their language but knew the word they shouted must be equivalent to Freedom! Freedom! Freedom!

They had reached the airport, said their farewells to the new ruler and waved him off as the Rolls turned back towards the town. Was it possible that after all, the worst had failed to happen? In the airport manager's office Harry Morgan changed out of his tailcoat and into his linen suit. The top hat travelled in its own box. The rest he had, with difficulty, to fold and force into his suitcase. It was the first time in many years that he had packed for himself.

There was hardly anyone to see them off. As many as possible of the English community, and some like the Sondheimers attached to the United Nations, had flown out during the week. The Wallers even had gone that morning. Only the Colonel of the regiment, the Ambassador to the Northern Province, and of course Wheeler, were there to shake his hand and wish him well.

Geoffrey walked with them far enough across the tarmac to be out of hearing. 'Well, you brought it off,' he said. 'You really did. You brought it off and not a drop of blood shed.'

He smiled, expecting that Morgan would smile back. But he did not. He was tired perhaps. He simply said, 'Only a little,' thanked Wheeler, wished him luck and turned to climb into the plane.

That evening in London Flo and Daisy changed into their woollen dressing-gowns and made their cocoa early while the new television set, well tuned in advance, chattered excitedly in the sitting-room next door. By nine o'clock, they were seated, mugs in hand, staring at the flickering screen. The final item on the evening news was what the announcer called, 'Another task of empire successfully completed.' There was a clash of band music. A frame of the Palazzo came unbelievably on to the screen, then a close-up of the Union Jack jerkily descending. 'The caretaker government of the tiny protectorate of Aderra was today handed over to the representative of the Northern Province, to which it is now federated as an autonomous state.' The new flag was hauled up. A new anthem played. There was Harry Morgan, the sum of so much that was good, standing to attention in top hat and tailcoat. 'Oh, doesn't he look wonderful,' Daisy cried, reaching out and squeezing Flo's hand. 'Oh, you must be so proud!'

Already it was over and another man spoke as eagerly about tomorrow's weather, which would be fine. 'That's nice,' Daisy Mayhew said in the same pleased tone. 'It's always nice to make a fresh start with the sun out.'

Tomorrow Flo was due to start her secretarial course. Her bag was packed for the morning, when Tommy Denbigh had promised to call round in a taxi on his way to work, to install her in the hostel. 'And just think,' Daisy said. 'Only nine months and if you work hard you'll be equipped to earn your own living and then you'll be free, Flo, absolutely free.'